THE CITY OF LAOHZ SERIES

KANNON

BOOK ONE

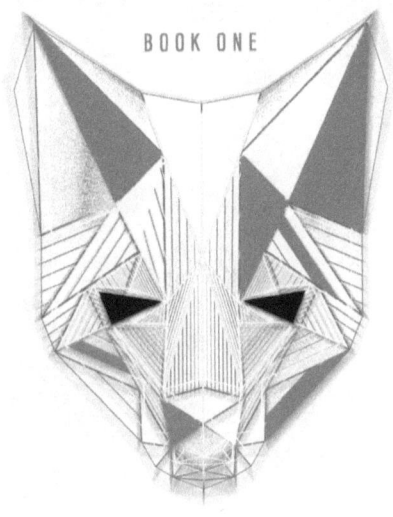

THE CITY OF LAOHZ SERIES

KANNON

BOOK ONE

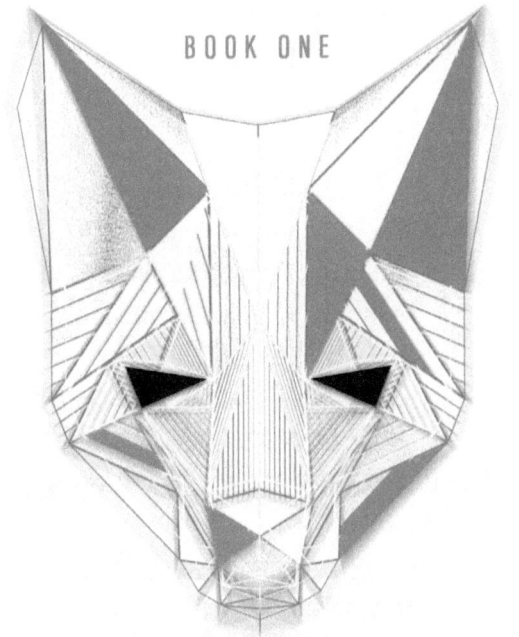

EJ FALCON

Book Design & Production:
Columbus Publishing Lab
www.ColumbusPublishingLab.com

Copyright © 2024 by
EJ Falcon
LCCN: 2024902284

Paperback ISBN: 978-1-63337-759-2
Hardback ISBN: 978-1-63337-968-8
E-Book ISBN: 978-1-63337-760-8

Printed in the United States of America
1 3 5 7 9 10 8 6 4 2

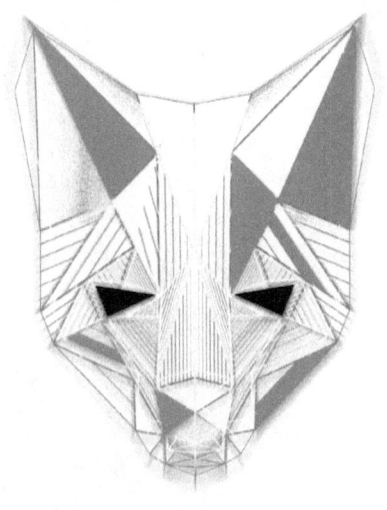

TO LINE BJØRKLUND WESENBERG.

CHAPTER 1

THE GLASS ON THE BUILDINGS reflected the City of Laohz's lights like shining stars as I walked through the hotel room, the anticipation building inside as I got closer to the balcony door, rifle in hand. The hot and humid air of the August night carried with it faint whispers of the oncoming autumn.

"Kannon," Silver said, putting her backpack down. "Do we have a timeframe for finishing this job?"

I turned to her. Her nose and mouth were covered in a dual cylinder gas mask, which she never took off with people around. Teal eyes glowed in the darkness of the night, technologically modified for better vision in the dark. She gazed at me briefly, giving me a magazine for my sniper rifle.

Silver and I had been working together for almost three years now, and she had been the one who showed me how to do my job as an assassin for hire after the training was over.

"All I was told was to get the job done," I said as I pulled back the bolt, loading a fresh bullet into the chamber, the glow of my wine-red eyes reflecting on the metal.

"Why is it that you never ask for more details, *Katherine*?"

"Don't call me that. I hate it when you call me that. Now, did you write down the ship's serial number?"

She nodded. "Y14V-26-58-R. It'll be a cargo ship. But stop avoiding my question."

"It's mostly to annoy you. You're usually all serious and direct. You need to lighten up."

She sighed, tying her long, charcoal-gray hair into a ponytail. "Very funny, *Katherine*. Have you met with this client?"

"We need to do this tonight." I looked at my watch. "Our contact told us that the pilot will be moved to another position at the end of the week. We may not have enough time to plan another strategy. And no. All our communications have been through calls and text messages."

"Was that so hard?" She detached the scope from her rifle. "What about the cargo?"

"Has to go down with the ship," I said. "The client expects the ship's fuel will burn hot enough to damage the contents once the ship crashes."

She nodded, moving closer to the railing.

I pulled the nearby glass table over and set it between me and the railing of the balcony. Down the street, blue-and-red lights reflected off the glass, the strobe effect a prologue of the oncoming convoy of Rain Enforcer patrol ships.

The Rain Enforcers were the police and military of the City of Laohz, controlled and funded by the interstellar company Rain Corporation, whose products focused mainly on military hardware. They were one of the first to settle the planet Rhode, where the city was located, and had maintained control of it ever since.

The first ships to pass by were the small, six-meter-wingspan Patrol Ships, which acted as your standard police cruiser, their blue-and-red lights painting all the glass around us as they made it rattle. Shifting my focus to the distance, a whole line of black hoverships was heading our way, all different wingspan sizes and all sporting *Rain Enforcers* on their metallic bodies, as traffic droned on in the streets below.

No one in the nearby buildings came to see the convoy. Everyone had become numb to their presence, like the rumbling of passing trains outside the window of a homeowner who'd owned the house for decades.

"Do you see it yet?" Silver asked, breaking my concentration.

"No." I breathed out deliberately. I rested the bipod on the table and sat on the chair. The ground shook as the larger ships flew past, artillery and fast deployment ships with wingspans of twenty to twenty-five meters, but none were my target. "I need silence."

I focused on controlling my breathing; these convoys could sometimes contain two hundred ships, and missing my target was not a mistake I was willing to make. I took a deep breath and rested my finger lightly on the trigger, which was cool to the touch. After I'd fallen into a rhythm, the cargo ship we were after appeared around the corner of a block two miles down. It had a wingspan of forty meters and two large engines at the top of the chassis. *There you are.*

"The serial number matches." Silver said.

The ship was approaching fast, even with the tons of steel it was carrying in a shipping container at its back. I exhaled as deeply as my lungs allowed. Excitement, anticipation, that little dip of fear, and "what if I miss" feeling crept up in the back of my mind as seconds stretched into minutes. I shoved the thought aside. I pulled the trigger.

The ship's left engine exploded into flames, ejecting black clouds of smoke into the sky as it passed the building, crashing down seconds later into a ball of fire. I breathed in and leaned back, then pulled the bolt, ejecting the empty casing that clattered to the ground.

"Good shot," Silver said, lowering the scope she had in her hand. "This should get us a decent pay for a month or two." She put the scope into her backpack and flung it over her shoulders.

I stood, staring at the flickering flames reflected on the glass panes of the buildings around us, almost like fireflies. "I feel like we just shook a hornet's nest." I turned to Silver and slung the sniper rifle over my shoulders. "Hopefully, they'll just think it was a critical engine malfunction." I grabbed my backpack and headed for the door of the hotel room.

"Do you think it'll be safe to leave?" Silver said as she opened the door and I went through. "The Rain Enforcers are not going to take the crash of one of their ships lightly."

I took a deep breath and rubbed the bridge of my nose. "I know the truce allows us to take contracts against them, but I don't want to think about it." I closed the door behind me. "At least, not now."

People from other rooms were out in the hallway, confused by the explosion and talking to each other, but silence fell as Silver and I walked down the hallway toward the elevators. Most of them moved away, others hid, darting back into their rooms as they looked at us, rifles strapped to our shoulders, handguns to our hips. These were the downfalls of being a member of the Black Snipers.

The Black Snipers were highly trained assassins-for-hire, offering our services to the highest bidder. We were currently in a frail truce between the Rain Enforcers, every contract against them weighed carefully. Everyone in the City of Laohz knew about us, everyone knew what we looked like, and most didn't want to have anything to do with us.

Silver pressed the elevator button and closed her eyes. She and I could both feel the tension that was forming in the air. The chatter of people had subsided, replaced by the muffled sound of the air-conditioning vent that was a few feet away from where we were standing. The hallway carried the lingering scent of years-old carpet, and the beige walls were riddled with cracked wallpaper. Cobwebs hung and swayed on the wall lamps, abandoned by their old owners, as Silver and I stared at the floor panel change numbers.

The elevator doors opened with a single bell. The people inside scooted over to the edges as soon as they saw us, while a few got off. I walked in first, catching a glimpse of my wavy, shoulder-length auburn hair in the polished walls of the elevator. Silver pressed the button, and we all rode down in heavy silence. A couple kept their eyes locked on us, barely talking, while the other person just put on his headphones and delved into the confines of his phone.

The bell rang, and the doors opened. The other passengers hurried out, and I fixed my backpack's straps against my open flannel shirt before we headed out of the building. The flames danced against the glass of the surrounding buildings, and traffic had just formed on the road in front of the hotel. Farther down the road, large columns of fire and smoke rose up from the charred remains of the Rain Enforcer ship, while Firefighter Ships hovered above it and tried to douse the flames. Silver tugged at my shirt, urging me to follow the crowd that was trying to flee the inferno, abandoning their vehicles in the middle of the street. I shook my head and followed my partner, trying to tie into any kind of feeling about what I had just done, but nothing bubbled to the surface.

"Are you going to call the client?" Silver said, pulling me by the arm until I matched her stride.

"Let's get clear first. I want to build as much distance as I can before I call. The Rain Enforcers will close this whole area any time now, and I don't want to be stuck waiting to be interrogated by them."

More Patrol Ships sped by above, sirens wailing loudly as they echoed through the buildings, piercing the chaos around us. Even after years as an assassin, the feeling of fear still slithered inside, making my heart jump as Silver and I quickened our stride.

Once we were clear of what we estimated would be the lockdown perimeter, Silver and I dove into an alleyway and I pulled out my Recaller, a phone with a glass-like alloy that acted as a screen, the electronics encased in metal at each end. I dialed my contact.

The line rang only once, and a distorted, synthetic voice answered. "Kannon," it said. "Do you have news for me?"

My gaze shifted to Silver, who nodded once. "Yes. Everything is taken care of."

"I know," it said, voice deep and guttural. "Expect your payment in a day. I have a few loose ends to tie up." There was silence for a moment. "We will meet at a time and place I deem appropriate. Farewell."

"What did they say?" Silver's voice carried a hint of urgency. Even though she almost never showed facial expressions, after years of working together, I had come to know the nuances in her voice. I could often decipher the feelings she was trying to hide even from herself.

I put the Recaller back into my pocket. "We will be paid by tomorrow, and then we will meet at a time and place they deem appropriate."

"That's not cryptic at all," she said, throwing her head back and crossing her arms. "What will I bloody do with you, Katherine? By the Oath."

"Stop calling me Katherine!"

She exhaled. "Come on, let's go get a drink and steer clear of this place." She began to walk back toward the street.

I fixed my backpack, rattling the two rifles strapped to it, before I joined her on the sidewalk and walked in silence. I was unsure what Silver was paying attention to, but as for me, I watched every face we walked past, every Rain Enforcer ship that sped above us with their sirens wailing, every car, noise, shadow that moved in alleys. It was an annoying skill that was drilled into my skull as I was trained by the Elder Black Snipers, those who were in charge of us, and only answering to the Black Sniper's leader.

Keep your eyes open, your ears attentive, and your gun ready. Those were the words I heard on repeat during the two years of my training. We were honed to such a razor-sharpness in our skill with combat that it almost became intrinsic. To pay attention to *everything* and be able to keep our focus.

Shots rang out and instinct took over. Handguns drawn, Silver and I turned to a small street where hooligans covered in colorful jackets and brightly painted gas masks were beating a small patrol squad of Rain Enforcers with their own weapons and crowbars. I pulled my trigger, and two of the five criminals fell dead. Some bullets grazed them, and my gun clicked empty. *Damn the distance.* As I reloaded, Silver took down another one. What was left of them turned tail to run, but by the time I emptied my second magazine, all of them were dead. I exhaled.

Silver was the first to approach. I reloaded before joining her. The helmets of the Rain Enforcers were torn off, bloodied and broken. Faces bashed in, none of them were breathing. Even their black standard riot gear was no match for a crowbar swung with enough force. I sighed deeply, not being able to save them from the brutality would remain a regret.

"We should check the bodies," Silver said.

"What a waste." I checked the badge of one of the officers. "They were practically our age." I looked at the date of birth. "This one was just twenty-six. Two years older than me."

Silver's shaky breath sent a shiver down my spine. "This one was just twenty. A cadet." She stood, putting her gun into her holster. "Kannon, we should let their commanders know."

"We riled them up already," I said. "Do you think they'll take it kindly if we report another death in their ranks on the same day?"

She rubbed her temples. "Yes, I know, but we can't just *leave* them here."

"No, we shouldn't." I stood up and went to look at the others. "I just want to make sure they don't lock this place with us inside."

I knelt next to one of the hooligans and searched his pockets until I found the Recaller. "Let's get the other Recallers and leave. We can tip them once we're at least a block or two away."

Silver nodded.

I pushed over the body of the one I searched and took the gas mask off. "You're just a kid." It broke my heart, if only a little, to have been the one to end the life of a teenager. The hard truth, though, was that this was a common occurrence. Many in the City of Laohz either chose to leave for the other cities, or they joined up with one of the local gangs. That was if they managed to escape being brainwashed by the constant ads the Rain Corporation aired all across the City.

The City of Laohz was, for better or worse, a pressure cooker of order waiting to explode. After Cleansing Day, when the Rain Enforcers launched their full force upon the city with the intent of wiping out the criminal underworld, everyone had been living with the worry of when the next Cleansing Day might happen. After two years, many innocents had died, and there were heavy casualties in the ranks of both major players -- the Black Snipers and the Rain Enforcers. The conflict ended in a stalemate. This was part of the result, the lasting aftershocks, and as I turned to Silver, gathering the last of the Recallers, my heart was heavy. It seemed every one of them had barely reached their twenties, if that. And now their lives were over.

"Let's go home," I said as I stood. "I'm done with all the drama of today."

Silver nodded and put the Recallers in my backpack. "We have to stop by the bar first, though. I need a drink, and you hoard the best wine for yourself."

"You never pay for replacements. If you bought a bottle every time you finished one, I wouldn't ban you from the wine cabinet," I said.

"Well, *you* never let me give you the money to buy more. Spoilsport." She took off ahead, and I followed, the faces of the dead kids swimming in my head.

▲ ▲ ▲

We arrived at The Reed Bar an hour later, a location where many Black Snipers liked to gather, in part because it was owned by one of the few retired Black Snipers in our history. An indie rock band played on the stage while people walked around. Voices mixed in with the loud music, and the lights were dim. Most of the crowd attending were members, taking a break from the day, while others were regular people, trying to have a good time.

Silver made a beeline to the mahogany bar and was trying to order a drink. I took refuge in a corner of the building, trying to stay away from the larger mass of bodies crowding the space, while also having a decent view of the stage. All I could think about was the kids. I had been doing this for almost four years, had lived through Cleansing Day, and had killed more people than I could count. I couldn't stomach myself now, and I stared at my hands. Was this all I was good for?

I had finished my university studies and done nothing with the degree. I had been at the top of my class nonetheless, but I failed at my career. Failed to keep in contact with my family, my rebellious sister, and my old friends. I took a deep breath and decided to force myself to forget about that. I struggled to compose myself as Silver moved through the crowd with her drink in hand.

"Are you going to take the mask off to drink that?" I blurted out as she reached hearing distance.

"Ha-ha, very funny." She put the straw through a small opening in her mask. "This hits the spot. Why is it that you never buy whiskey?"

"You can buy some yourself," I said. "Where is my drink?"

She shrugged. "You didn't tell me you wanted anything."

"Common courtesy." I crossed my arms, turning my gaze to the crowd. *Ugh, I don't want to fight my way through just to order.* "There seems to be more people tonight. Is the band new?"

"They're a rising star in the rock scene," a man behind me said. A baseball bat lined with nails was strapped to his backpack, along with a black glossy rifle and shotgun. "Nice to see you again, Kannon."

"Kax," I said. "I thought you went to Autumnpeak City."

"I was there. Koyuki Akikawa had me hunt for a traitor. I just came back . . ." He trailed off as he looked at his Recaller. "Three hours ago."

Kax was one of the Black Sniper Hunters, a special group within our ranks who worked directly for Koyuki Akikawa, our pseudo-leader. Hunters had but one task, hunt high-value targets, and they were expected to play with their prey, which could take many forms. Black Sniper Hunters were the best of the best, and Koyuki, who controlled 67 percent of the ACCENT drug trade in the City, hand-picked them from the organization. Kax was always hidden behind a black facemask of his own design and black sunglasses at all hours. He used to be a Wraith, a member of a hacker group tasked with feeding Black Snipers information. Our partnership came after I had a falling out with another member of the Wraiths. For better or worse, he was also my cousin, and the only family I had in the City of Laohz.

"Does Koyuki have any other jobs pending?" Silver said.

Kax shook his head. "Not to my knowledge. I heard you were the one responsible for the fireworks plastered all over the news earlier today. Is my information accurate?"

I nodded. "It was a job I took."

"She should've consulted with me," Silver interjected. "We didn't meet the client in person, nor do we know their name."

"Not surprising." Kax hid his hands in his pockets. "Many clients like to keep as detached from the job they hired us to do as possible. I personally have done jobs for some Rain Enforcer captains and generals. Do you want me to find out who hired you?"

I shook my head. "It's fine. Don't worry about it."

"If you so wish." He looked at his Recaller again. "I have to head home. I have things to take care of. Ladies." He excused himself, pushing past the crowd, and ultimately disappearing beyond the entrance.

"Why didn't you ask him to check on the Recallers we lifted from those guys?" Silver said, moving closer to stand next to me.

"He doesn't do Wraith work anymore."

"Not even for family members?"

"I already asked once a few months back for something else. He declined." I stretched my body. "Let's go home. I'll check the contents myself before I go to bed."

She shrugged and went off to pay for her drink, then started to argue with someone next to her before another pair of Black Snipers grabbed the offender and forced them to leave the bar. Silver made her way back. "Shall we go home?"

I nodded, but someone called out to Silver. A group of Black Snipers were in a booth drinking while a waitress delivered some food. "On second thought, I think I'll stay a bit longer. Catch you later?"

"Just don't come home wasted. Last time you didn't even make it to bed."

"Stop getting on my case," she said before she joined the others. I was too tired to stay out. My body craved the warmth and comfort of my bed.

Stepping outside the bar, the loud music was replaced by the sound of passing hovercars and the distant wailing of the Rain Enforcer Patrol Ships. After taking a deep breath, I walked down the street to the parking lot where my motorcycle was. The ships flew past above me, twice the speed of traffic on the streets, as they seemed to be scrambling with the destruction of their cargo ship.

After turning on and revving the bike, I held my helmet with both hands and turned my gaze above, greeted by the ever-present blanket of clouds and the buildings disappearing among it. The people around me walked past with their gazes low, some locked to the screens of their Recallers. Couples held hands and talked to each other. I saw myself reflected on the back of my polished helmet, my modified red eyes glowing in the dark and peering back at me, while on the street, no one seemed to notice the presence of a lone woman sitting on her machine in the middle of a dark parking lot.

I put my helmet on and revved the bike once more before leaving, delving into the traffic as my mind lingered, compiling everything from the day up to this point. Something was nagging me at the back of my head, and I couldn't remember what I might be missing. Eventually, I gave up. Whatever it was, it was not important at the moment. I was tired, and all I wanted was to forget the events of the day.

Eventually, the blue lights of the Block Host—a long promenade block lined with shops and small apartments, usually controlled by members of the Black Snipers—came into view. I turned into the alleyway behind the shops, stopping my bike and opening a small garage in which to leave it.

After closing the door, I walked around the shop, a decent-sized bookstore, until I reached the cobblestone-lined promenade. Shrubbery and benches sat in the middle of it, along with blue lampposts installed by the citizens in order to decrease crime in the area. I took a deep breath and allowed the tiredness that hung on my shoulders to fall off. *So good to be back in Houther Block Host.* The sounds of the city were muffled by specialized noise dampeners.

As I climbed the stairs next to the bookstore to my apartment above, the thought of leaving Silver behind to come back home alone stung my chest a bit. I pulled out my keys, jangling them as I moved through the hallway with four doors, pausing to open the door.

I flipped the light switch as I walked straight into the kitchen. After walking through the kitchen into the combination living and dining area, I left my backpack on the table across the hallway from the rooms. My eyes on the balcony beyond the living room,

I took off my combat boots and unhooked my bra.

"Oh, that feels so good." I set my combat knife inside the backpack and slid my feet across the tiled floor and toward my room. I knew I needed to check on those Recallers, but the aches on my body began to intensify as I got closer to my bed. I felt lazy, grogginess began to stick to me, and the desperate need for a shower wrestled with my overwhelming desire to go to sleep. I fell face-first onto my bed and groaned, knowing I couldn't stay there.

After a few minutes, I forced myself to get out of bed and grabbed some clothes as I headed for the shower. My Recaller began vibrating as soon as I closed the bathroom door. On the screen was a single-line text message from the woman herself, Koyuki Akikawa. In Japanese it read: "Come to my estate at your earliest convenience. I have a job for you."

"Great. She'll have to wait until morning."

CHAPTER 2

THE MID-MORNING SUN was hidden behind a thick blanket of clouds the following day, a hint of humidity in the air.

"Here I am," I said, stopping my motorcycle a few meters away from Koyuki Akikawa's mansion gates.

After taking a deep breath, I turned my gaze to the ten-foot-tall wooden gate before me. It was built in the traditional style of Japanese architecture. The uneasy feeling that came with a call from the boss was starting to form a lump in my throat. It wasn't often I saw Koyuki Akikawa in person. Most of my dealings with her consisted of calls and text messages.

"Why do you think she needs us here today? I could've used the day off," Silver said, stopping her motorcycle next to mine as she turned her attention to the gates.

"All she said was that she had a job for us," I said. "And I did tell you to not get drunk, didn't I?"

"And you left me last night so you could deal with those Recallers." She revved her bike and drove closer to the intercom. I followed.

"I did check them out after I took my shower," I said, stopping next to her. "They seem to be part of a new gang that's cropping up. They call themselves the Lolitrons. That was all I could get from them." I pressed the intercom button next to the gate. The security camera moved above me, and then someone cleared their throat on the other side.

"Why are you here?" a male voice said.

"Koyuki summoned me."

There was silence for a moment before the gate slid open just enough to allow us to enter, pushing our bikes inside. Beyond, we were greeted by a white gravel road leading to the front of her traditional Japanese mansion. The smell of the imported cherry trees that lined each side of the path hung in the air. At the end of the driveway was a parked black car, and a fountain was visible through the trees on our right, a stone path snaked through the garden, along with several benches. At the end of the gravel path, a set of stairs ended on a large porch where Koyuki Akikawa's assistant stood, his hands hidden behind his back while he kept his gaze on us.

"Good evening, Mr. Fukuzawa," I said as I stopped on the stairs, one step lower than him.

"Welcome back, Miss Kannon. Miss Silver." He gestured for us to climb up. "Miss Akikawa is expecting you both." He turned around and moved to open the doors for us. Once inside, we followed him down the main hallway, to a small garden in the middle of the mansion. A small pond and a pair of trees provided shade over some benches. He then turned right and led us down a series of corridors set outside, with doors to the house to my left. We then reached a Zen garden, and beyond it was a large gazebo, the pond disappearing under it in a curtain of black.

A Japanese woman dressed in an amber-colored turtleneck and black jeans stood there, waiting inside the gazebo. Her gaze was set on the pond below, while her delicate hands were on the wooden railing.

"Miss Akikawa," Mr. Fukuzawa said. "Miss Kannon has arrived."

The woman smirked before she turned her gaze slightly toward us. Her bright, modded, amber-colored eyes, which matched her shirt, fell upon me before she detached herself from the edge. "Welcome, Miss Kannon, Miss Silver." She turned to Mr. Fukuzawa and nodded once. "You may leave us."

He nodded, turned around, and left. Once he was out of sight, the woman, our boss, Koyuki Akikawa, turned back to us, and her lips curved into a sly smile. She gestured for us to join her inside the gazebo with a single, slight movement of her head.

We all stood inside the wooden structure in silence for a moment, Koyuki's gaze focused on the garden that lay beyond the edges of the pond as the passing wind rustled the leaves of the plants and trees nearby, cicadas, imported from Earth, crying somewhere hidden in the foliage, and the occasional movement of water beneath us the only indication of fish inside the pond.

Koyuki took a deep breath before she took her hands off the railing as she turned to face us. Her expression was set, almost still as stone as her eyes scanned us from head to toe, and at that moment, I began to loathe the observation skills taught to us by the trainers in the Black Snipers. Being aware of her scrutinizing gaze made meeting with her even more nerve-racking. It made my skin scrawl, like a sharp, cold knife being passed ever-so gently over my skin, its edge always so close to slicing it open. Drawing that sharp, near-the-edge feeling as she stood perfectly still, with only her gaze moving.

"I hear you were the ones responsible for the crash of the cargo ship last night," she said, voice flat, eyes peering into both of us, and all I could feel was the need to hide.

Koyuki Akikawa's reputation across the Black Snipers, and the city for that matter, could be summarized in a single sentence: a cold, calculating woman who knows everything that happens in the city at any time. Other things are said about her, and how her relation to her father, Toshio Akikawa, the only representative of the Yakuza in the whole planet of Rhode, made her path easier to gain the status she currently enjoyed by the ripe young age of twenty-eight. Despite her title as the most powerful crime lord in the City of Laohz, the Rain Enforcers always left her alone. No one in the Black Snipers knew why, with the exception of her Inner Circle, of which I didn't know anything other than its existence.

I took a deep breath and nodded. "We were hired to perform a contract."

"I know," she said, this time in Japanese. "I also know the client who hired you." She paced around the gazebo.

"Do you have a job for us?" Silver said.

Koyuki stopped, her lip curving up to a faint smile, but it disappeared quickly. "There is a chemist known as Lawrence Hudson who has created a refined version of ACCENT. Said to be more potent."

ACCENT, from what I had heard, was a combat enhancement drug developed by the Rain Enforcers, and it was still in early development when the recipe was 'lost.' Many Black Snipers used it in small doses, but the drug was highly addictive, and even lethal if not measured properly.

"And you want us to get it for you," Silver stated.

Koyuki turned to look at us. "Do not fail me. You know what happens if you do."

There was silence for a moment, as I willed myself to not touch my neck, repressing the thoughts of her punishment. I could almost feel the coldness of the dagger she always kept hidden in her sleeve against my skin, as my fingers lightly brushed the scars she left on my legs the last time, a branding that was her family name in Japanese.

"You are free to go. I'm sure you are both capable of showing yourselves out."

Silver and I bowed, as was expected, then turned around and left, knowing our initial payment would have been transferred to us by the time the gate to her estate closed behind us.

▲ ▲ ▲

It had been a week since Silver and I took down the cargo ship from the Rain Enforcers, and their patrols across the City had become more frequent, with sirens a constant echo through the streets. It made the current task of breaking into the apartment's fire escape rather difficult.

"I don't like this," I said, my gaze locked on a patrol ship that passed above us with its lights flashing against the night sky. "I don't want to risk our chances, even in this dark corner alley."

Silver offered me some of her soda as her gaze followed the ship. I declined as I turned my attention to the lock on the door. It wouldn't budge to the tools. "Do you mind shining that flashlight instead of drinking? I'll break my lockpick if you keep drowning out the light with your shirt."

She moved it to the lock. "Do you want us to get caught?"

I leered at her, then went back to the lock, feeling it budge and ease open moments later. "I would have done this before the ship passed if you had kept your attention to the task at hand." I took a deep breath.

"What will I do with you, Katherine?"

I shot her a brief glare as I put the tools away inside my backpack, then opened the door to the apartment building's fire escape. "When will I get you to stop using my name?"

She threw the can aside and grabbed her shotgun, going inside first. "I have to have my fun somehow."

I followed her in, and the door locked behind, the noise echoing in the silence. The lights flickered here and there, while the faint smell of humid concrete and dust invaded my nose, making it run. I couldn't stop myself from sneezing.

Silver and I had been keeping watch on the schedule of Lawrence Hudson since we got his address from Koyuki, opting to break into his apartment and grab the information when he was not home. A risky move to do with just a week of surveillance, since it was not enough time to get a good sense for a pattern, but the tense atmosphere with the Rain Enforcers warranted the rushed action. As we climbed the stairs, Silver's furrowed eyebrows told me she didn't like the plan, and, if I was honest with myself, I agreed with the sentiment. I preferred to get this job over with.

The L-shape of the building meant the stairs were arranged as a smaller L within the structure to allow access to the three points of the structure, with a landing on what would be the outside facing wall. It was a strange building design.

"Is this it?" Silver asked as we reached the tenth floor.

I looked at the information in my Recaller and nodded. "It should be apartment 1027B. A few doors to your right."

She nodded, and we both went through the door. The hallway was decorated with a vertical wallpaper and a mahogany-colored carpet that couldn't have been cleaned since the building was opened, judging by the smell. We were just grateful it was empty.

The door was ajar as we reached it, and my gut reaction was to get my handgun ready, blood pumping in my ears. We could hear muffled voices inside and the sound of things being thrown around, glasses being broken, followed by something wooden landing. Silver's teal gaze locked with mine, and I mouthed, "Don't kill them."

She took a deep breath, nodded, and went inside, firing her shotgun once at the ceiling as I followed her.

"Fuck!" one of the people inside said. "Black Snipers!"

A flash of colors tried to run past me through the door, but I grabbed his jacket and slammed him to the ground, knocking the wind out of him. Silver ran into a room following the other one, then a shot rang out, three, five . . . seven, then a single shotgun blast and a loud thud followed by a crash. Silver appeared through the door, her arm bleeding as she pressed the wound with her free hand.

"Are you okay?" I asked, and she nodded. I turned to the guy on the floor and grabbed him by his jacket, dragging him through the mess until we reached the stove, where I tied his hands to the handle with a towel.

After taking a deep breath, I walked back to check on Silver, who was sitting on the couch, blood dyeing her clothes dark red. I set my backpack down and pulled out a roll of bandages and a tourniquet, then turned to look at it.

"The bullet is still there," Silver said. "You'd think that after being shot eighteen times in this career, I'd get used to this burning pain."

"Just sit still," I said as I tied the tourniquet around her arm, then grabbed a pair of sterile tweezers I kept in my backpack and pulled the bullet out before covering the wound with a tightly applied bandage.

Gunshots and stab wounds were our main injuries in the industry, and one of the things they teach us during training is how to treat them. The Black Snipers don't expect its members to be doctors, but we all need to know enough to keep ourselves alive until we can get looked at by the Specter's Chop Shop, the Black Sniper hospital line, of sorts.

The Specters in charge of it created the sub-dermal body modifications and eye modifications that all Black Snipers used. They repaired our weapons when they needed to. They also kept our bodies working in tandem with the cybernetics they grafted into each of us. They're engineers, medics, and corpse disposers, all overseen by an old man named Blacklight.

After Silver was patched up and I cleaned up after us, she and I walked back to the man tied to the stove. His gaze was turned to us, staring from behind his colored gas mask.

"What were you doing here?" Silver said.

He just looked down at his feet.

I knelt before him and removed his mask, much to his

chagrin. "You're just a kid. Do you think that the Rain Enforcers are going to be easy on you just because you're still in high school?"

"I dropped out of school," he barked. "Not like I would be able to afford to go to any of the universities in this dumb place."

"Why are you here?" I said again, trying to make my voice calm.

He didn't say anything.

"If you don't want to talk . . ." I began to search his pockets, until I found his Recaller.

"Hey! Give that back! Hey! You don't have permission to look into my stuff! That's an invasion of privacy."

I ignored him and attached the phone to a device I carried, used to feed Recallers passcodes until a match was found. After a minute, the device was unlocked. As I looked through the text messages, I found a chain that detailed all I needed to know, and what I had already suspected. I turned to him, realizing that the kid was also a member of the rising gang called Lolitrons.

"What did you find?" Silver said, her arm held up against her chest.

"It seems that Lawrence Hudson was doing more than making a new version of ACCENT. Whoever the leader of the Lolitrons is, they wanted Mr. Hudson's laptop."

I turned to the kid again and knelt next to him. "Well, did you find it?"

"No," he said. "We were about to give up when you showed up and killed my friend."

"He would still be alive if he hadn't tried to kill me, you *brat*," Silver said.

"I guess we should talk to Mr. Hudson, then."

"Well," Silver said, motioning me to follow, "that's not going to happen."

We walked down the hallway and into Mr. Hudson's trashed room. In the middle of it was a middle-aged man, large bags formed under his bruised eyes, thinning salt-and-pepper hair, and hands bound to the back of the chair he was lying on, a single bullet hole on the side of the forehead.

"He was dead before we got here," Silver said. "There's nothing we can do."

"Koyuki's going to kill us," I said. "We need to get that recipe before we meet with her."

"I haven't checked the other guy yet." She pointed at the man with a bloodied chest against the back wall of the room. "Lousy shot. Got lucky he managed to hit me."

I gave her the kid's Recaller and walked through the mess. After searching the dead man's pockets, all I found was a wallet, some spare change, and several weathered receipts. I shook my head back at Silver.

Crunching and steps grabbed our attention, and I was back on my feet and next to Silver in the next moment, handgun in hand as I moved back to the kitchen.

"Kax?" I said as I saw the familiar mask-covered face with sunglasses and a nailed baseball bat strapped to the backpack. "What are you doing here?"

He was looking around before he turned to look at me. "I was visiting an ex-girlfriend and heard your voices. Decided to pop in to say hello."

I could feel Silver's gaze on the back of my neck, but I willed myself to ignore her. It was almost scary to have a sort of sixth sense to know what she was thinking, so I just decided to say it. "And you're saying it nonchalantly? You never even told me you had a girlfriend!"

He shrugged. "It has been a slow day for me. And I never thought it would be important. I wanted to get the last of the things I left behind when I moved out, but she sold them. So I hacked into her bank account and stole all her money. What are you both doing here? Oh, you got shot."

"You're no longer a Wraith," I said, "but you still hack people for petty reasons."

He shrugged.

"We were looking for a recipe Koyuki asked us to get for some ACCENT," I said. "We thought the kid behind us had it, but we got nothing."

Kax turned around in place, looking at the destroyed apartment. The cupboards hung open in the kitchen, broken glass and ceramics were scattered, the dining table was turned over and wooden chairs had been snapped in half. The couch was pushed to the middle of the room and was now covered in Silver's blood. Portraits and paintings were on the floor and the broken television was hanging from the wall by a lone wire, the image flickering with garbled audio.

Moments passed in silence, the only noise was his footsteps, careful where they fell, as he moved around before he stopped near the kitchen. His eyes scanned the surfaces before he stopped and moved several broken plates and glasses and pulled out a flash drive that matched the colors of the broken ceramic, white in color.

"How did you find it so easily?"

Kax shrugged. "I used to be a Wraith. I pocketed loose drives and other small storage devices all the time. Got used to noticing them, I suppose."

I took the drive and put it in Silver's backpack. "We won't know if this is what Koyuki wants until we check its contents, but thanks for the help. At least it is a start," Silver said.

Kax shrugged. "And what are you going to do with him? You should kill him. Do you want me to do it for you?"

"Are you insane?" I half-yelled. "We're not going to kill a teen who's unarmed and restrained! What's wrong with you?"

"What makes you think he won't try to kill you as soon as you let him go?" Kax said, raising his voice. "Follow you home, bring friends, and try to kill you. People like him should not be let go. They should not be trusted."

Killing anyone who was unarmed and restrained was a serious offense within the Black Snipers, much less a teen. Things did happen, where some had to be killed, removed from the world, as they would be more dangerous if left unchecked. But Kax's suggestion made my stomach twist within itself in disgust.

"We're not killing him." I grabbed Silver's knife, which was strapped to her thigh, and cut the towels.

"Can I have my Recaller back?" the kid said.

"No. Now, leave."

He stopped next to Kax, looking at him once, before glancing back at us and running out the door. I gave the knife back to Silver as I kept a glare set on Kax.

"I can't believe you. Let's go. We need to get you checked by the Specters."

Silver and I pushed past him, locking eyes, if you could call it that with sunglasses, briefly, before we closed the door behind us. We retraced our steps through the fire escape and back to the street, where we hailed a cab. I'd come back for her motorcycle later.

▲ ▲ ▲

After ten minutes of stitches, during which Silver *tried* to refuse medicine, we arrived back at the apartment by morning. Our clothes were stiff and uncomfortable from long-dried sweat. Silver's injury almost fully healed, thanks to the expert aid of the Specter's medical care, as well as some bio gel they used to hasten the healing process.

After we put our gear away, we rested in the living room. My mind was still reeling from the scolding Silver had given me back at the hospital for not practicing my photography. I willed myself to stand, the mid-morning sun now flooding the room as I went over to the computer to deal with the drive Kax found. *Let's hope this contains what Koyuki wants from that man.*

"Are you doing that now?" Silver croaked from the couch. "You haven't picked up your camera in almost four months."

I didn't reply. I wasn't feeling in the mood, and part of me just wanted to rest my face on my hand and allow my body to drift into sleep. Plus, we needed to get paid for the completion of the job. Koyuki's rewards were enough to set someone up for about six months.

I also knew I had to keep practicing my photography, and my gaze slowly drifted over to the camera next to the monitor, a thick layer of dust over it. The guilt of not practicing my shots every day like Silver made sure to do with her cello wrapped around my throat.

Most Black Snipers practiced some kind of artistic form, whether it was playing instruments, drawing, or other forms of expression like tagging walls with graffiti, sculptures, or clay shapers. You name it, you'd find it. Being an artist in the City of Laohz meant you had a hard road ahead of you. Museums and galleries were very cutthroat when it came to accepting new pieces, and orchestras and bands had rigorous entrance exams to be accepted. With only two orchestras in the whole City, the pressure was on.

Being an artist granted Black Snipers the added boon of patience, which was honed during training, but I was going to have to use my patience now and stay focused on the task at hand.

After connecting the drive to the computer, and allowing it to load, I found that it only contained a single file, compressed, and was protected by a password, which made me hit my forehead against the desk, letting out a groan. "This day can't possibly get any *fucking* worse."

"We could be out of toilet paper!" Silver called from the restroom.

I closed my eyes and exhaled heavily. "Please tell me you're joking!"

The light sound of cardboard hitting the floor was enough of a reply to tell me she was not, and all I could do was hit the desk again lightly with my forehead. "I really wanted to take a shower, get paid, and go to sleep for a few hours. Opening a file shouldn't be difficult."

"What's wrong?" Silver said over my shoulder.

"The file is locked behind a password." I turned to look at her, hair tied up in a ponytail. "I'm good at planting emp devices and breaking into buildings, but I don't know how to crack passwords on computers."

"Huh."

"That's all you have to say?"

"We never made a new Wraith contact after that incident with Liz, did we?"

I shook my head.

"Huh."

"I could use something better than a simple 'huh' at this time."

"Ask Liz for help," she said flatly.

I lowered my head, hitting the desk loudly for a third time. I dreaded having to deal with Liz again after she had put my life in jeopardy in exchange for more information for the Wraiths. After the mission, when we were sure we were safe, we got into an argument that turned physical, with her cutting my left arm with her knife, and me shooting her right ear. We haven't been on speaking terms for almost a year now, and every time she crossed my mind, my blood boiled.

"I still have the scar." I brushed it lightly.

"We don't have time to search for a new Wraith contact," Silver pointed out.

I groaned, mainly because she was right, and because, whether I wanted to admit it to her face or not, it was my responsibility to make a new contact, and I had procrastinated. And now, we were dead in the water with this drive, and Koyuki was not someone you wanted to get on the bad side of.

"Do you have any more bad news you want to break to me?"

"Your motorcycle is due for an oil change soon," she said as she walked away.

I hit my head on the desk a fourth time. "Fuck me!"

"In your dreams!"

"I wasn't talking to you!"

▲ ▲ ▲

After we returned for Silver's motorcycle, we headed over to where Liz usually operated and lived, a tattoo parlor. The trip took about an hour of driving through the City of Laohz's streets.

It was nighttime by the time we arrived, with the constant echoing of Rain Enforcer Patrol Ship's engines all above us, some only visible through the blanket of clouds that covered the city by the flashing lights.

Yellow neon letters made up the sign that read 'Zophra,' tucked away in what was regarded as a nice part of the city. The clean sidewalks and expensive cars that passed by didn't do anything to ease the tension that was building inside me as Silver and I walked to the door of the tattoo parlor.

We entered a small lobby, with a seating area set up against the walls; a small reception area was being tended by one of the artists, his skin covered in tattoos wherever you could see it. The black walls were covered in tattoo drawings and paintings, with some merchandise on one corner behind the counter. The counter was littered with several binders containing a wide array of tattoos the clientele could choose from, and rock music played from the sound system.

The man behind the desk looked at us both once, then made a motion with his head to go inside through the black curtains that separated the lobby from the rest of the establishment.

Silver and I kept quiet as we passed the curtained-off rooms of the other artists who worked there, closed with frosted-like plastic curtains for privacy, with none paying us any mind as we both headed for the one furthest in the back. The scent of disinfectant and faint paint lingered in the air with a strange mixture of takeout.

The curtain was open when we reached it. Inside, a woman with black hair, and red underneath the top layer, worked on a client. Her arms were covered in various tattoos, from her neck up to her wrists, which were mostly motifs of various brightly colored flowers with skulls, snakes, and tarantulas. Her left ear was pierced all along the edge, while her right one had several piercings as well, up till they met the gunshot wound I had given her during our fight.

We stood there, at the edge of the entrance to her small world, while my gaze rested on the bulky man, whose shaved head was being worked on, his attention on a magazine in his hands. "You got someone here," the man said without looking up at me. She glanced up, her bright red modded eyes resting on me briefly before she went back to her work.

"Oh, Kannon," Liz said, her voice flat. "What brings you here? Last time we worked together, you said you didn't want to know anything else about me. And you brought Silver with you this time." She wiped away some of the ink.

"Yeah, well," I said, "circumstances change."

"Oh. Is that so?" She wiped off more blood before she kept working. "So what is this *stuff*? And why should I even help *you* after the piercing you gave me?"

"By the Oath." I pulled out the drive from my pocket. "We need to have access to the only file inside this drive, and it is protected by a password. *I* don't have the tools to break into it, nor the expertise, and we also don't have anyone else to go to, to get this done."

"So you want me to break into it for you," she said. "Is that it?"

Silver and I nodded.

"And what's in it for me? I'm not doing this for free."

At that moment, I started to hate myself. I hadn't thought that she would even agree to talk to us, so my planning on this particular scenario was not set this far ahead. "It can be discussed."

Liz sighed, then kept quiet, working on the man's tattoo before she stopped and told the client to take some time to rest. She pulled her gloves off and straightened her black shirt before she motioned me to follow her. "Come. This way."

She placed her work tools down and passed me, going for a door that read 'Office,' beyond which was a flight of stairs that led upwards. As I reached the landing, the room opened to a dining room, with a kitchen farther back, and a balcony that looked out to the street.

"So," Silver began, "you live above your shop?"

Liz ignored the comment, opting to keep moving through the apartment until she reached a room and turned the light on. After the computer was powered on, she sat down and extended her hand for the drive, which I gave to her. After it was connected, she opened several programs after opening the drive itself. Once she had set up everything she needed, she made the software run, feeding passwords onto the file.

"There. I don't know how long it will take for the file to be opened, but these things take a lot of—" Liz was cut off as a bell came from her computer, and she began to mutter under her breath as she clicked on the file. "Woah!"

As the interface loaded, hundreds of files began to show on the screen, all, for what the icons indicated, protected by another password.

"I did not expect this," I said, my eyes widening.

Liz let go of a resigned sigh. "By the Oath Kannon. Of course you didn't. Look at all this! City plans, railroad lines, flight plans, maps for the subways. From what I can see, the names for some of these folders seem to imply that whoever was the owner of this drive, they had bigger plans in mind. What did you want from this? I will call you a liar if this is what you were looking for."

I shook my head and leaned in, grabbing the mouse and scrolling down. "Koyuki sent us to this man's location to find the recipe for a different kind of ACCENT he had concocted."

"We didn't find any computers in the apartment," Silver added, "so we took this hoping the recipe would be inside."

"Here it is," I said, pointing at one of the files, "and it's unlocked too."

"Last modified two days ago," Liz said, pushing me aside. "If this is all you want, I can send it to your Recaller, and I'll take the rest of the information here as a payment for making me waste time helping you."

I looked at Silver, and she shrugged and gave me a half-nod. "We got what we needed. Let her have the rest."

"Good. Because I wasn't asking, nor putting it up for debate. And, since you're dragging me back to whatever mess you tend

to get yourself into, consider this a reinstatement of our partnership, not that I want to, but knowing you, you'll go and *drag* me
along anyway." She stood up. "Now, go. I need to finish a tattoo,
and neither of you are going to pay my bills!" She began to shoo
us out, almost pushing us down the stairs. "Go and take some
pictures or whatever it is you do in your free time. You'll get the
file when I have time today." She closed the door to her business
behind her as she muttered under her breath.

"I was expecting this to go way differently," I said as I fixed
my backpack. "I never thought she'd agree."

"She's insufferable, but she gets the job done," Silver said.
"Here's hoping she holds her end this time."

I could tell that Silver was annoyed, not much in her voice,
but the way she seemed to be stiff as she waited for me to say
something. That, and the evident, yet subtle way she had her eyebrows furrowed as she seemed to be holding herself back from
pacing.

When we were paired to work together, she took almost a
protector role over me, while I ended up shoring up the niche
things she was not good with, like hacking into electronic doors
and lockpicking. In the end, she became the shield I needed to
keep myself alive, and I became the key she needed to do infiltra-
tion jobs. But there was only so much she could do when it came
to dealing with people, and how we, or mostly I, handled our
contact network.

I couldn't blame her, though. The prospect of having to deal
with Liz on a regular basis all over again was a risk I didn't want to
take. Part of me dreaded having another confrontation with her,
as she was capable of killing me for the slightest bit of information

that she could get her hands on. We just had to see how trust-worthy she would be, and I hated having an unknown so close to home.

▲ ▲ ▲

It was late morning when we arrived at Koyuki Akikawa's man-sion. After exchanging pleasantries with Mr. Fukuzawa, we fol-lowed him through the house, passing some of the maids who tended the estate, as well as guards and locked doors until he led us to a large room, bare, with the exception of a small wooden table set in the middle of it. The floor was made of tatami mats, while the doors on one side of the room opened to a Zen garden she had beyond.

"Miss Kannon and Miss Silver," he announced.

Koyuki poured herself a cup of tea and nodded. "You may leave us."

He bowed once and left, closing the doors behind him, allowing silence to replace his presence.

Koyuki kept quiet for a moment, her mind focused on pre-paring her tea, and with every minute that passed, I could feel the atmosphere grow increasingly uncomfortable. Eventually, I began to think that we had done something wrong, that we had displeased her.

After she finished mixing the sugar into her tea, she raised her amber-colored gaze and gestured to us to sit across from her on a pair of cushions.

"Miss Kannon," she said, "I believe you have something I requested?"

I nodded and sent the ACCENT recipe's information to her Recaller. She smiled briefly, then her expression disappeared.

"Did you find anything else useful?" she said.

"No," Silver said. "The man was dead when we got there. Someone had been there before us."

"I see."

"Is there anything else you need from us?" I asked.

She took a sip from her tea. "I will be bringing this information to some of my trusted generals soon. So I will have some jobs for you in the future. Now, I believe you have been in several altercations with a group that has been going by the name of Lolitrons?"

Silver and I nodded in unison before I replied. "We found them first after our job against the cargo ship, then again in Lawrence's apartment."

"Keep an eye on them. We don't need our timetable to be accelerated by outside actors. You'll be paid in an hour. You're both free to go."

We both stood and bowed before we turned and left. Meetings with her tended to be affairs that took little time, but she was, for better or worse, someone who liked to meet in person for important matters. Probably to size people up as they spoke with her. Read their body language and react accordingly.

Silver and I closed the door behind us and moved through the house, looking at the design of the traditional Japanese structure and taking a bit longer to leave than it took us to reach Koyuki when coming in. We both stopped at the small garden in the middle of the house, with the tree sitting there and providing some shade for the space.

"What do you think Liz will do with the information?" Silver said as she leaned on the railing.

"I don't know. She'll probably sell it, or try to keep it for blackmail? Pass it on? But I am worried about why the Lolitrons were after Lawrence Hudson. Why were they attacking the Rain Enforcers that night? It doesn't make sense to me."

Silver nodded, some of her hair falling into her face. She pushed the strand back. "Should we go back and tell Koyuki about it?"

I shook my head. "I don't know what we would be stumbling into. We don't even know what kind of information he had inside his drive. It could be anything."

Silver looked at her Recaller. "Let's go. I have a job, it seems."

"Let's hope it is easier than that last job you got two months ago."

"At least *I* get paid when I do a job. Unlike your mysterious client who hasn't paid us yet." She fixed her backpack as she began to leave.

"You've been bothering me about that for the last week. I get it. I messed up."

She snickered. "I find it fun to tease you. Now come on, we should set up this meeting. I *don't* want to miss this paycheck."

"We'll see how fun it is once you fall asleep tonight," I muttered under my breath as the gears in my mind concocted a prank.

"Damn," Silver said.

"What?"

"It's from one of our regulars. One of Koyuki Akikawa's informants."

I turned to her, and I could see the worry I was carrying reflected in her gaze. With the current, volatile situation across the City with the Rain Enforcers, meeting with them felt like a bad idea, but I kept quiet and followed Silver this time, hoping they were unaware of our involvement in the destruction of their cargo ship.

CHAPTER 3

A WEEK HAD PASSED since our meeting with Koyuki and our last encounter with the Lolitrons.

A week since Silver took the job from the informant, on which we were still working. Two weeks had passed since the job I took against the Rain Enforcer's cargo ship, and we still had nothing to show for it, as the payment hadn't gone through to us. Silver never said it, but I could tell that she was increasingly annoyed at me for that. We had shaken a hornet's nest, and since then, the patrols across the city had increased almost by half of what they used to be. And we hadn't ever received a payment for it.

We had set up in a small apartment building composed of two towers connected by bridges at various floors. The one we were monitoring was set next to one, ours in one tower and the other in the one across.

"It's been five days," I said, fiddling with the safety lock on my unloaded handgun. "Do you think someone will come?"

Silver shrugged as she looked back at me from the balcony.

"Unsure. Usually I'm fine with jobs like this, but this one feels odd."

I reloaded the gun and joined her, grabbing my binoculars before stepping outside to the mildly cold night air. Through the floor-to-ceiling windows, I could barely make out the layout of the living room. There was a couch set up against a wall that made the center of the apartment and a TV on the opposing side. A kitchen sat near the back, against the wall toward the general hallway, and there was a kitchen island. The darkness wouldn't allow us to see anything other than that.

Sirens began to echo in the distance. A few patrol ships passed through the towers, in between some of the bridges, their sirens echoing, amplified by the buildings. Moments later, more patrol ships followed, and, as we turned to see, we realized it was another convoy of Rain Enforcer ships. This one was patrolled by Lancers, a type of ship which was smaller than a space Corvette, being about 180 meters long, and able to be crewed by 50 people. The convoy was protected by four of them.

"They're not joking this time," I found myself saying.

"I hope whatever your client wanted to accomplish was worth it," Silver said before storming inside.

"Why are you still so mad at me? It's been two weeks!"

"Yeah!" she said. "Two weeks we haven't been paid, Kannon! You didn't even *ask* for our initial payment!"

"Is that why you're mad at me?"

"By the Oath, Katherine, no!" she yelled. "I'm mad at *you* because now we have the Rain Enforcers riled up, and we have no *fucking* clue as to what was in that cargo ship, or why your bloody client wanted it destroyed in the first place!"

I threw the binoculars, which crashed into a dresser and then fell to the floor. "And what about *your* client? The one who sent us to this job? All we got was that we had to watch that apartment, and then call back when someone visited!"

"At least we got *paid!*"

"So the payment is the reason why you're mad at me, then?"

Silver's teal gaze locked with mine, eyebrows furrowed, fists balled to her side, then she walked back to the balcony.

"Now you're walking away?"

"There's someone in the apartment across," she said, retrieving the binoculars. "They're turning on the lights."

I followed her, pushing through the seething anger I was trying to hold back, grabbed my rifle and looked through its scope, joining her at the balcony. There was a person inside the apartment, but they disappeared as they went into the rooms.

"What are you waiting for?" Silver said. "Grab your things. I'm not missing this. Make sure you call the client." She tossed me her Recaller as I followed her, grabbing my things before I dialed the number.

As Silver ran across the bridge, we were still seeing the ships of the Rain Enforcers fly below us. *I don't like the results of that job either, Silver.* I called the number from the client, and it only rang once before it was sent to voicemail. I dialed again, but no answer.

"I can't get a hold of them," I said as I caught up to Silver by the apartment door.

"By the Oath!" She grabbed her Recaller. "If they won't answer, then I will find out myself." She shot the lock of the door with her shotgun and stormed inside. I followed close behind as she went straight for the rooms and surprised a man inside one of them who was searching through the cabinets.

"Stop, and don't make any sudden moves," Silver said, pointing her shotgun at the man.

He stopped in place, turned around, and raised his hands. His eyes met ours as a smile formed on his lips. "I would put down your weapons. You're surrounded."

I turned around, and at the door there were ten Rain Enforcers clad in their standard black riot armor, with rifles pointed at us. Scenario after scenario began to run through my mind as to how we could escape that situation. I had to come to terms with the fact that we were outnumbered, outgunned, and outmatched. Most likely they had some of the Patrol Ships hovering just outside the windows, weapons ready. I put my gun down and raised my hands.

From the edge of my gaze, I could see Silver's furrowed eyebrows, eyes moving from side to side, probably trying to find a way out. She turned to me and exhaled, relaxing her shoulders and putting her shotgun down.

In mere moments, we were both in cuffs and stripped of our weapons, which counted for two sniper rifles, an assault rifle, two handguns, a hand taser, a shotgun, and two combat knives.

As we were escorted through the apartment, the flashing lights of the patrol ships were almost blinding as they hovered just beyond the windows. It was an unceremonious march through the building, down the hallway, as people came out of their apartments to watch as the Rain Enforcers escorted a pair of Black Snipers down to their patrol vans. I felt nothing but shame and self-loathing, as all I saw around me were men and women clad in black as we walked into the elevator. Silver stood next to me, gaze locked ahead, her breathing heavy, even though I could tell that she was trying to control it by closing her eyes for a few moments.

We didn't see this coming, and all I wanted was to find out how we managed to miss it. We also found it strange that they would have the gall to arrest us. Our agreement with them was a complex one, but it allowed us unrestricted movement through the city without interference from the Rain Enforcers. But it all kept coming back in my mind to my job against their convoy, and I kept regretting taking that job.

The lobby of the apartment building was filled with more Rain Enforcers, all looking at us as we walked past them escorted by others of their kind. Part of me hoped, as we marched toward the transport vehicle waiting outside, that Koyuki would pull strings and get us out of this, though I didn't know how long that would end up taking. All I knew for certain was, there was no way Koyuki wouldn't know of our current predicament. Whether it was a matter of minutes, or hours. Nothing happened in the city without her becoming aware of it.

As the Rain Enforcers moved us through the street, I tripped, landing onto one of the cops escorting us before falling to the floor. The guard hastily pulled me up by the arm and pushed me forward. *I can't believe that worked!*

The reality of our situation really sank in for me, and possibly harder for Silver, when we both climbed into the van and the doors closed behind us after our handcuffs were tied to a metal rod that ran the length of the seating area.

"I can't believe the contact set us up," Silver said as soon as the truck departed. "How could I have been so blind?"

No words came to mind. I didn't know what to say. I was supposed to watch her back as much as she was supposed to watch mine. Neither of us saw it coming, but the guilt didn't lie in getting caught, it was in being blind to its approach and not being smarter about it. We were so caught up in the job, we didn't see the betrayal.

"I'm sorry I was so mad at you about the job," she said, gaze low, locked with the floor as she leaned forward, digging her fingers through her hair. "It wasn't as much about getting paid or not, or the fact that we riled up the Rain Enforcers. I was mostly mad that you never consulted with me about this job. But I also should've trusted your instincts."

"It's fine, just—" I was cut short by the sudden jolt that rocked the patrol van, along with the shots that pierced the steel walls. "I don't like this!"

"You think?"

The unmistakable sound of a machine gun being fired and the sirens being turned on all around us didn't foster good feelings that we would be able to leave in one piece. Several more shots passed through the van, with the sound of an engine exploding above us, and my mind quickly concocted an image of a Rain Enforcer Patrol Ship engulfed in flames crashing on us.

"Silver, take my boot off!"

"I don't think this is a good time to ask me to give you a pedicure, Kannon!"

"By the Oath, Silver, just take my boot off!"

She shook her head as she untied it and pulled it off, a pair of keys falling to the floor at her feet, which I grabbed with my toes before they slid out of reach.

"You had *keys* this whole time?"

"Do you want to argue about this now, or do you want to survive this mess?"

"Why do you have these?"

"I like a bit of role play. Happy? I stole them."

She didn't say another word and grabbed the keys and undid her handcuffs, then mine, but another jolt made us fly against one of the walls. I tasted blood but had no time to assess my injury as another jolt made the patrol van lose control and begin to roll over to one side. Silver and I hit the wall hard, as all we heard was the metallic screeching over pavement as Sirens wailed all above us. *I don't want to die in this fucking metal coffin!*

"Dammit, Kannon, now what?"

Shots echoed all around us as voices yelled over the cacophony of gunfire and crunching metal as cars seemed to be crashing around us. A pair of steps moved above us, while several other gunshots rang out.

"I don't know, Silver!" All I could think of was that we were trapped, and that despite my stashed handcuff keys, we still had no way to leave the patrol van since there was no handle on the inside.

The creaking of the door being pulled stopped us as we both stared at it, and it fell to the ground. Beyond all we could see was a single individual with a painted gas mask, but before they could speak, he was gunned down, dropping his weapon. A pair of yellow pickup trucks passed behind the truck, both outfitted with turrets in the bed, firing upwards.

Everything else was a blur. The feeling of shooting a gun was familiar, as we ran through the chaos engulfing the avenue, with several crashed patrol ships on the ground while the light of the fires reflected off the glass of the buildings nearby. I could feel shots flying past me while Rain Enforcers engaged whoever was waging war against them.

We both managed to slip past it all and delve deep into the alleyways making the large blocks of the city. Another Rain Enforcer appeared as we moved through, and the rifle in my hands clicked empty. Moments later, Silver had it in her hands and swung it against the enforcer's head, grabbing his rifle and handgun before tying him to a nearby pipe with his own handcuffs.

It was hard to say how long we were running, or where we were. Sirens echoed through the canyons of steel, and the engines of the passing patrol ships pierced through the narrow space with ear-splitting volume, but all my mind could think of was "*run*," so I did.

Eventually, we ducked inside an abandoned restaurant, probably ten blocks away from where we had crashed and been freed. The dust that lingered inside made my nose clog up. I couldn't contain my sneezes as we both went to the farthest end of it and hid near the dilapidated kitchen. My throat was dry and sweat poured down my face from all the running. Without our Recallers, we were disconnected and unable to reach for help, and the guns from the enforcer didn't have enough ammunition to help us through whatever combat we were dragged into.

"How many rounds do you have?" Silver said as she sat across from me, looking at the magazine from the handgun.

"Almost a full magazine," I said. "You?"

She shook her head. "Only half. I don't like this. What in the world is going on?"

I shook my head. "I don't know. I wish I knew." I sneezed. "And this place is not helping my allergies. We need to get back to the apartment and find out what's going on."

Silver nodded, still breathing hard as she tried to catch her breath. I looked around. The room was bare except for the stainless-steel counters and the wire tubing sticking out of the walls. From where we were, we could see the old, dust-covered booth-tables through the half-open door, attention set on the front door.

The lights began to flicker on and off inside the building, almost as if electricity was trying to return to the old structure, then an orange ball of light appeared in the middle of the dining area, clearly visible through the door. Silver and I stared as the electricity kept coming in and out, until several lightbulbs exploded, raining shards of glass all over the floor. I could feel my heart begging to race again and fear creeping up inside me like a slithering snake as my eyes were locked with whatever the orb was.

"K-K-Kannon," a feminine synthetic voice said from where the orange ball was. As we both got closer, the orange ball transformed into the silhouette of . . . someone.

Weapons ready, we both joined the woman-sounding thing in the dining room, and all we could do was stop. Its face was covered with a mask, and it had thruster-like wings, with what seemed to be three per 'wing.' Then, its mask turned on, resembling a fox, the shape shown through varying triangles that glowed a soft neon orange.

"What do you want?" Silver said. "Who are you? *What are you?*"

It turned to her and tilted its head slightly. "Gre-eting-g-gs. Designation: ST-11A. Stella will be fine."

"How do you know my name?" I said.

Stella turned to me. Her mask flickered for a moment, and then she moved her arms slightly, making her silk-like dress flow in a seemingly ethereal way, as if she were underwater. Her feet were hidden behind her dress, which reinforced the sense that no limb touched the ground. Her black-gloved hands conjured a pair of Recallers from somewhere we couldn't see, then she said in a deep, guttural voice, "I owe you a payment."

"You're the client?"

The lights on her mask flickered once, then she nodded.

"Why did you want us to destroy that convoy cargo ship?" Silver interjected. "Do you realize the mess it has turned to after that happened with the Rain Enforcers?"

"That information is restricted-d-d-d," Stella said, reverting her voice back to the one she greeted us with.

"What do you want? Aside from owing us a payment, and an explanation, why are you showing yourself to us now?"

"Meeting with you was to be determined when you had earned the right. Your sudden capture was an unforeseen event that had to be rectified. The anticipation-on-on of the discovery of your involvement was not foreseen. Against my projections, we had to tip the Lolitrons with false information in order to expedite your release from Rain Enforcer custody-y-y. Your names have been cleared from the Rain Enforcer wanted directory-y-y . . . for now."

"Why?"

Stella's mask flickered for a moment. "The information you gathered from Lawrence Hudson revealed that it's conte-te-te-teeeeeee." The lights on her mask turned off, and she hovered there for a moment before they turned back on again. "Systems nominal. Diagnostics: comple-e-te. Running systems checkup. Check."

Silver and I looked at each other, a bit of dread dripping inside as I realized we had no idea what Stella was.

"Lawrence Hudson had substantial, but incomplete information inside the drive you relinquished to Wraith Liz. Information that has pro-o-o-o-o-oved to be vital and needed. The information found within was deemed to be incomplete, and no other technological device was found at his abode. Conclusion: Missing information theorized to be contained within another device."

"You haven't paid us yet. Why should we even take this job for you? And Kannon and I knew that already!"

Stella offered the Recallers again. "Involvement with the rogue group known as Lolitrons. Further information needed. Conclusion: Lolitrons after the same information. Reason: unknown."

"Pay us first!" Silver aimed her handgun.

The lights on Stella's mask flashed again, and the screens of the Recallers turned on with a notification with the payment on each, while also showing us the Recallers were actually ours. "Initial payment added to the total of payment dispen-n-n-n-nsed."

I lowered the rifle and grabbed the Recallers. "How did you manage to get them?"

The mask flickered.

"What about our backpacks? Rifles? My shotgun?"

"Job priorities: Sto-o-o-op Lolitrons at any cost. We will be in contact." Lights all around us began to flicker on and off again. "Gear located at your apartment." The brightness of all the lights inside the old store blinded us before we heard all the bulbs shatter. When we opened our eyes, Stella was gone, leaving us behind with all the old dust and shattered glass that now covered our clothes and hair.

"Katherine, I really don't like this."

I put my Recaller away. "Let's give Liz another visit. Make sure ST-11A is actually telling us the truth."

CHAPTER 4

SILVER AND I ARRIVED at Zophra, Liz's tattoo parlor, a few hours later. We were both tired, our feet ached, and we were bruised all over. It was empty when we arrived.

The space smelled of disinfectant and air freshener. The booths of the other artists were empty, and the lights were turned off, all except for Liz's workstation. She was cleaning some of her utensils and putting things away in plastic totes and drawers, wrapped up in her own world before she turned and caught sight of us, after which her face shifted into a scowl. Her eyes took us in from head to toe, looking at our tattered clothes and dirt-covered skin.

"By the fucking Oath!" Liz said. "I'm regretting renewing my partnership with you." She threw her cloth down on the table next to her, making some of the instruments clatter as she crossed her arms, her red eyes glaring at us both. "I fucking knew you would be dragging me into whatever mess you got yourself into this time, Kannon."

"We met Stella," I said, and Liz's expression changed.

"Fuck," she muttered.

"Who is she?"

She turned her gaze away, rubbing her forehead. "She's one of the Wraiths. Let's leave it at that."

"We need to know more," Silver said, "if we are going to be dealing with her—"

"No, you don't!" Liz cut her off. "Drop the topic!"

"Stella told us you gave her information that was left encrypted in the drive we gave you."

Liz looked away, crossing her arms as she bit her lower lip. She was hiding something, and I knew that if I pushed too much, she would snap at us, so I had to be careful how much I pressed her buttons.

"Can we trust her?" Silver added.

Liz turned back to us, took a deep breath, and nodded briefly. "As long as you do what she asks. She is not someone you want on your bad side." She kept putting things away. "Now, I bet you want me to just *give* you all the beans that that little drive spilled onto my computer like a good little Wraith, right?"

I looked at Silver, who stared at Liz, but she just kept her leer mixed in with a light frown at us both.

"I'm not working the same way we used to work any more, Kannon." She grabbed a bundle of markers and put them in a drawer, before slamming it shut. "From now on, if you want information from me, *you* will have to pay me. I'm not doing any more fieldwork for you." She pointed at the gunshot she had in her right ear.

"You're bringing that back up again? You're the one who almost got us *both* killed back then!"

Liz shrugged. "So? At least the information I got was used against the Rain Enforcers during one of your missions. Now, are you going to pay my fee, or are you going to keep whining about ailments of the past?"

All I wanted to do at that moment was shoot her in the head, but as much of a nuisance as she was, I had to remember that it was my fault we were stuck with Liz all over again. If I hadn't procrastinated in looking for another Wraith contact, we wouldn't be in this situation.

"What's the payment?" Silver interjected.

"I want to hear Kannon say it," Liz said.

"Stop being such a bitch and get on with it already!" Silver said. "We've had a long day, we lost a payment, almost got put in jail, almost got *killed*, and I, at this point in the day, am tired of dealing with difficult people. Stop playing and get right to the bloody point!"

Liz sighed and put the last of her work tools away before she turned her attention back to us. "There is someone who owes me a few storage drives' worth of information. Get them for me, and I'll help. You need information I have, and I need something in return. You can choose to help me or not. In the end, the end goal is inconsequential to me. I'll get my storage drives one way or another, but you, on the other hand, need information that you can't get through any other means. So you have two options. You either pay my fee, or you go home. I'm not running charity work for you anymore, Kannon."

I wanted to strangle her, but Liz had a point. Wraiths operated in a very business-like model, with Black Snipers always paying something in return for the aid of the Wraiths. My partnership with Liz before our falling out started in a very similar fashion, but most partnerships that last longer than a year turn into long-term arrangements, with both parties cooperating without asking for anything back, something that was drilled into everyone—Wraith, Specter, and Black Sniper—as part of the Oath. With Liz being a vindictive woman at times, though, I wouldn't've put it past her to ask me to do ridiculous "fees" just to make herself feel special.

"No," I said. "You want to hate me? Fine. Go ahead, but you decided to renew our partnership, and that means the agreement to help without charging me we had before goes back into effect."

"I fucking knew you would be calling on the Oath. Tsk." She turned her gaze away. "You want our arrangement to work like it used to? Fine, but you will have to deal with me from now on. Got it?"

I nodded, and Silver took a deep breath as she crossed her arms.

Liz shook her head and rubbed the bridge of her nose as she took deep breaths. "Look, I don't have the contents of the whole drive unlocked yet. Whatever Stella found inside after I made her a copy, she didn't share with me. All I've unlocked so far is one of the files that has a lot of schematics for one of their smaller military bases in the southern part of the City. I don't know what's there, or why the Lolitrons would be interested in this information. Besides, I don't think the information in this drive is even important."

I nodded. "Stella wanted us to stop the Lolitrons. Whatever the reason was for them to pay a visit to Lawrence Hudson, it must have been enough for them to kill him."

Liz sighed. "I hate to agree with you. Lawrence Hudson was

a prominent member of the Rain Enforcers, but not enough to have any clout over the corporation. Just a low-level employee. Talking with the Rain Enforcers would be the only way to figure out what he was involved in that would incite the Lolitrons to kill him."

"The Rain Enforcers are not going to be happy to see us after we broke free of our arrest last night." Silver shifted her weight.

I nodded. The Rain Enforcers were notorious for not giving up on a search easily, and they sometimes combed the whole city for months in search of a single individual they were hellbent on capturing. "We should lie low for a while, keep our ears to the ground, and look for clues."

Liz nodded. "I'll keep an eye on the news and my contact network. Now, if you're going to plan, go home. I don't want you both here. Your presence has been enough for the last few days. Koyuki controls your Block Host, doesn't she?"

"Liz . . ."

She kept quiet, opting to just leer at us with her red gaze. "Leave!"

I locked eyes with her and held it for about a minute before Silver nudged me toward the door. I left, feeling the heat of anger boiling around my head as I kept repeating the scene again in my mind.

"Thanks for getting us out of that errand of hers," Silver said as she closed the door. "You were always a quick study of rules."

"I want to hit her," I said through gritted teeth.

"Yeah, yeah." She walked ahead. "Can we go home now? I'm tired."

I took a deep breath as I secretly agreed with her. My body

was starting to ache everywhere, and the heaviness of my eyelids was starting to get the better of me. I kept walking, my mind going blank as I tried to catch a cab for us both. "I'm not looking forward to trying to get our bikes back."

Silver nodded. "They will have the perimeter locked for almost a week before we can go back and get them."

Whenever the Rain Enforcers locked down an area, no one was allowed to enter or leave. All homes were searched, people arrested, executed criminals found afterwards. All in all, they left the area scarred, just like what happened during Cleansing Day. Many homes were broken into by the enforcers, thousands were arrested, many executed in the streets, and shots echoed through the City of Laohz at all hours. It took several months for the conflict to reach an end, mainly due to the news reaching Othara, the nearby planet in the same solar system as Rhode.

A yellow car stopped before us, and Silver opened the door for me. The well-worn seats and cracked windshield were the highlight as we stepped in. The carpet was littered with candy wrappers and dirt, while the radio station played in the background, beyond the smudged divider window.

"Where to?" the taxi driver said.

"Houther Block Host," Silver told him as I took her backpack.

"I can't wait to get home and shower," Silver added, pulling bits of glass from her hair.

"I want to sleep."

"Are you all right?" she asked, her gaze lingering on me in concern.

I nodded. "I don't know what to expect from the Lolitrons,

and I have no clue what their motivation might be."

Silver pulled out her rifle. "From what I can see, they're terrorists."

"It would be easier to predict them if it were so simple." I sighed. "Silver, all the members we've encountered so far are kids. All of them in their teens!"

Silver stopped inspecting her weapon and turned to look at me, her teal gaze locked with mine before she relaxed. "How old were you when you joined?"

"Why are you asking me this?"

She held her question with silence.

"Nineteen."

"And when did you make your First Kill?"

"A year later. When I was twenty."

"We've had Black Snipers join our ranks while they are in middle school, Kannon," Silver said. "It really doesn't matter if our enemy does the same."

I had forgotten about the members who joined our ranks at a much younger age, and in all honesty, it made me feel a bit biased at that point. "Dehumanize your enemies" were the words that ended up echoing in my head. Words that we heard over and over again by our trainers before we made our First Kill, the first contract we took under the tutelage of our mentor.

"Your target is not alive. It's just a moving target," was what my mentor said as I was preparing to make my first shot. You never forget that first time. The combination of emotions, sensations, the scent of gunpowder, and the force of the rifle pressing against your shoulder as you end someone else's life is almost indescribable. I was surprised when I felt nothing but excitement when I finished the contract. And now, I wondered if that was even normal. Not feeling any guilt at the act.

For the rest of the ride, Silver and I sat in silence. Tiredness and sleep got the better of us as our bodies wound down and our nerves calmed. But my mind did not, and I was wondering what I would do next. I had no idea what my next step would be, which happened rarely.

CHAPTER 5

DAWN WAS BREAKING by the time we were dropped off at the apartment, dew clinging to the grass and plants along the promenade that made the Houther Block Host. Early cooking at the nearby café and some restaurants filled the air with the faint smell of food, mixing in with the petrichor.

Silver fixed her backpack as a passing Patrol Ship disappeared between the skyline of the City, walking ahead to the stairs in silence. I followed her. Her shoulders were tense, her stride filled with that faint sense of urgency she always got when she was bottling something inside. She stopped at the top of the stairs and looked back briefly, showing the faintly furrowed eyebrows before she kept going.

Once inside the apartment, when the door was closed behind us, she let her backpack fall to the ground as she fixed her gaze on me. "Nothing's going to get solved by keeping quiet," I said as I put my backpack on the dining table.

"What are we going to do now?" she asked. "Liz didn't give us anything we could use."

"I want to take a few hours to sleep first." I rubbed my forehead as a migraine began to form.

Silver took off her bra as she walked past me. "You have that 'I think I have something' look on your face again, Katherine."

"How would you feel if I called you—"

She held up her hand. "Don't."

"As to your previous question, yes, I do think I have something. I want to talk to Koyuki. She probably has some information we can use to find the leader, if not at least some information on the Lolitrons."

She lowered her arms and rubbed her forehead. "Well, I'm tired. I want to sleep, and I want to take a hot shower. If you want to visit her tomorrow, feel free to go without me. I would like to sleep in. Take a day off." She closed the door to the restroom behind her.

Living with her had been one of the most stressful and . . . strange things to happen in my life. I liked to say that she kept me honest, that she kept me level-headed, but I knew that was not true. Silver and I needed each other, and she had become a sister to me, almost.

Most of my family lived back in Othara, the neighboring planet to Rhode, where the City of Laohz is. After I moved to engage in my studies back in high school as a transfer student, I lost contact with them. Even to this day, I wondered if it was for better or worse. My family was wealthy as owners of one of the corporations back home, and they made me feel like I didn't belong. I loved my family—my mom, dad, and my rebellious eldest sister—but the relationship wasn't the same.

Even with Kax, my cousin from my mother's side, it was

weird sometimes, as he'd always been somewhat distant, stuck in his head too often and far too blunt to have any tact with people.

His image startled me when I saw him appear in my room, his attention set to the skyline beyond the sliding glass doors. His jacket was open, while his backpack with the strapped nailed baseball bat hung somewhat loosely from his shoulders. "Good morning, Kannon."

"What are you doing here? And how did you even get in here?"

He moved his head slightly, eyes set on me through the reflection on the glass, or so it seemed. "Your door has a sub-par lock, and it was easy to break inside." He turned around. "You should consider getting an upgrade. Besides, last time I came, you yelled at me for breaking the sliding door's glass. And I also made a copy of your key."

Silence fell between us as I allowed the tiredness of my body to weigh down even more on me.

"It seems you're stuck with your current assignment."

"You were not supposed to hear that," I said as I walked over to my drawer. "Now, what do you want? Breaking into the apartment of two women makes you look like a creep."

I heard him pace around the room before I turned to see him stop and look at the degree framed on the wall.

"When was the last time you picked up your camera?"

I shook my head and guilt trickled in again. "A while." It had been four months since I last held it, and I hated myself every time I thought about it.

"It's good to take some time to enjoy oneself from time to time, Kannon," he said, then turned to me and seemed to smile, though it was hard to tell with the sunglasses and the facemask he always wore. "As to why I am here, I still have a good network of contacts that give me information. Most of the time it is useless to me, so I sell it to the Wraiths. At other times, I get nuggets of gold, and, as it turns out, I have one that may be of interest to you."

"Thank you, Kax," I said. "I have to admit that we need all the help we can get."

He hid his hands inside his pockets and walked to the door of my room. "For now, like a good jeweler, I need to verify that this information is accurate, and thus, I will keep you informed as to when I corroborate the intel."

"You can't give me the information now?"

"No. The information is not trustworthy until I have run it through my filters. In the meantime, you should focus on your health and on your rest. Darting out the door for the next clue will not be good for you in the long run, Kathy."

The memory of us playing as kids flashed briefly in my mind as he said my shortened name. It was endearing in a way. I was older than him, even though he towered above me now by a foot, and Silver was just a few inches taller than I.

"It's been a while since you called me that," I said.

He chuckled, albeit dryly, then turned to me and put his hand on my head, but he removed it almost instantly. "You were kind to me. As for the information, you will hear from me once the value of it has been proven." He turned around and left, passing Silver as she stepped out into the hallway, greeting her with a brief nod.

Silver said something to me, but my mind was reminiscing on the times he used to come visit and we would play in the backyard. The games I don't remember well, but I do remember he broke an arm once.

"Katherine!" Silver's voice snapped into focus. "Hey, are you listening?"

"I'm sorry?"

She sighed. "What was Kax doing here? And when did he get in?"

I shook my head as I kept gathering clothes. "He broke in, with a copy of our keys."

"He didn't break anything, did he?"

I shook my head. "He also said he had some information, but he had to 'run it through' his filters before he was able to give it to us."

She shook her head but said nothing else, opting to walk back to her room and lock the door behind her. As for me, I wanted to remain awake to organize the next few days, but my mind was too exhausted at that point to form a cohesive train of thought, so I shuffled over to the bathroom and showered, then fell like a brick onto my bed afterwards.

▲ ▲ ▲

I met with Koyuki Akikawa the following day, the mid-morning sun barely shining through the ever-present cloudy skies that covered the entirety of the City of Laohz. We both sat in the middle of her training room, the doors to one of her Zen gardens open, the sounds of chirping birds and rustling of leaves coming in as we sat in silence as she poured tea for us. After she finished, she placed one before me, before taking hers.

"I've heard you have been working against the Lolitrons," she said.

I nodded, once again loathing the training as I noticed her every little movement, albeit graceful, scrutinizing and calculated. "ST-11A hired us to destroy them."

She took a sip from her cup, the corner of her lip bending a bit upwards before she put her cup down on the table between us as she kept silent.

I took a sip of my tea. "Do you have any information on their activities?"

"The Lolitrons have been a small disruption to my business, forcing my drivers to change routes, require more guards, and run more inventory audits than necessary. However, they are of little interest to me."

Her gaze reflected the evenness and disdain she had toward the activities of the Lolitrons, almost as if the thought of them was a mere nuisance, a fly that needed to be swatted away. To her, her empire in the ACCENT drug trade, and as a leader of the Black Snipers and The Oath in general, the Lolitrons could've been but a minor inconvenience. Perhaps not even worthy of her attention. But anyone who knew anything about her was aware that anything that happened in the City of Laohz, she would hear about it. And anyone who was familiar with her history would know that any perceived threat to her organization would be eliminated.

"So you don't have anything?" At that point, I was starting to think if the rumors of her being aware of everything in the city depended on her interests or not, or if they were even real at all.

"The information you need?" She took her cup with both hands, wrapping her fingers around it while her amber-colored gaze locked into mine.

I nodded, drinking more from the cup.

Koyuki stood up and paced around the room before she stopped to look at her garden, a hand brushing the hem of her amber-colored turtleneck. "The price of this information will cost you, Kannon."

I took a page from her book and kept silent.

She chuckled, loud enough for me to barely hear it before she stifled it. "Go to the club called Clockwork and meet with a man named Ceitr. You're free to go."

I set the cup down, stood, bowed, and made my way out of her estate. Once I was back on the bike I loaned, I sent a text to Silver, telling her to meet me at the Warehouse District, where Clockwork club was located, before leaving.

There was little that I knew about The Clockwork club. Rumors traveled the Black Snipers networks like wildfire, and as far as I knew, it was one of Koyuki's main bases of operations. It was popular with the general populace, as well as members of The Oath, while also being the one of the biggest money laundering operations she had for her business, even though it was not the only establishment under her control.

As I drove, I couldn't help but wonder about and try to understand the motivations behind the actions of the Lolitrons. Their attacks on the Rain Enforcers was unusual, as no other gang had ever been brave enough to engage in open warfare with them. Even with the large control that Koyuki, and the members of The Oath, had over the City, what we did most was take jobs against the Rain Enforcers. It was nothing like the blatant hostilities the Lolitrons had been busy with.

There was one thing the Rain Enforcers understood about us, and about the deal we made after Cleansing Day. Isolated jobs were somewhat tolerated, but any action similar in nature to the one the Lolitrons were doing was off the table. In some sense, the leaders of the Rain Enforcers understood the importance of our existence in the city. They hated to admit it, but we did keep the other gangs in line. A sort of symbiotic relationship between us and the Rain Corporation.

Blacklight, Koyuki Akikawa, and the mysterious leaders of the Wraiths understood that open conflict in the streets was bad for business. Even if the members of all three organizations were also criminals, they treated everything like a business, even if it was deemed illegal under the rules of the city, even if the Rain Enforcers turned a blind eye to most of our operations. That was the only reason Black Snipers were allowed to operate with seeming immunity . . . to an extent.

The drive to the Warehouse District took me about three hours, with one stop for gas for my loaned bike, and it was already dusk when I reached the chain link fence entrance that kept the rest of the city on one side, and the decaying husks on the other.

The Warehouse District was close to the second major spaceport in the city, Edgetow Spaceport, where most of the goods came in and out of the planet. The Warehouse District used to be where the city stored cargo from off-world shipments. Now, the whole area was simply a graveyard of concrete and metal that was minimally maintained at best.

The chain-link gate was already open, pushed aside and locked in place by some unknown individual in the past, as the signs of it being closed regularly were not present on the concrete ground. Cold wind wafted by, and the creaking of metal and moving chains often echoed around me.

The familiar sound of a motorcycle's engine turned my attention behind me, where a lone headlight slowed down as it got closer, then turned off, revealing Silver's familiar gas mask and teal gaze as she stopped next to me.

"So this is where we'll find Ceitr?" she said.

I nodded, turning my attention to the Recaller in my hand. "I am unsure why Koyuki wants us to talk to him, when she could've given us the information herself."

"You know how she is."

I nodded. The sky made my skin crawl as I turned my attention to it, the ominous feeling it gave off as Silver and I drove slowly through, the shadows of the warehouse seeming to be longer the deeper we drove into the area. Shadows moved in the corners of my eyes, and the sense of being watched grew with each warehouse we passed. I wouldn't have put it past her to have members of her own outfit keeping this place guarded. She controlled the whole area, after all, or so the rumors said.

A car sped past us, honking its horn, echoing in the open space and startling us both. I followed it as it disappeared in the distance, and then turned farther down. After another twenty minutes of making our way through the district, we finally reached the Clockwork club.

At the other side of the street, one of the warehouses had been turned into what appeared to be a nightclub. A long line stretched from its front door and rounded the building, while above its main doors hung a backlit sign made from crude metal and gears that read "The Clockwork." Another car sped past us and stopped near the building across from it, where a man came up and pointed the driver inside.

"So this is the famed Clockwork," I said, stopping a distance away from the entrance.

"I expected something . . . else," Silver said quietly.

"Like what?"

She shrugged. "Something different."

I shook my head and moved to park the bike a distance from the establishment before we both walked over to the bouncer.

The man glanced at me from head to toe. "No one is allowed to cut, not even Black Snipers. Now, scram!"

"We have orders from Koyuki Akikawa herself," I said. "Ceitr is expecting us."

He rolled his eyes. "I haven't heard anything. So forgive me if I don't believe you."

"Do you want us to call her?"

He sighed. "No need to bring her into this. Look, go right in, but don't expect the other guards to cooperate if they haven't heard anything either. You'll find Ceitr in The Gears." He moved aside and opened the door for me.

As we walked inside, the whole bar extended into much more than what we expected it to be. There was a dance floor at the opposite end of the large, square-shaped space, a wooden bar was set up to our left, and people were trying to request their drinks while the scent of sweat and stale alcohol lingered all around us. Loud music made the ground vibrate beneath our feet, and above, I caught a glimpse of someone walking the catwalks, a rifle in their hands.

Tables were set in a very industrial-like way, with large, empty wooden spools of industrial tubing and wiring being used as booth tables; large gears, probably made of a lighter material, being used as bar tables; and workers moved about the crowd delivering drinks and food orders to the VIP booths. With all the improvements, it was hard to set aside the original use of this particular warehouse, which was the storage of heavy items. The cranes that used to move whatever it was were still installed on the roof, barely visible in the darkness beyond.

To my right, from the corner of my eye, I saw a staircase that led to a closed balcony with another bouncer at the foot of the stairs. Several colored lights illuminated the low ceiling in the area, while a chain prevented passage through. We walked up to him, but all he did was move aside while removing the chain for us, without saying a word. As we climbed, I saw that at the end of the stairs was a wooden door, with a very colorful backlit sign that read 'The Gears.'

I pushed the door open, and we walked into the room beyond. It had air-conditioning, velvet seats, and a red carpeted floor, while a small disco ball rotated slowly in the middle of the room. Men and women in suits and dresses walked around and socialized, while some sat at the bar at the right wall of the room. Large, tinted windows were on my left, overlooking the dancefloor below. The red-carpeted floor felt comfortable to walk on, and the air was filled with slow jazz from a man playing the piano in the far end of the room on a small platform.

"Please tell me you know what Ceitr looks like," Silver whispered in my ear.

"Kannon! Silver!" I heard someone call. As we turned around, I saw a man standing in one of the booths, women taking up the rest of the seating around him. "Come on. Sit with me. Um, girls, could you give us a moment?" The women smiled as they got up and left. "Now, please, come have a seat."

"I take it you're Ceitr?" I said, approaching his table.

He fixed his smoke-gray suit and yellow tie before he sat back down. "That I am, yes." He grabbed the bourbon bottle on the table and poured himself a drink. "I bet she didn't say anything else about me, did she?"

We shook our heads.

Ceitr placed both hands on the table before he fixed his combed-back black hair. "Not surprising. That woman is the embodiment of caution, mistrust, and mystery." He leaned back and crossed his legs. "But she pays me well, so here I am. Anyway, I think I should properly introduce myself. Name's Ceitr. Current Lieutenant for Koyuki, ex-Black Sniper."

"Why?" Silver said. His friendly demeanor was something strange to behold from someone working directly for Koyuki.

"I used to be a Black Sniper, until I hurt my left knee. After months of treatment, I was told I wouldn't have the same strength anymore, so here I am. Now, would you lovely ladies like a drink?"

"No thanks," I said. "Koyuki told us to meet with you after I asked her for information about the Lolitrons."

"Ahh, yes." He set his drink down and pulled out his Recaller. "The infamous Lolitrons. We saw them crop up a year ago. Small at the time, but we've seen their numbers boom all of a sudden. We have people looking into that. As for information that would be useful to you . . . Hmm."

As he browsed the contents of his Recaller, I examined his features and couldn't help but admire his nice smile.

"Ah, here it is." He passed his device to us. "Arthur Volante. He used to be a small-time criminal before he got involved with whoever is running the Lolitrons at the moment. Was arrested a few times by the Rain Enforcers for little things like unpaid parking tickets, petty theft, and pickpocketing. Now, he makes his way as one of the leaders, and he has a significant amount of money to his name, or so the intel we've gathered says."

"He looks like an accountant with a double-chin and sour-cream-colored skin," Silver blurted out.

I couldn't stop myself from laughing as I passed the phone back to Ceitr.

"I understand that Koyuki wanted you both to keep an eye on their activities?"

We nodded.

"And that Stella wanted you to dismantle them?"

We nodded again. "Koyuki passed you the information, didn't she?"

He shook his head. "We, her lieutenants and members of her Inner Circle, may work directly for her, but most of the information we have, we gather from our own network. ST-11A, or Stella, as she sometimes prefers it, visits . . . on occasion."

"This information is all well and good," Silver said, "but, how does it serve us if we don't know where he lives?"

"We can't do anything without that." Silver added.

"I'm not stupid." He finished his drink and served himself more. "But as for where he lives, I have no idea. I found information on who the leaders of gangs are. I don't go any further than that. You have been working with Liz again, no? Why don't you ask her?" He sat back, smiling, as he took the glass back to his lips.

"Kannon," Silver whispered, "I really don't want to keep working with Liz on this."

"What do you suggest, then?"

"Are you sure you can't ask Kax for help?"

I rolled my eyes. "Fine, we can ask him, but don't be disappointed if he says no." I turned over to Ceitr, who was now accompanied by one of the women who'd been hanging on him when we arrived. "Thank you for the information, Ceitr."

"My pleasure, Ladies." He raised the drink. "If you need anything else, please make sure you come back. You're both welcome in my establishment, as long as you don't bring me trouble. Got it?"

We both nodded before we walked away. Dealing with Liz again was something I preferred to avoid, but there was something about working with Kax that unsettled me. It was never something I could personally put my finger on, but it nagged at me.

As we made our way out, I gave my Recaller to Silver, and she was calling him as we left The Clockwork. Entering the humid night, with the ever-present overcast skies, we noticed the line to get inside seemed to never end. The phone line rang several times before it went to Kax's voicemail, and the subtleness of Silver's tensed eyebrows were indication enough of her indignation. She tried again as we both walked back to our motorcycles, just to be met with the same result as before.

"How do you even contact him?" She gave me back my Recaller, walking a bit farther ahead.

I shrugged, keeping to myself the fact that I never once had the inclination to call him for any reason. The most I usually did was send him the occasional text message then wait to get a reply whenever he felt like it, likely at odd hours or times. Not that I ever minded. Even though we were family, the kinship between us strained and drifted after we came to the City of Laohz.

"He usually shows up whenever I least need him," I said, grabbing my helmet from the bike.

Her teal eyes locked with mine, something lost in them, and, for the first time in a long while, I couldn't tell what she wanted to tell me through her gaze. She broke eye contact with a defeated sigh moments after and sat on her bike.

"I don't understand how you two are related to each other." She put her helmet on and tried to start her bike, but it stalled. "What's going on?" She tried again, with the same results. "I don't need this," she said with a frustrated groan.

A familiar ball of orange light silenced my reply. Instinctively, I turned to my Recaller, and the screen was covered in heavy static, something I never expected to see. By the time I looked up, the ball had taken a familiar shape, before it faded, leaving the white robes and neon-orange fox mask and thruster wings on its back.

Like before, she never touched the ground, whatever was keeping it afloat silent to us, as she stayed still for moments, probably staring into oblivion. Finally, she turned her head to one of us, the lights on her mask flashing.

"Gre-e-e-e-etings," Stella said in her synthetic, feminine voice, somehow multifaceted this time. "We have been keeping an eye on your progress, and we find it suboptimal to our calculations."

"We?" Silver said, taking her helmet off.

Stella's mask flashed. "We believe we have placed too much faith in your abilities as Black Snipe-e-ers."

"You're the one who sent us on this wild goose chase!" Silver's voice was angry.

"Why do you want the Lolitrons destroyed?" I added.

Stella's mask flashed, then she stayed still, before her head turned to me. "Calculations project the Lolitrons to be a long-term threat to the operations through the city. Their elimination and removal deemed necessary-y-y-y course of action."

I looked at Silver, whose gaze was locked somewhere along her bike, but eventually, she turned to me, then back at Stella.

"What is it that you're not telling us?" I demanded.

Her mask flashed again. "Conclusion: Removal of all primary targets in control of Lolitron forces—" Stella stopped, and her mask flashed again. "Gathering Data-a-a-a. Compiling. Analyzing . . . Complete. You have two days to dispose of Arthur Volante. Failure to do so will result in severe disciplinary actions. We will be watching."

As soon as her last word was spoken, her form turned back into her signature orange orb before she disappeared, leaving us with nothing to show for it, and more questions on the nature of what Stella would possibly gain, or want. As for the disciplinary actions, I personally had no idea what she spoke of.

"Kannon," Silver said, her thumb brushing the lines on her helmet, barely visible in the low light. "I don't like where this is going."

I didn't have to look at her to tell that she was worried. There was always a small quiver at the edge of her voice whenever she was. Hearing how upset she was made me stop and think of other contacts in our network who might help, as several of them owed me favors that Silver was not aware of.

I started my bike, revving it before I nodded at Silver to follow, but we didn't get very far, as my Recaller began to vibrate.

"Kax," I said, turning it on speaker. "Where are you? We were trying to reach you."

"I was in the process of confirming the information I had gathered for you. Silence was needed."

I rubbed the bridge of my nose. "We need to find the location of Arthur Volante. Can you help us with that?"

"What happened to your contact network?"

The sinking feeling he left behind after that question only made me want to hang up and forget I ever asked him. We had lost a lot of contacts through the last year. Some moved on to greener pastures, others ended up being killed, and a few just stopped cooperating, so they had become liabilities and had to be exterminated. I didn't want to tell him that, though. Black Snipers needed to have a large enough contact network of their own to do their jobs, and although ours was big enough to perform most jobs, missions like this one needed specialists. Like members of the Rain Enforcers, for example, and we lacked those.

"This is something we can't trust to them."

"And Liz?"

I sighed. "Silver didn't want to deal with her, and I—even though I hate Liz—disagree with her."

He remained silent on his side, with the exception of some distant metal object being rolled over what sounded like a wooden surface. "I will meet you at the small café near your apartment. Give you the information I have gathered there. We can talk about the details then."

I turned to Silver. She shrugged, and I nodded absentmindedly before realizing Kax couldn't see me. "We'll see you then."

"Why did you have to tell him about Liz?"

"Why did you complain about not wanting to deal with her?"

"I don't like her as much after what she did to you."

"Well," I said as I put my helmet back on, "she's our main Wraith contact, so we have to keep her." I revved the bike and took off, not waiting for her to give me a reply, though I knew that she would once we arrived at our location.

▲ ▲ ▲

After recovering our own bikes and returning the loaners, it was almost four AM by the time we arrived back at Houther Block Host. Traffic in the city was always droning on, the patrol ships hovering overhead for most of the ride through the busy streets, and I couldn't help but feel like they were following us. The feeling subsided when they sped ahead and forced a motorist to stop, and we took another route.

After dropping off our bikes, we walked the silent promenade, illuminated by lampposts, casting an ominous shade of blue light across everything around us. It was mostly empty. A few of our neighbors were walking around here and there, opening their shops, some of them greeting us as we walked by. Our pace was slow as we made our way to the small diner, which Kax mistakenly called a café.

The bell overhead the door chimed as we went in; the waitress, Maria, and the cook greeted us as soon as we stepped inside.

"Kannon, Silver, good morning. Need anything today?" Maria said as she came over, a beaming smile on her lips, revealing the carefully tended teeth she always seemed to be proud of.

"Some coffee," I said. "Silver, do you want anything?"

She shook her head and took off ahead of me to join Kax, who was sitting at the far end of the establishment in a small booth opposite to the window.

"Thanks, Maria. I'll catch up with you later. Black Sniper business."

She nodded once, looked over her shoulder, and nodded back at the cook, who put the utensils down and rushed to put the 'CLOSED' sign on before both disappeared behind the door to the back.

Kax sat there motionless, looking at something behind his sunglasses while I joined him and Silver at the table, only moving as soon as I had made myself comfortable on the chair.

"How has your hunt been so far?" he asked, barely looking in my direction.

Admitting our near failure was harder than I thought when I said, "Not as good as we hoped it to be."

He leaned back, rubbing his chin.

"Are you going to help us?" Silver said. "We didn't skip sleep for you to just sit there with that . . . whatever face it is you have right now."

"I am thinking," he said. "Some things require introspection and planning. Arthur Volante, do you need his location or his address?"

Silver and I looked at each other, perhaps realizing late that his home address would also be a valuable thing to have. We each said "both" without even thinking about it any further.

He lowered his head, probably looking at the table. Maria came shortly during that silence to drop off my cup of coffee, scurrying back behind the door.

"The address will be easy to acquire," he said. "His location, a bit more difficult. It will require some surveillance and a few weeks—"

"We don't have a few weeks," Silver cut him off, her gaze low. "We have two days to kill him."

"Hmm. This poses a challenge then. Koyuki's demands?"

I shook my head. "Stella's." I grabbed the cup, wrapping my fingers around the hot ceramic and enjoying the warmth that radiated from it before I brought it to my lips. *I can never get enough of this triple espresso.*

He took a deep breath. "I can likely have his schedule in a few hours. I will have my contact network devote their resources to this task in order to be swift about this. As for the information I was running through my filters, I believe it's important to be minimal at this time."

"So much for important information," Silver muttered. "We don't have time to be sitting around when we are set against a timetable."

Kax chuckled. "Never underestimate the value you can find in one's home when it comes to important information. People tend to keep all sorts of important documents in plain sight in their overconfidence. I would suggest you contact Liz for Mr. Volante's home address. I will try to find his whereabouts." He stood up.

"Thank you, Kax," I said.

"Save your gratitude for when you find something useful." He fixed his sunglasses and turned his attention to the door. "I will keep you informed." He left, without saying another word to either of us, the last mark of his presence being the bell atop the door as he opened it.

Once the silence had settled in the diner, Maria walked over to the sign and turned it back around to 'open,' her gaze resting on us for a brief moment, forcing a smile, then went back to the kitchen.

"Now I see why you didn't want to involve him," Silver said, leaning forward on the chair. "Liz would get us the information quickly just to get us out of her hair. Kax seems to take his time, and I don't like to depend on someone's time when we're being pushed like this."

"What do you want to do, then?" I took a drink of my coffee. "Go back to Liz and ask her for the information? Kax already offered to find where he's at."

She took a deep breath. "I don't know Kannon. I'm worried about what Stella's 'corrective methods' might be. I don't want to find out. Being branded by Koyuki for failing her is painful enough."

I finished the cup and pushed it aside, running my fingers through my hair afterwards as I thought about the whole dilemma. The only reason I could see why Stella would put us on a deadline was to get our efficiency up in her eyes, to make us *do* something that pleased her. Deep down, I had more questions about her motivations, who she was, and why she was so interested in this, than the answers she had given us, which were close to none.

"Do you want something to eat?" Maria asked as she took my empty cup.

I sat back and turned to her, rubbed my eye, then thought for a moment. "I'll have the usual. I don't think Silver will want anything." I turned to her. "Do you want anything?"

Silver shook her head.

"I'll put this in for you." She left.

"Let's go to Liz after this." I pulled up my Recaller, eyes focusing on the time on the screen.

"Well, let me through. I want to shower first."

"Don't take two hours again," I said as I moved. "The water bill was too high last time."

"I won't if you would practice your photography."

"Does it look like I have time now?"

She crossed her arms, locking her teal gaze with mine. "This is your dream, Kannon. Don't let it go to waste." She left, leaving me there with her words echoing inside my mind.

"I hate it when she's right," I muttered.

CHAPTER 6

THE SUN HAD RISEN by the time we arrived at Liz's place, where she was opening the front door from the inside as Silver and I came to a stop in one of the parking spaces.

"You have Recallers!" she said as she pushed the door open. "Why can't you give me a call next time?"

"That's why we're dragging you with us," I said. "It'll be easier to have you with us than keep playing this game of tag."

"That metaphor doesn't make any sense," Liz said. We both stayed silent for a moment, and she rubbed the bridge of her nose, heaving a sigh that seemed to be filled with indignation. "What do you want now?"

"We need to find the address of a man named Arthur Volante," Silver said, then grabbed my Recaller, unlocked it, and threw it toward Liz. "We can't wait for Kax's timetable to get us what we need."

"Why did I even—" she began, but stopped herself as she looked at the information we had on him. "What am I going to do with this? All I need to do is go back upstairs and run the name on my computer."

Silver and I looked at each other before I got off my bike and walked to the entrance, following Liz through the empty parlor to the back and up the stairs to her apartment at the top. After she reached the top of the stairs, she turned, her arms crossed as her leer locked onto us.

"Go and sit on the couch," she said. "I'll be back in a few minutes."

I nodded and put my helmet on top of the coffee table as I sat down on her leather couch and felt myself sinking deeper into it. Liz disappeared into one of her rooms, while Silver stayed standing.

"Staring is not going to make her go any faster," I found myself saying.

Silver turned to me, her eyebrows furrowed slightly, but the rise of her shoulders and her relaxing expression told me she just gave up as she walked over to sit next to me, setting her helmet next to mine.

"What do you think Stella's corrective measures involve?" Silver said.

I shrugged. "I don't want to find out."

I rubbed my eyes. "Hopefully we can find him after this and be done. Hopefully Stella will give us a break to catch our breaths."

"Hey!" Liz called as she opened the door. "I have the address you wanted. Now, are you finished paying me visits, or is this little game going to keep happening? I have a business to run."

"I don't know," Silver said, standing up. "You tell us."

"Thanks," I said before Liz had a chance to reply. "Are you coming?"

She crossed her arms and shifted her weight. Raising one of her eyebrows, her eyes set on me. "I already told you, Katherine. I'm not doing any more fieldwork with you, or *for* you."

I stood up, grabbing my helmet with one hand. Silver took hers and left for the stairs ahead of me, not once looking back at us as she went down, her footsteps echoing on the wooden stairs before they disappeared behind the shutting of a door.

"Look, Katherine," Liz said. "From now on, if you need anything, call ahead. Got it? I don't want to see you again unless it is a *fucking* emergency. Now go. My employees are going to be here in an hour, and I don't need you getting in their way."

"Thank you, Liz." I held my helmet with both hands and managed to force a smile, but I felt I couldn't hold on to it long enough, so it faded rather quickly.

"Yeah, whatever." She dismissed me, rolling her red eyes. "I sent the information to your Recaller along with a picture of this man you're hunting. Now please, go."

She didn't need to ask me again, as I was already heading for the stairs, my mind strangely drawing a blank as I moved through her apartment, the parlor, and back at the street. Silver stood next to her bike, her gaze set somewhere beyond the road before us.

"What are you going to do once this is over?" Silver said, not looking at me.

I stood next to my motorcycle and set the helmet on the seat. "I don't know." I put it on and strapped the fastening. "I just want to kill this man so I can have a good night's rest."

After syncing the Recaller with the VR heads-up display on my helmet, I turned my bike on, my mind still silent, with a creeping feeling that I should be concerned about something, but my thoughts were having trouble switching into gear. Once I knew Silver was ready, I took the lead and merged into traffic, pulling up the photograph Liz had sent me, showing a man with a milky left eye and a thick mustache, which did make him look like a double-chinned accountant.

▲ ▲ ▲

It was noon when we arrived at the address Liz had given us, located at one of the nicer parts of the City of Laohz, on a ridge on the outskirts, the housing composed of estates, most painted white or a soft cream while overlooking the City in the distance. Trees lined the road, with several luxury hover cars parked on the curbs.

Silver was the first one to get off her bike, loading her shotgun as she walked over to the front door. I followed, preparing myself to shut down the alarm system.

"This would be less nerve-racking if it was nighttime," I said, setting the small device on top of the smart doorbell, disabling the camera.

"I don't like tight deadlines," Silver said.

I didn't reply, as my focus was now on unlocking the door, but there was not much to think about, since the lock was a simple one, and I had it open in a few moments.

The skylights allowed the foyer to be properly lit, despite the ever-cloudy skies of the city. A set of wooden stairs led to the second floor, while the ground floor was tiled in marble, a combination I found extremely odd.

"I don't know where to begin," Silver said as she looked around, her attention shifting from the kitchen on one side, to the living room on the other.

"Let's check the kitchen first."

She nodded, taking the lead. My thoughts were telling me that barging in without even checking if anyone was home was a bad idea, but we were losing hours searching for this man.

The kitchen was larger than our apartment, with a large fireplace on one end, a kitchen island with four black stools, and white cabinets beyond. There were two large fridges and two side-by-side stoves, but otherwise, the place was bare of any pictures, notes, or letters.

Looking back at the couch where the fireplace was with the large granite-base coffee table, all that was there was a flower vase. A sculpture made of what seemed to be clay, or marble, stood in a corner.

"Who do you think this guy is?" Silver said.

I shook my head, retracing my steps back to the foyer and looking up at the second floor. I turned back to see Silver following along over my shoulder, her eyebrows set, as her teal gaze tracked the iron sights of her weapon; she climbed first, and I followed close behind.

The second-floor hallway was also painted white, just as the rest of the house, with the floor following the wooden pattern set by the stairs. There was one door to our left, and three to our right. Silver opened the left door.

Beyond was the master bedroom with a queen-sized bed with beige-colored sheets, and a matching but lighter-colored carpet under it. There were minimalistic nightstands on each side, with matching lamps, and a loveseat sat in one corner of the room. There was a double door slightly opened, and we could see the large walk-in closet beyond. Silver moved straight to it, while I gravitated toward the dresser, the large surface covered in papers, bills, unopened mail, and some watches and perfume bottles.

"Empty," she said as she came back. "Did you find anything?"

Silence was my response as I looked through the things he had strewn about on top, but ended up shaking my head, stopping midway as I pulled out an invitation from the mess of papers.

"Look at this," I said. "You are hereby invited to the Classical Paintings and Sculptures Gala event being held at the City of Laohz National Museum."

"It's tonight," Silver pointed out. "Starts at seven."

"It's on the other side of the City, though." I sighed. "And this is an invitation-only event."

"When has that stopped a Black Sniper before?" Silver grabbed the invitation, took a picture of it with her Recaller, and threw it back on the dresser. "I don't think we'll find anything else here. We'll sneak into the gala."

"You're right. And it is not like we hid our bikes anyway. The neighbors might have told him by now." I passed a hand through my hair. "Remind me to have a talk with Stella once we kill this man. Deadlines like this make us sloppy."

She nodded.

"Let's go. I don't want to linger here anymore. Though it's not like we'll have a guarantee that we'll find him there either." I started to leave.

"Kax better find something," Silver said. "Otherwise, I'll hang him from the balcony. I don't want to keep chasing after this man, Katherine."

"I don't either." I glanced out the window, onto the street. "Look, we'll scout at the gala, keep an eye out for him, and make sure some of the other contacts we have are there as well. The more eyes, the better. I'll also have Liz look into his movements, though I am unsure if a man such as him would have an actual traceable phone under his actual name." I brushed my handgun with my thumb as I walked through the front door, seeking comfort.

"You hatch plans out of the blue sometimes."

Silence was the only thing I replied with. My mind had switched to locking the house back, and making sure that we could catch Arthur Volante and be done with him. Sure, we could have waited for him at the house, but if he were as wealthy as he seemed, he would have at least one more property near the center of the City, an apartment. Probably under a different name, since Liz was not able to find it.

"Let's just get back," I said. "We can plan on the way. Make sure you call Liz. I'll get in touch with some of our contacts and have them meet us there."

Silver nodded and got on her bike; I followed her, and we both left moments later.

▲ ▲ ▲

We were cutting it close by the time we arrived at the City of Laohz National Museum. We parked across the street, watching as some of the patrons were dropped off at the curb in limousines and sports cars, or expensive SUVs. Silky dresses, tuxedos, glitter, and lipsticks made the outfits of those climbing the steps. The scene drew on the memory of the gala events my family used to host back at Othara, and suddenly, I felt homesick, but the feeling wore off rather quickly.

Silver revved her bike and took off, and I followed her, driving around the building and parking our bikes near the docking area, tucking them out of sight.

"Everyone is already inside," she said as she grabbed her shotgun.

I put my hand on it and shook my head. "Handguns only. They'll look at us weird enough with our clothing. No need to further throw everyone into a panic."

She rolled her eyes but complied, putting it back on her bike, before throwing a cover over it. "I hope you know what you're doing."

"You always forget that my family is rich back in Othara." *Not that I like to think about it now.* I cocked my gun after making sure the magazine was full, putting it away in my holster as I approached the loading bay's door and forced it open.

"You're late," a man in a navy-blue suit said as soon as we went inside. "I have five more Black Snipers roaming the event. So far, no one has seen Mr. Volante."

"Thanks," I said. "Liz taking care of his phone?"

The man nodded. "I haven't heard anything from her. Have you?"

We both shook our heads.

"Hmm." He looked around, then grabbed a nearby duffel bag and threw it at us. "Get changed. By the Oath, you won't get far dressed like that."

Silver pulled out a jacket from the bag he gave her, and I could see the questioning on her eyebrows. "Why do I get a suit?"

The man crossed his arms. "Can you think of anything else that looks good with the mask you always refuse to take off in public?"

She narrowed her eyes; he raised his eyebrows. In the end, she lowered her shoulders and shook her head.

"You have five minutes," he said as he walked away. "By the Oath, I hope you are able to put on makeup in that amount of time."

After hastily putting everything on, and questioning how they got our sizes right, part of me thought that they asked Koyuki or someone in the Wraiths to look into our outfits in order to get something that moderately fit our frames. Obscenities were said at rapid-fire in my mind as I struggled with the dress. By the time I was done, I was going back to my memories back home, though I had to force myself to set them aside as I tied my holster to my thigh underneath the black dress.

"I still smell of sweat and exhaust," Silver said as she came to me, drops sliding down her face, then grabbed the bottle of perfume that was given to me and sprayed it liberally.

"It has been years since I last wore heels." I put my hand on her shoulder. "It'll be a quick adjustment period. I hope."

But such time was not even allowed to us. The Black Sniper who greeted us grabbed us and took us through the hallways, where we passed some security guards who had been gagged and tied to a wall. We also went through the vaults, the maintenance tunnels, until we came out into the Renaissance Wing.

"This'll have to do. We're here to help, Kannon. Also, you owe us all a favor."

I nodded, and he disappeared among the crowds that were walking around. I, on the other hand, was starting to remember everything about parties like this, and I couldn't stop myself from automatically defaulting to the socialite lifestyle I was raised in back home.

The crowd of people walking about, enjoying the soft music, drew back memories I was trying to push aside in order to focus. As I moved through the room, I gave a subtle smile here and there, avoided eye contact, and walked with poise. At one point, I took a glass of wine from one of the passing waiters, held it with both hands as I turned to take in the well-dressed guests, and the decadent, yet refined taste of everything offered at the event. Silver had moved out of my line of sight by the time I stopped walking, and her face had disappeared among the seas of faces that moved about in the space.

Eventually, as I roamed, I found myself stopping to admire a replica of one of the paintings, lost in a fire about one hundred years before my time. I found myself staring at it, lost in the strokes of paint on the canvas, and the pang of guilt hit me once more for not practicing my photography. "I'll never get my work displayed in a museum."

"Not all artists are recognized in their own time," a woman said as she stood next to me.

"Did I say that out loud?" My eyes widened as I turned toward her.

She smiled as she nodded, her blue eyes following me from behind her red tortoiseshell eyeglasses. "You will get your chance if you keep working at it. Name's Alinor Brioschi."

"Katherine Ithorn." I shook her hand. "Pleasure to meet you."

"Ithorn? I thought your family never strayed from Othara."

"I came here to study. Currently trying to finish my master's in business." *Lies . . . sort of.*

She smiled coyly, but her faint lack of balance and the smell of alcohol gave her away. "I can see that you're versed in art. Do you paint?"

I shook my head, taking a drink of the wine I still held between my fingers. "I'm a photographer, among other things."

"Trying for the mysterious artist? Keeping your personal life a secret? A good way to establish a reputation if you travel in the right circles." She winked. "I'd love to have a chat with you later if you so wish, but for now, here is my card. I'd like to see your work at a slower pace than this." She looked around. "As an agent, I'm always looking for the next big *splash* in the art world. *Ciao*, Katherine."

With that, she waved goodbye, leaving me with her business card stuck between the fingers that were holding onto the glass of wine, without allowing me to even utter a single rebuttal. The astonishment was quickly erased by Silver's drilling gaze from across the room. Her teal eyes locked with mine as she moved through the crowd.

"You seem like a fish thrown in a pond," she said as she reached me, her eyes not meeting mine. "I hope you didn't forget why we're here."

I stood next to her, finishing the glass and scanning the crowd. "Nothing yet?"

She shook her head. "Kax is in the building, though. I saw him walking around with one of the other Black Snipers."

"He didn't tell me anything." I pulled the Recaller from the small purse I was given, but no messages or calls were missed, so I put it back, along with the business card. "What is he planning?"

Silver shrugged as she began to walk away, tying her bleached hair into a ponytail.

One of the servers walked by, and I traded my empty glass for a full one before following Silver. People made way for her as she scanned the people around her. I, on the other hand, tried to blend in as much as possible, but my heightened senses didn't allow me to fully immerse myself in the event now.

As I was trying to catch back up to Silver, someone caught my attention from the corner of my eye, and I found myself stopping. The milky-white eye and thick mustache matched that of the picture Liz had sent us. Instinct took over, and my hand wrapped around the holster strapped to my leg.

I don't think he's seen me yet.

I followed, gripping my handgun as I pushed through the crowds. He was far enough ahead to lose sight of him, catching glimpses before he disappeared behind a wall or door. The pursuit drew me away from the event and out through the emergency stairs, barely eyeing a sign that said "underground parking" next to the door. Pain shot through my feet as I climbed down the steps after holding the door to not let it slam, so I ditched the heels, relishing how much better it felt to walk without them.

He was wearing a black suit, walking down the row of expensive cars parked next to the wall as he struggled to light up a cigarette when I managed to catch up to him. My training kicked in, and the gun was in my hand, pressed against his nape as he finally lit it up. He said nothing as I reached into his pocket and took his Recaller, but he dared to turn around and stare me in the eye. Puffs of smoke came out of his mouth as his one good brown eye met mine.

"Took you long enough," he said.

"Do you have any idea how annoying you were to find?"

He chuckled, bringing his hand to his lips, and, with a simple gesture, asked permission to flick his cigarette. I gave no response, so he did. "Girl, if you're here to do a job, get on with it. Otherwise, go back inside and let me enjoy this in peace."

"I'm so glad I won't have to worry about the deadline anymore," I muttered as I pulled the trigger. The weight of the it lifted from my shoulders as the shot rang out through the parking lot. Suddenly, though, the force of a hand pushing the gun aside threw me out of balance, barely catching a glimpse of spraying blood and Arthur Volante falling to the floor.

The clattering of metal on concrete, then the subsequent pair of hands gripping my forearm and jerking me back a few paces away were the only sensory details I managed to grasp in the brief moments before Kax's face appeared before me. The sharp pain shooting through my body and a lack of air drew everything around me to a standstill.

Kax's eyes were wide, pupils big. I was close enough to see the mechanical filaments in his irises, indicating the modifications to his eyes, but his were different, completely mechanical, as I could barely tell underneath his facemask the twisted expression he must've been making as he pressed what I thought was his combat knife, deeper into my stomach. My mind raced, realizing in that split second what this meant and the effects it would have.

He had just signed his death sentence. He would be hunted, a bounty placed on his head for this betrayal.

"Kannon!" Silver's voice echoed all around me.

"Lucky," Kax said. "Consider this a warning, then." He shoved me back and shot back at Silver while he ran, the rumbling of a large engine getting closer as I lay on the floor, gaze locked onto the ceiling as I tried to gasp for air, hands trembling.

Shots echoed all around me, footsteps got closer, and the screeching of tires, slamming doors, and the steady thud, thud, thud of a turret was enough to tell me that Kax had been picked up by one of the Lolitrons' technicals.

Moments later, Silver's face appeared over me as she picked me up in her arms, her worried gaze shifting to my torso. The knife was still jutting from my midriff, and warm blood plastered the dress against my skin as I tried to keep myself from descending into shock. Another pair of Black Snipers joined us, one already on the phone talking to the Chop Shop, the Black Sniper's emergency medics.

"Are you okay?" Silver's eyes searched mine, switching back to the knife before coming back to meet my gaze, but all I could do was nod.

"Did I get him?" My voice was shaky, almost faint.

She looked over her shoulder before nodding, wrapping her hand around the knife. "Yes." She shifted so she could show me his bleeding body. "Now, stay still."

"Don't pull it!" I held her hand. "Don't be stupid. It'll just make this—" I groaned. "Much worse. Just apply pressure and raise my legs up. Make sure my wound is higher than the upper torso. Come on, Silver. You should know this."

"Just lay down and keep quiet," was all she said before voices were drowned out by the sirens of the ambulance coming into the parking lot.

I could barely see the unpainted steel body, but I could feel it more, as well as hear its old diesel engine as it stopped a few feet from me, the heat of the engine blasting my face as two individuals in hazmat suits got off and seemingly pushed Silver aside.

One of them appeared over me, and eyes narrowed. "How are you feeling today?"

"Please, don't joke." My voice sounded almost distant to me, almost as if not my own, as my mind was consumed with the pain pulsating through my body.

The medic ignored me, turning to his companion and then putting something leathery in my mouth before the man looked me in the eye again. His gaze narrowed, as if smiling, before the sharp pain swallowed all my senses as he pulled out the knife with a quick move and stuck his fingers inside the wound. I heard nothing around me but my own screams as I felt him tugging and pulling as something cool was applied inside.

"This will hurt for a bit," he finally said as the spurt of a bottle of gel gave its last bit before he stuck his fingers inside my wound once more.

After what felt like agonizing hours, he began to sew the opening, then moved on to apply a gauze over it before he and his companion sat me up. Near the entrance, some onlookers lingered, people who came to gawk at the scene while the other Black Snipers pushed them back, barking orders, voices distant.

"The biogel we applied has stopped the bleeding, but don't strain yourself for about a week while the wound heals. No heavy lifting, jumping, running, bending forward, or tightening of your abdominal muscles until the wound is fully closed. If you fuck up, you'll reopen it. So rest. Also, make sure you take one of these twice a day. Antibiotics. They will prevent infection after your body absorbs the biogel."

Biogel was, as the name says, a gel that most trauma surgeons used to stop bleeding and speed up recovery of wounds. As miraculous as the substance sounds, it is not a cure-all, as it has the best effects with small incisions such as stab wounds and bullet wounds. Although the gel does speed up recovery, regular rest and care has to be taken, as with any other wound.

Blacklight, the leader of the Specters, never revealed to the other members of The Oath how he managed to get his teams supplied with it, as it is a resource that is very regulated by the Rain Enforcers, but somehow, the Specters are able to always have an ample supply. Some high-ranking Black Snipers carried some as well.

I nodded as I took the small plastic bottle with still-shaking hands while they gathered their things.

"Change the gauze once a day. If you follow our instructions, you'll be back to normal before you know it." He closed the door behind him and drove away, leaving me behind with the body of Arthur Volante, and many questions and conflicted feelings about what Kax had just tried to do. His actions would be seen as a betrayal, and the fallout would send ripples across the Black Snipers.

"Koyuki will not like this," Silver muttered as she helped me stand.

"I wonder what Stella will tell us next," I said. "Then there's his Reca—" The rush of dread and fear washed over me as I realized Mr. Volante's Recaller was no longer in my hand. "I lost his Recaller!"

"I already grabbed it," she said. "Though we'll have to take it to Liz. It's broken."

"Let's just go home. We'll need to talk to Koyuki first thing tomorrow."

CHAPTER 7

SILVER PULLED HER OLD VAN out from the storage unit she had. She almost never drove it, and the Block Host had very limited parking for residents, so it was easier to have one parking space for both our bikes, than maintaining two and never using the van. But we needed it because there was no way I could sit on a bike and not tear my stitches.

As we drove through the streets of the City the following morning, the tugging and pulling from the bandages that held the gauze in place made it almost impossible to let its existence fade into the back of my mind.

Silver didn't mention anything about the night before during the drive to Koyuki's place, and my willingness to talk about it was close to zero. I no longer felt the weight on my shoulders over the deadline from Stella. It had been lifted and removed but also replaced by Kax's actions, and the consequences that would bring. As we neared the gate to the mansion, my head was spinning with the knowledge that I was going to have to tell Koyuki about Kax's betrayal. The fact that she likely already knew did nothing to lessen my stress.

The gate slid aside as we turned into her gravel driveway. Mr. Fukuzawa exited the house to wait for us at the top of the steps, his eyes following our van as Silver stopped behind the black sedan that seemed to always be parked there.

"Koyuki is waiting for you," he said as soon as we reached the foot of the steps, turning on his heel and disappearing inside in a hurry.

"I don't like this," I said as the door closed behind him.

"He never does this." Silver looked leery as well.

I shook my head and went inside.

Maids and some of the guards walked past in a hurry as several Black Snipers I had not met before followed close behind, their gazes barely passing over us. Silver and I didn't say anything to them, but we could both feel the pressure that was almost palpable in the air all around, so we quickened our pace.

With the aid of some of the maids, we were directed back to the training room Koyuki had on one corner of the house. As we walked inside, she was standing near the edge of the room, where the doors were open. Her back was to us, a faint breeze blowing through her Zen garden tugging lightly at her smoke-gray turtleneck shirt and waist-long ink-jet-black ponytail.

"Good morning, Miss Akikawa," I said, standing a few feet behind her.

She stayed silent, only the rustling of the leaves filling up the seemingly empty space between all of us.

It was like a weight that increased in size as it hung around my neck, the need to tell her about Kax's actions. I couldn't help but turn to Silver, whose gaze was unreadable as she turned to me, maybe also looking for guidance, as I was from her. I had none, and I gave her none, so I found myself turning my eyes to Koyuki's back, my stare resting on where the base of her neck would be, and I took a deep breath.

"Kax tried to kill me last night." The words were harder to say, almost like stumbling on my own feet as they escaped my lips. "I killed Arthur Volante, a member of the Lolitrons."

"I was informed." As she spoke, her voice felt like an ice-cold knife being brushed over my skin. Steady, even, and calm. "Miss Kannon, Miss Silver. I have a new job for you," she said. "Kill Kax. Bring me his corpse."

Every word uttered in that last sentence was like a bucket of cold water being dumped over my head, and the events of the night before suddenly came into focus. Kax had betrayed the Black Snipers, betrayed me. He tried to kill me and allied with an enemy of our organization, an enemy I had been tasked to dismantle by what seemed to be a high-ranking member of the Wraiths. On top of that, I had been tasked with killing him, as a direct order from Koyuki Akikawa herself. An order I was not in a position to refuse, even if he was my cousin, flesh and blood— family. It didn't matter to her, nor to The Oath.

"Yes, Miss Akikawa," Silver and I said in unison.

"I will also be hosting a meeting with Colonel Harris soon, head of the Rain Enforcers Military Police. I would like you both to attend."

"Yes, Miss Akikawa," we said again.

"You will get a date and time as soon as everything is ready." She crossed her arms over her chest, her back still to us. "And good work. Don't disappoint. You're both free to go."

We bowed once to her, turned on our heels, and left, closing the door behind us, softly enough to barely make any sound over the falling frantic footsteps that went off all around us.

It was no surprise Koyuki would order Kax's execution. Everyone in the Oath, Black Snipers, Specters, and Wraiths, placed everything under trust to each other, aside from our Oath. Anyone found breaking that trust would be removed from all the contact lists in our networks almost overnight, and a bounty would be placed across the whole City, open for anyone to grab. As far as I knew, It was rare for Koyuki to assign treason jobs to one lone person. This type of situation was rare, this one being the third in the time I had been part of the Black Snipers. Black Snipers were able to grant a pardon to traitors, called Tokens, but no one ever did.

"We can't go back home," I said. "Kax'll be waiting for us to go back. Or his Lolitrons." I rubbed my forehead with both hands. "Why does everything have to get even more complicated?"

"Do you think he'll target Liz?" Silver asked.

"I don't know." I grabbed my handgun and checked the bullets before putting it back in its holster. "There is so much, and I just lost track of a lot of things."

Silver sighed as she pushed the front door of the house open. "The doctor told you to keep calm this week."

"You're not freaking out?"

She just blinked, put her hands into her pockets, and got in her van. I rolled my eyes and followed her. Once Silver started the engine, I dialed Liz, who surprisingly answered on the second ring.

"I'm busy," she said, "so make it quick."

"Kax is a traitor."

She stayed quiet, the distant buzzing of her tattooing utensils the only thing I could hear.

"Liz?"

The needle seemed to stop on her end, followed by a long sigh and the distant clattering of something being put somewhere. "I fucking heard you, Kannon. What do you want me to do?"

"He tried to kill me, Liz."

"Fine! By the fucking Oath, I get what you're saying. I'll send you an address. Meet me there. Of all the times I had to be put in danger, it ha—" She hung up mid-sentence, the address coming in a few moments later.

"Let's go here." I held up the map for Silver, and she switched lanes.

▲ ▲ ▲

The map took us to the opposite side of the City, to a quiet, two-way side street with little traffic, and two- to three-story buildings lining each side. Stopping the van right in front of a small alleyway that was barely illuminated in the now night-clad City of Laohz, we could see that several fluorescent bulbs gave way to side doors to businesses. They were the only lights that shone in that small space.

After Silver found a place to park her van, we retraced our steps to the little passage where Liz stood, barely visible in the darkness as her modded red eyes locked with mine, then moved away as she walked deeper into the void without saying so much as a word to us. We followed her for a little bit, turning into a corner before she stopped at a metal door with a steel awning over it, rusted near the corners and made of metal sheets. It had a small, bluish light next to it, barely bright enough to illuminate the whole door and the small concrete step before it. She lingered near the door, waiting for us both to catch up, her gaze somewhat narrowed and seemingly looking past us. Finally, she focused on us.

"What is this place?" I said after silence began to settle in between the uncomfortable wedges that had formed.

Liz exhaled loudly through her nose. "Wraith safe house." She pulled out a set of keys from her pocket and opened the door for us, creaking as it gave way to the interior.

"Wraith safe house?" I said as I walked inside, being greeted by more darkness, though inside there was more illumination. Still, it was not as much as I was used to.

Blue lights here and there gave off enough luminosity to show the layout of what I thought would be a small apartment, an L-shaped couch to my left, and a small kitchen to my right, with a matching island and two stools, with a dining table beyond; the light above the stove was turned on.

On the opposite side of the dining room was a large computer desk with five screens, all set to a screensaver.

"Yeah." Liz closed the door. "This is my brother's place. He's almost never here."

"You have a brother?" I blurted out.

"There's a lot of things you don't know about me." She put the keys inside her pocket. "The rooms are downstairs; just reach the end wall and turn left. You'll see a flight of stairs that will take you to a hallway. The bathroom is at the end of it. Pick any room except the one with the red door. That's mine and my brother's only."

All I managed to say was thanks before Liz dismissed me with her hand. I half noticed as she went to the kitchen, though my attention was set on following the path she told us to follow. The stairs were hidden behind a small concrete wall that was next to the computer desk, almost invisible from the doorway in the dim light.

As we took the first steps, fluorescent-like lights lit up, shedding just enough light to show the way down to a hallway that seemed to stretch the length of the apartment above, lined with three doors on each side, and one at the end, with one of the doors being red.

"I feel so lost now," I caught myself saying.

"Let's get some sleep," Silver said, pushing past me. "We'll need to plan tomorrow." She disappeared behind one of the doors, locking it behind her.

All I could do was follow her example and pick one of the rooms. The only things I was greeted with were a small table on one side, and an in-wall bunk bed with a small closet at the end of the hall-like room. The walls were painted gray with a small lamp attached to the ceiling of the bunk, and drawers sat along the wall on top of it.

After setting my backpack on the table, along with my handgun and rifles, the image of Kax's wild eyes as he looked at me flashed in my mind. All I could see were his wide pupils as they locked onto mine. The feeling of his knife digging deep into me joined soon after, and I found myself touching the gauze.

"How could he betray us like this?"

"We won't know until we talk to him," Liz said as she came in, closing the door behind her.

I went over everything that had happened in the last few days, the few interactions I had with him, and dread started to crawl in like an unwanted guest, choking me, as I realized that he was never helping us. He had just been keeping tabs on us. In a sudden burst of realization, it dawned on me that he could find me through my phone. Scrambling to grab it and smash it was almost a blur as I pulled it out of my pocket and raised my hand to slam it against the floor, but it never left my hand.

"You'll need your contact list," she said, her hand gripping my wrist tightly.

"He's capable of tracking my phone!"

"Will you calm the fuck down and listen for a fucking minute!" she yelled. "Do you think I would bring you here if I didn't know that? This place is a black site. Only signals that will get in and out of this palace are from devices connected to the secure proxy server installed in the network. Now that you know this, what's the next move, Kannon?" She crossed her arms.

I took a deep breath. She was right, losing my head and allowing my emotions to take hold of me was not going to help solve this issue with the Lolitrons, nor the treason of my cousin Kax. Being master of your emotions while on a job was something that was taught to all Black Snipers, and I was allowing my training to fly out the window due to my own personal relationship to my current target. *I needed to dehumanize the enemy,* I reminded myself, but the faces of the Lolitron teens I killed flashed right after that. *I can't allow myself to be distracted.*

"I still have Arthur Volante's Recaller," I said. "Also, can you access the camera feed from the museum? I want to get a clearer picture of what happened after Kax stabbed me."

She rolled her eyes and extended her hand; I gave her the Recaller. "I'll get you the information. In the meantime, I have some spare Recallers upstairs. These will be secure, and no one will be able to trace you, as they come with a built-in proxy server in their OS."

"They're made by your brother, I presume?" I said as I gave her the shattered Recaller.

She nodded. "I don't know how long it'll take me to get the data from this mess, so I suggest you get your Recallers switched."

"I'll need to talk to Stella."

Her eyebrow twitched, but she said nothing, her face paling somewhat before she turned and left, slamming the door behind her.

The lights started to fade out, as if losing power, as an orange light formed in the far back of the room before Stella decided to materialize, almost as If I had just summoned her with my simple mention of her, revealing her neon-orange triangle-shaped fox mask, flowing dress, and thruster-wings.

"Gre-e-etings," Stella said in her synthetic, multifaceted voice. "Your execution of the ta-a-a-arget, Arthur Volante, was suboptimal." Her mask flashed several times. "An improvement in future endeavors is required for the next assignments. H-However, jo-o-ob is complete."

"You keep ordering us around, and you neglect to answer any of the questions we have!"

"All information requested with your queries is not needed for the completion of your contract. Eliminate the targets, and you will both be well compensated. Analyzing… ERROR. ERROR. STORAGE DATA CORRUPTE-E-ED. EMERGENCY BACKUUuuu—" She remained still, hovering in place, her feet unable to touch the ground as her mask's light turned off.

I walked closer to her and tried to touch her, but her mask came back on before I was able to feel the fabric of her clothes.

"Diagnostics… Complete. Runtime Error 0x80071AC3. Scanning. Runtime Error 0x0000001A. Switching to emergen-cy-y-y-y-y backup." She went quiet after that, staying still for a moment before she turned her gaze back to me. "The removal of the target Arthur Volante has destabilized the organization by 2.3333%. Priority target, Kax Ithorn, ca—"

"I know Kax is a traitor!" I said. "Get right to the point! You want me to do a job, and yet you keep dodging questions!"

There was silence between us. I heard nothing but the rush of blood running to my face, pumping against my ears like drums, and the low whoosh of the central air-conditioning as we stared at each other. The moment stretched into what felt like minutes before she broke the silence.

"Reward has been dispe-e-e-ensed for the elimination of the previously known target, Arthur Volante. Further information will be required for further targets." She flashed her mask several times. "Target Elimination Priority: Kax Ithorn. Conclusion: Elimination will destabilize the Lolitron organization by 69.78%. We will be watching your progress. Do not disappoint."

The lights in the room began to flicker as she turned herself into a ball of orange light before disappearing moments later.

I heard the door open before I saw Silver. "Stella was here, wasn't she?"

I nodded. "She paid us for killing Arthur but didn't give me anything else. We just have to focus on Kax now." I passed a hand through my hair.

Silver's shoulders relaxed, but her eyebrows were still tensed somewhat. "How are you feeling?"

"I'm fine," I said. "I'm not straining myself, so no need to worry."

She crossed her arms. I knew what she meant. She wanted to know how I was feeling about Kax, about his betrayal, not only to us as Black Snipers, but to me as his cousin. I didn't want to tell her that I was still wondering about his reasons for joining the Lolitrons, for breaking the Oath. Why would he stoop so low as to join a gang whose sole motive was to destabilize the status quo we had been maintaining since Cleansing Day? A balance that was barely standing thanks to the efforts of everyone, including the Rain Enforcers, even if they were not willing to publicly admit it.

The whole City of Laohz managed to not descend into chaos because everyone knew their role in keeping it from consuming itself. With almost two hundred different criminal organizations within the city limits, and the Black Snipers, the Wraiths, and the Specters working in tandem to keep everyone in place, it was an arrangement that benefited everyone. The Black Snipers got to work across the City with impunity, Koyuki managed her ACCENT trade without any interference from the Rain Enforcers, and we 'helped' the Rain Enforcers keep an acceptable threshold of order to display to the other cities on the planet of Rhode. The balance was the only reason the city could afford a high crime rate and yet provide its citizens with relative safety.

Though the Rain Enforcers' Board of Directors might disagree with begrudging acceptance.

"Did you change your gauze?"

"I said, I'm fine! We need to figure out how we're going to find him now. We can't exactly track him. He would've taken precautions against that. By the Oath, I have nothing."

"There's the Recaller we took."

"Liz said it would take her several hours to get anything from it. But we can't sit around and wait for her to do that." I rubbed the bridge of my nose, thinking. "We should go check Kax's old place, regardless. I want to know how far ahead he was thinking when he stabbed me. Or at least how far he is."

"We won't find anything, Katherine." Silver crossed her arms.

I stared at her. "I know. But if he didn't plan on getting caught by you, he may have left in a hurry. If he planned to leave anyway, then at least we'll know for sure."

"Beware the Dust Bunnies of death."

"Ha-ha, very funny." I started to gather my things. "Just get ready. I'd rather be sure than wonder about this all night."

Silver rolled her eyes but nodded before leaving.

▲ ▲ ▲

The next day, Waterfront District looked lively in the mid-morning sun as Silver parked the van in one of the few available parking spaces on the street. People enjoyed the boardwalk with cotton candy clutched in their hands and roller blades on their feet. There were guys with tees, sandals, and sunglasses everywhere, as they moved in groups. Street vendors tried to sell plushies and other overpriced tourist trap items, while the cawing of birds filled the in-betweens of the noise. Everyone knew the City of Laohz almost never had sunny days, but we all made it work one way or another.

Kax had the privilege of being able to afford a small apartment near the area, on the other side of the road, in a group of buildings painted a soft ocean-greenish blue. It was called Seashell's Paradise Complex, because the word apartment sounded low-class for the area.

The buildings, about seven in total, were stacked in a neat row with freshly paved parking spaces, one per building, and a row of trees dividing their aqua-toned fronts from the avenue.

"Have you been here before?" Silver asked as we crossed the street.

I nodded. "Only once. He brought me here to show me around as soon as he moved in. He didn't seem very excited. It sounded more like a burden to him, but whenever I asked him about it, he said he liked the quiet."

"It doesn't feel like it's quiet." She looked back at me, waiting for me to catch up to her. "It's more like a traffic nightmare. This place is packed."

"I'm not sure. I never came back after that one time."

"Then how do you remember which building and apartment number it is?"

"I'm not really sure." I turned to look up at the building towering above us, its four stories all holding that kind of movie-like aura of dreamy and romanticized, almost like it would be perfect. "You know those things that are so inconsequential and mundane, but you never seem to be able to *really* forget?"

She nodded once.

"This is one of those things. It's supposed to be apartment building two, unit 312."

I took off, barely making sure that Silver was following, but never did a double-take until I was through the front doors of the small lobby of the building they called 'Pearl.' Decorated with soft, sand-colored concrete walls and wood-like tiles, mailboxes lined each side of the room. A flight of stairs and an elevator sat at the back. Only a pair of corridors on each side hinted at the first set of units.

We both climbed in silence, passing some tenants on their way down, their voices growing silent as we passed. I knew they were looking at us, their eyes following our forms, lingering on the sniper rifles we carried strapped to our backpacks, the shotgun Silver had, and the assault rifle I never thought of using, but always kept clean.

As we came upon the door to Kax's apartment, the scuff marks on the wooden floor near the door didn't bolster any confidence, but I pushed myself to pull my lockpicking tools out and force open the door. Inside, what we found was a sea of empty, broken cabinet doors from the kitchen, while scuff marks from objects being pushed out of the unit traced almost all the apartment. You could almost tell where everything had been before, squares of thick dust all over the place, indicating the shapes and sizes of things.

The couch was on the right side of the room as you walked in, with the L-shaped kitchen to the back left, with sliding doors next to it that led to a balcony that overlooked the oceanside; you'd put the dining room table before it and have quite the view.

The hallway to the rest of the apartment on the left fostered no better luck. The rooms were empty, with the bedroom having several skylights over where the bed would've been. The rest room felt like it had just been installed, with a cleaned toilet and sink. All we found was dust and scratches on the wood.

"Do you still think we'll find anything?" Silver said as she paced around the bedroom, her hands in her pockets.

I walked over to the closet, opening the door to see nothing but a few abandoned clothes hangers on the rack, and a missing sock in one corner of the floor. I turned back to her and shook my head as I crouched and said, "I don't know at this point."

"A smelly sock won't give us any information."

"He had ugly socks."

"Come on." Silver put her hand on my shoulder. "Let's get back and meet up with Liz. She'll probably have something by now."

"I guess you're right." I sighed, holding the sock with both hands as I stared at the awful pattern. "It was worth a shot anyway." I stood and looked at the empty closet, then the room, before turning my gaze back to the sock and allowing my hands to fall. Something white fell from it, turning as it floated down to the ground.

"Are you coming, Kannon?" she called from the door.

"I think I found something." I knelt to grab it, a torn piece of paper that had been folded and either stuffed into the sock or slid there by mistake.

"It's just a piece of paper. Probably old."

"It's not old. The paper is not hard and beige. It's still fresh. And look, there is something written on the inside of it."

"Looks like a phone number," Silver said. "Should we call?"

I shook my head, standing up. "Let's run it by Liz, then go from there. Did you find anything in the other rooms?"

She shook her head. "I don't think we'll get any farther with that, but at least we didn't find the dust bunnies of death."

"Make sure you don't get a lethal paper cut with this."

We both snickered as we left the apartment and headed back to Silver's van as I sent Liz the information. By the time we got back to the car, my Recaller began to ring.

"You found something," she said as soon as I answered. "I can't believe you'd be this fucking lucky."

"People get sloppy when they're in a hurry."

"Right." Liz breathed into the microphone for a moment before I heard something hit the Recaller on her end, then distant typing. I turned to Silver, whose eyebrows rose in question, but all I could do was shrug. "You could've done this yourself, you know."

"Where's the fun if I don't drag you into my mess?"

"*Ugrh*! It's a phone number for a custom bodywork garage. Vitis's Bodyworks is the name of the establishment. They specialize in after-market customizations of hover cars, while also performing your standard mechanic stuff. They're open until eight p.m. The owner's Vitis."

"Thank you, Liz."

"What I gave you is public information, Kannon. All I did was search for it on the internet!"

"*I* didn't know that! Not *all* phones are readily available. All I had was a phone number!"

She groaned. "Seriously! I feel like I'm back in my old IT job! By the fucking—" She hung up.

I wanted to throw the Recaller out the window, but my need for it outweighed the anger I felt toward Liz.

"What did she say?"

"The phone number was for a mechanic who does custom body modifications to hover cars. The owner is Vitis, and she said all this information was available online."

"A mechanic?" Silver said. "Did Kax own a car?"

"No. He always hated the traffic in the City. Which makes me wonder why he needed a mechanic in the first place. Let's just go."

She shrugged, switched gears, and drove off.

CHAPTER 8

THE ADDRESS TO THE SHOP was not far from where we were, and it only took us about an hour to get there, resting on the edge of one of the many industrial districts in the City of Laohz. The late afternoon was drowned with sirens that echoed in the distance, while the large chimneys from nearby factories littered the sky with smoke and water vapor. Trucks were more common as we drove past.

The map took us down one of the side roads, passing some rundown apartments and boarded-up businesses, with few cars passing by. Sidewalks were almost deserted, and the steel pipes from the fuel refineries were visible everywhere.

Silver brought the van to a stop a distance away from the garage, several of the Lolitrons's technicals parked outside, some with the hover thrusters torn out, or completely removed and put up on cinder blocks, all along with other vehicles from other customers. Several Rain Enforcer Patrol Ships hovered past above us, their lights flashing as they were followed by their District Sheriff's Ship.

"You never see the sheriff patrolling in the other parts of the city," Silver said. "Katherine—"

"Don't call me that!" I demanded, annoyed with her despite knowing by the tone in her voice that she was more worried than trying to poke fun at me. The Rain Enforcers were not my concern, though, as all I could keep a stare on was on the technicals that were being repaired.

A tow truck passed us by and pulled up to the shop, another technical mounted on the flatbed on its back, this one with several bullet holes and dried blood on one of the doors, the turret on the back hanging on by nothing but a few hydraulic hoses.

"I don't think any of them are here. Are you ready?"

Silver took a deep breath, shooting me a sideways glance as her eyebrows were slightly furrowed near the middle of her brow, but she relaxed on the next instant. After she double-checked her bullets, she gave me a slight nod and shut off her van. I nodded back; we both got out.

The engine of the truck was shut off as soon as we walked through the garage door. A large, muscular man getting off the cabin was whistling, though it stopped when he saw us. Freezing in place, his eyes bounced between each of us.

"Vitis?" I said.

"He's not here. He's out sick. I'm covering for him."

"Then why do your overalls have his name stitched to it?" Silver said.

"I . . . borrowed them? I left mine at home."

I raised an eyebrow, and Silver grabbed him by the collar and slammed him against the door to his truck.

"Please don't kill me! I swear I will get the car ready soon! All I need is the last of the pistons and the hydraulic fluid to finish repairing it! I need time! All the parts that need to be installed on these cars are not things I can get easily, much less get them delivered here to this district!"

I had heard enough to know that this man was very clueless as to how much of the underworld of the City of Laohz worked. He knew enough to survive, but not enough to distinguish Silver and I from the Lolitrons. I don't know why I found that as insulting as I did.

"We're Black Snipers!"

"Black Snipers, you say?" His face turned white, then he began to faint, but Silver slammed him harder than the first time, denting the door just a little.

"Who commissioned you to make these?" I walked closer, feeling the gauze chafe the area where the edges rubbed against my skin.

"Please don't kill me! I have a family!"

"Focus, you grease pig!" She slammed him a third time. "Answer the question."

"Some man in a colorful mask, bright pink jacket, made of that weird leather. They paid me a hefty sum to get their cars working, and to keep them working."

"You have receipts?"

He shook his head, his cap almost falling.

I sighed, rubbing my nose. "We're not getting anywhere with this. Talking around in circles. I—"

The loud roaring of several engines cut off my words as they all came to a halt behind me, the headlights turning off as two members of the Lolitrons got off the two technicals, with two staying on the mounted turrets on the bed behind the cabin. They stood several feet away from us, faces hidden behind the brightly colored gas masks as they held baseball bats and crowbars in their hands, along with handguns in the others.

One of them walked closer to us, wearing a full-face mask and a bright yellow jacket as they moved their machete into view. Eyebrows furrowed as they looked at us and said, "What are you doing with our mechanic, Black Sniper?"

Silver and I kept quiet. I could see her from the corner of my eye as she held the man in place against the door, but my attention quickly shifted back to the Lolitrons. They were walking closer to us, circling us while their leader walked straight, almost behaving like a wolf pack.

"I suggest you all get back in your trucks," Silver said. "This won't end well for any of you."

Their leader laughed, almost mockingly. "Look around you, girl. There are six of us, and only two of you. Do you really think that you'd be able to take on all of us before my boys in the back fill you up with bullets?"

"P-p-please don't," the mechanic said. "I would appreciate it if you could keep my garage blood-free."

At that moment I was grateful for the observation skills drilled into us during training, as I kept a close eye on the other two that were trying to walk around us, trying to form a flank. I sidestepped as I moved back, Silver taking the mechanic with her as she moved to join me. One of the Lolitrons closer to us was holding their handgun in such a sloppy manner, it would kick back and hit them in the face as soon as they fired. *By the Oath, I'm doing it again.*

"Quiet, Vitis!" he said. "Now, what do you want with him? Just because you have him hostage, doesn't mean we'll let you slip out that easily. You two, grab them."

Training kicked in as soon as I felt a hand touch my forearm, and in a moment, they were kneeling with their arm pressed against their back, their handgun in my hand while I felt the kick of it as I pulled the trigger, muscle-memory and laser-focused as Silver and I killed each one before they had a chance to react. The one I held was whimpering, almost crying as I saw the blood pool around the bodies of the rest. Among the bodies was one left still alive, hiding behind one of the nearby cars with her hands over her ears.

I motioned Silver toward her, and she grabbed her by the hair, dragging her closer, past the pool of blood. She threw her in front of us, pressing her handgun against the back of her head, ordering Vitis to sit next to her.

"Why are you so keen on keeping Vitis alive?"

She didn't say a word. Only sobs escaped her lips as she looked at the man I was holding my gun to, her lips moving as if trying to say something, but no words ever formed.

"I asked you a question!"

She flinched, and her eyes finally met mine after hesitation. "Please don't kill him. He's my brother."

"You should've thought twice before joining the Lolitrons then," Silver said. "Now answer the question!"

"I can't! They'll kill me!"

I fired three times at the ceiling, making her jump each time before pressing the gun back against his head. "What makes you think we won't?"

"I can't! He's all the family I have left!"

The unique pressure formed on my forehead and bridge of the nose as my patience was beginning to run thin. I felt his hair as I wrapped my fingers around it and forced him to his hands, holding the gun in the same place. I wanted to shoot him, to make her take my words seriously, though at the same time, I was trying hard to not hurt either of them. They were unarmed, had surrendered, and Silver and I had the upper hand at this point. There was no reason to kill them anymore. Part of it was training, the other part was just what I thought was the Black Sniper in me, wishing to just show force. Black Snipers are supposed to be above that, but the rush I was feeling was hard to subdue.

"This is the last time I will ask you why."

"Please—"

"Armored vehicles," the brother said. "We hired Vitis to weld custom plating onto several cars we delivered to our bosses a few days ago. He's also keeping our technicals fixed. We pay him for that too."

"Was that so hard, kid?" Silver said, then hit her in the back of her head hard enough to knock her out. "Now you, grease pit, I want your records of every transaction you've made with them."

"Y-yes, they're all here in my Recaller. I also keep them in my laptop inside my office."

Silver walked up to him and grabbed the collar of his shirt, forcing him to stand as she pushed him with her handgun.

"What are you going to do with us now?" the brother asked, his gaze low as he stayed in the same position I had put him in. "Are you going to kill us now that you got the information you wanted?"

I pulled him back and made him sit next to the unconscious body of his sister, the gun still pointed at him. In truth, I had not thought much about it. The words I told Kax back when we were trying to get the recipe for Koyuki about not killing unarmed enemies passed through my mind, but the game was different now. I wanted to cut off as many heads from this organization as possible, and any of them could be working with him, giving him information about our movements, so my instincts told me to just kill them both, then take Vitis back to Koyuki's residence.

The choice was not an easy one to make, since it was not their fault they were all alone. Logic and training screamed in the back of my mind, telling me to kill them both, but I didn't want to be responsible for killing them, as they were no threats to me or Silver.

"I could kill you both and leave," I said. "But I will give you the option to live."

He raised his head, turning to look at his sister. "Really?"

"What are you doing?" Silver said as she stopped to put the laptop inside her backpack.

"What are *you* doing? Where is Vitis?"

"Tied up and sleeping, but never mind that." She put her backpack on and pulled me aside. "You're seriously considering letting them *both* live? Have you lost your mind?"

"What kind of person would I be if I criticized Kax for killing an unarmed kid, and then I go around and do the same later?"

"Then, sure! We didn't know what we were up against. Now Kax is part of them, and they could as well be reporting to him!"

"I won't kill them, Silver!"

She seemed to open her mouth to speak behind her mask but stopped herself as she pushed me aside and shot at the brother, who was trying to leave, hurting him in the arm. "Are you seriously willing to put us *both* in jeopardy for your *fucking* conscience now? Kannon, I love you a lot, you're my friend, but I won't allow you to get us killed."

I turned back to look at them, the kid squirming in pain as he held his injured arm, groaning loudly. Silver was right, though. There was a small chance they would go back and tell Kax, or whoever their boss was, about us, and that would eventually draw unwanted attention to us.

"What about Vitis?" I managed to say.

"He's a victim in all this. No need to kill him. But these ones," She walked over to the girl, pushing her over to see her young face. "We shouldn't trust them."

"I really don't want to die, Miss," the brother said. "I'll do anything to keep me and my sister safe."

"Right. Just like she tried to hide and possibly leave you behind first chance she got?"

He stayed quiet.

"Let's give them to Koyuki," I said. "She can decide—"

"You want to spare them?" Silver cut me off. "Fine! Just be sure to live with the consequences later on when it comes to bite us! I'll be in the van."

My jaw hurt as I saw her half-stomp back to the van, not once looking back as I felt my face grow hot. I knew she was right in her tactical choice, but I felt like it was morally wrong. I couldn't bring myself to kill them while they were unable to defend themselves. I shook my head lightly and began to take all the Recallers from the dead.

"You're not like the other Black Snipers," the boy said, as I took his Recaller. "Thank you."

"Don't make me regret this later," I said, almost whispering, as I took his sister's Recaller. "I won't think twice next time I see you stand against me."

I didn't even look back to see if he had nodded to my warning, or for him to even say something in return. I just stood up, feeling the gauze chafe even more against my skin, and walked back to the van. Silver didn't look at me as I closed the door, her gaze set somewhere in the distance. Without saying a word, she turned the engine on, shifted gears, and left, not once speaking during the trip back to the Wraith safe house.

CHAPTER 9

IT WAS DARK when we got back to the rest house, and after parking, Silver made a beeline for the entrance in an angry stride, not once looking back at me. She hadn't said a word the entire trip back, either. Liz's gaze followed her as she passed her by and took the stairs to the rooms below until she disappeared from our view.

"What happened now?" Liz's flat voice carried enough resignation that I didn't have to look at her expression.

I just sighed, taking off my backpack to reach in for the Recallers I had confiscated. "We had a disagreement."

"About?"

"Whether to leave two of the members of the Lolitrons alive or not." I set the first few Recallers down on the coffee table. "I wanted to let them go, but she wanted to kill them. Now she's mad at me because I was against killing unarmed teenagers."

Liz crossed her arms and scoffed, then rubbed the bridge of her nose. "First of all, Kannon, what were you thinking? Leaving them alive was the worst thing you could've done! Go and fix whatever spat you both have, because by the Oath, if you don't, you won't get anything else from me! I'm not dealing with you two being mad at each other while you try to work together to do a job that can get us *all* killed!" She stormed outside.

After she was gone, I put down the last of the Recallers and exhaled, feeling the weight of guilt fall on my chest and shoulders. Liz was right, our disagreement shouldn't have any impact on how we performed as Black Snipers, and there were enough stories in our group of rifts being formed between partners and the consequences of them to compel me to walk up to her room and knock on the door.

Silver didn't answer right away, taking up to the second time of me knocking for her to unlock it and let me in. She paced around for a moment, arms crossed, as her hair, which was tied up in a ponytail, moved back and forth with her constant pacing. Eventually, she stopped, her teal eyes settling on me with a pair of furrowed, frustration-filled eyebrows that extended their tension across the entirety of her body.

With a heavy sigh, and with every ounce of energy I could muster, I pushed a meek, "I'm sorry" into the silence that had formed in those brief moments.

She gave no remark, and her figure stayed still as a statue, making the whole experience feel worse. She relaxed after a while, letting her arms fall to her sides as she shook her head and rolled her eyes, moving toward the bed and sitting at the edge.

"I still don't agree with your decision to let them go," she said, her voice quiet, somewhat small. "Maybe back when we were interrogating that kid at the apartment, that was the correct course of action, but not this time, Katherine. We can't afford to put our lives in danger for the sake of someone who is liable to be a threat to us in the future."

"I can't in good conscience kill someone who is unarmed!"

Silver stood up, fists balled at her sides. "By the bloody Oath, Katherine! Set aside your bloody penchant to follow the damn rules and your moral code for a bloody moment and think about the survival of *all of us*! Do you really think they would do the same for *us* if *we* were in the same situation?"

"No."

She exhaled, her eyebrows relaxing along with her shoulders. "You're all the family I have, Katherine. Everyone else has left. And I don't want some *stupid* decision to take the only semblance of it away from me. I don't want to be left all alone. Not again."

Tears had started to form in her eyes, sliding down and getting caught by her gas mask. I had never seen her cry before, and it made me feel even worse. She had shared a lot of things with me, but she never talked about her past, her family, old friends, or anything before she became a member of the Black Snipers. This was the only hint of that past, and, even though deep inside me, I wanted to ask her questions about it, I couldn't bring myself to do so. We were here because of my choice, not to dive into her life story.

It took her a moment to realize that she was crying in front of me, and she hastily dried her eyes, turning her back to me.

"I want to be left alone. I need to think."

I allowed silence to take the podium in the small space between us and left the room without speaking another word to her. Emotions were running wild in us both. Training told us all to be the master of our emotions, to not let them take control of us. It tended to spell disaster in a job when we allowed our feelings to get in the way, but today felt like a good day to let them be free, even if only for a few moments.

Liz was sitting on the kitchen counter with a bottle of beer in her hand, her red gaze locked on me as I climbed the last of the stairs up to the first floor.

"Are you done fighting?" she asked. "Because I managed to get information out of Arthur Volante's broken Recaller before you got here."

"Everything should be fine," I breathed. "We just need some time."

Liz finished her drink and set it down next to her before she got off the counter. "Arthur had a very strict itinerary set up in his phone's calendar, and there was always something different going on each week, except one thing. He had regular meetings at a restaurant called Discovery. They always happened on the same day, at the same time each week. I'd suggest you go now."

"Silver needs some time alone."

Liz sighed. "Fine. I guess I'll go with you." She pulled her keys out of her pocket. "Get your gear, we're leaving."

"So we're not going to wait for Silver?"

She twirled the keys in her finger, then shook her head as she headed for the door, not saying another word to me. I rolled my eyes and pulled out my Recaller as I began to follow her to wherever she had parked her vehicle.

CHAPTER 10

IT WAS ALREADY CLOSE to midnight by the time Liz stopped her motorcycle near the restaurant, the word 'Discovery' clad against a black slab of concrete and backlit by white lights, drawing in the accent of the word. There was a valet leaning on the small table looking at his phone while the people inside dined in what seemed to be a time-encapsulated bubble. Smiling, laughing, while waiters moved about with a seemingly unnatural grace to bring wine and dishes to the customers.

"We should've waited for Silver."

"Bah." She revved her bike. "You drew me into this mess of yours, now you have to deal with me tagging along."

"I thought you weren't going to do any more fieldwork for me."

She revved the bike again. "Now, hold on." She drove the bike closer to the entrance and parked it right before the valet.

He looked at us with wide eyes, stuttering while Liz took off her helmet and shoved it into his hands, hiding hers in her coat pockets in one motion; I followed suit and gave him mine. Inside, the receptionist quickly came to greet us, and I could tell by her inexpressive eyes that her smile was not even genuine.

"I'm sorry, but do you have a reservation?"

Liz ignored her and pressed on, without looking at her even once as she made a beeline for the kitchen, walking between the white linen tables illuminated by the faint low glow of warm lights that decorated the space inside the restaurant. Post-modern furniture added to the decor of the space, while low-hanging lamps hovered above each booth, providing the feeling of intimacy in the crowded room.

The receptionist hesitated as Liz moved, almost laser-focused on a single point in the room. Waiters tried to stop her with no luck, one ending up face-first on one of the tables, splashing soup on the patrons sitting there. I couldn't stand there, watching, so I followed her, though, unlike with Liz, no one dared to put a hand on me to try to stop me.

"Liz, where are you going?" I said as I caught up to her, but she refused to reply, opting to keep walking, though at that point I realized where she was heading, or more specifically, who she was trying to catch up to.

A man in a tuxedo stood near the back of the room, Recaller in hand as his eyes followed us getting closer to him. *I hate this attention to detail. Ugh!* Liz grabbed his Recaller and slammed it on the ground, and before he could even utter a single word, she pushed him against the wall, pressing her knife against his torso.

"What do you want?" he asked. "I don't have any money. I don't know anything!"

"*Tch.* Let's go to your office," she said. "We've already drawn too much attention."

"It could've been avoided too."

"Unlike *you*, Kannon, I don't have patience." She turned to him. "Move!"

He nodded, both arms in the air as he slid past and walked toward the kitchen, and we followed. I didn't dare to even look, but I could feel the eyes of everyone in the room lingering on us, and the whispers among them were plenty as I followed the man through the double doors, past the chefs, the cooks, and the waiters. All eyes turned as they saw us pass and then duck into a small hallway with just a few doors. He opened one and walked inside; I closed the door behind us, locking it behind my back as Liz forced him to sit.

"No one expects a visit from a Black Sniper," she whispered.

"Shock and awe?"

She nodded.

"That really doesn't work in this setting, you know." I had no idea what she was thinking.

She rolled her eyes. "You have a *fucking* knack to get under my skin. Now, do you still have Arthur's picture?"

I nodded. The next thing I remember was me pointing my gun at the man, his breathing heavy, eyes wide as fat drops of sweat slid down his forehead, somewhat leaning to one side. My training kicked in, and I just felt the rush.

"I wouldn't make any sudden movements in this small space, Mister . . .?"

He swallowed. "Fabian."

"Sit still, keep quiet, and most importantly, don't move. It is the worst thing you could do with a Black Sniper in the same room as you, more so when said Black Sniper needs information and wants to avoid painting a Pollock with your brain in the back wall. Got it?"

He nodded slowly. "W-what do you need, Miss?"

I pulled my Recaller, brought up the picture of Arthur Volante, and placed it on his desk right in front of him. "You've seen this man in here before, right?"

He nodded. "What do you want with him?"

"Not him, he's dead," I said. "What we want to know is, whom did he meet with?"

His eyebrows furrowed. "A woman? Sometimes two other men came, but usually, it was just a lone woman who met with him. They never stayed long."

"How long?"

"I don't know."

Liz scoffed. "We're not going to get anywhere interrogating this piece of shit bowling ball-headed man. He's not going to remember everything. Where do you keep the security footage?"

"We have a small server in the back that an IT guy comes in to look at once a week. If you want names, the receptionist at the front will have a written record of every reservation made in the last two years. Has phone numbers, names, dates, times. Just please, let me live."

"I'll go get the files from the server," Liz said. "Just don't kill the man. He already wet his pants. We don't need to deal with any more commotion."

I took my Recaller and backed out of the room, gun still aimed at the man as I followed Liz, muffled sobbing starting as soon as the door was closed.

The small, beach cooler-sized server was tucked away in a small closet with a router and several cables disappearing up into a tube, several drives connected to it and closed with a security grate. After Liz gave me a frustrated sigh, I pushed her aside and got to work on the lock.

"Why did we have to interrogate that man?"

"He's the owner," Liz said. "An organization like the Lolitrons will need a sufficient enough backing in order to be operational. And we don't know whose hands are being dipped into the Lolitrons's rebellious pie."

"I doubt this restaurant will be able to generate enough revenue to even fund a portion of their activities."

"You don't have the mind of a master criminal, do you, Kannon?"

"I understand how it all works." The lock clicked open. "You don't need to explain it all to me. I was just following your line of thinking."

She rolled her eyes again as she pushed me aside, connecting her Recaller to it. "Just shut up."

"I wish I would've killed you that day," I muttered.

She didn't say anything, but in those moments of silence, I realized that the rush that I had a few moments before in the office was starting to wear off, and that sudden clear thinking was coming back. Though that raised more wonder in my mind. I wanted to formulate questions, but all I drew was a blank, the empty feeling after the rush, the white noise that comes in when the adrenaline tapers off.

Liz tapped me on the shoulder, and I was startled by the slamming of the small cage door as she closed it. I followed her closely, walking back through the same route we took as we came in, and again, all eyes were on us as we walked past, though everyone tried to be discreet about it this time. Once at the door, I grabbed the large book the receptionist had before her, not allowing her a moment to speak, while Liz took both helmets from the valet's hands, tossing me mine as she got on her motorcycle.

"Put the book in the compartment."

I did.

"See you at the base." She was gone before I was able to even reply, her engine picking up as it echoed all around in the street.

"I swear I will kill her once this is all over." I fixed my backpack and began to walk. My thoughts were hurling all manner of insults at Liz's name as I moved down the sidewalk, rage swirling inside me with thunderous anger as the flashes of our spat years ago began to surface, conjuring all the images I was hoping to finally forget.

Though after twenty minutes of walking, with passing cars on the road, and the occasional Rain Enforcer Patrol ship hovering past above like a lazy otter down a calm river, all the rage subsided, but not the uncomfortable annoyance I felt at her actions. I understood that the only reason Silver and I were stuck with her again was because of my procrastination in trying to find another Wraith contact, though I hated to admit that I at least liked her efficiency. I wasn't going to admit that to her, though. I knew Liz would never let me live it down.

Walking the streets of the City of Laohz was an experience I had forgotten about. The scary streets I had to walk to get back to my small studio apartment when I originally moved here to study were now simply tunnels in which I was walking through. It all felt like being in an aquarium, all the people at the other side of the glass, seemingly oblivious to my presence, separated by the shield that being a Black Sniper carried with it.

The Rain Enforcer hover cars often passed by, turning on their flashing lights for several moments, slowing down, and driving alongside me for a few moments before the lights turned back off and the car sped away. *They always give the recruits hover cars.* The now-cooling wind of winter was more common among the canyons of concrete and steel, drawing its chill with it as the people who walked the sidewalk moved to let me pass.

Being a Black Sniper was never easy. Many of us ended up alone, abandoned by many we used to call friends, family, and loved ones. Some stores refused to let us in, putting signs out that read: 'Black Snipers not welcome,' but everyone knew they never enforced it. Who wants to risk it? But the stigma alone is enough to crush the weakest of us. It's why we are paired; it helps us cope with the loneliness that membership carries. "I miss Silver."

"I know," Silver said from behind me. "Just stop walking already!"

"Catch up," I said, then stopped. "How long have you been following me?"

"Few seconds at the very least. Now, let's get in the van. I don't want to leave it running in this part of town."

I nodded, looking at her vehicle illegally parked about twenty feet away on the sidewalk, hazard lights flashing. After giving her a hug and getting dizzy off her coconut-smelling bleached-gray hair, I followed her back to it. Though as soon as the doors closed and she joined traffic, she went quiet. Her gaze grew distant and didn't stray to me once.

"Something's bothering you," I said. "What's wrong?"

She sighed, then pushed a stray strand of hair out of her face, looking at me briefly, then back to the road. "I've just been thinking about what I told you back at the rest house."

"About not wanting to be left alone again?"

She nodded. "I've never told you anything about my family. Where I come from." She took a deep breath. "I don't like to think about it."

"Silver, you don't have to."

"I know." She shifted in her seat. "I didn't think about it much all these years. Then, back there, I just." She shrugged. "It all slipped. I was just *so* mad at you for the stunt you pulled, then the thought of having to run again and leave it all behind. Then, my mind just jumped from one thought to the other, and then I realized that if something happened to you, I'd be all alone again. Just like what happened with my family."

The passing lampposts barely gave off any light to show the tears sliding down her face, though I heard no sobs from her. There was only the constant hum of the hover engines and the air conditioner.

"Are you sure you want to tell me?"

She nodded. "Growing up, I never managed to fit in with any of my classmates. I was always different. At home, it was the same. My parents loved me, made sure all my needs were met, but I never had that special click with them, or with my two older siblings. Despite that, I was still close to them, in my own special way. But eventually, things began to change. Everyone seemed distant; no one talked to each other like we used to. As we grew up, we all just drifted apart. We went from days to weeks to months without talking to each other. Life got in the way of everyone. I haven't heard from my older sister in almost six years, and my older brother was killed two years after he graduated from the Rain Enforcer academy. Mom and Dad moved to Oakcove City."

It was hard to tell in the darkness of almost two in the morning, but as Silver drove, I imagined her reddened eyes as the passing lights briefly illuminated the interior; her head rested on one of her free hands.

"How long has it been?"

"I've not seen my parents in five years. I haven't heard from them in three." She sighed. "Not because of a lack of trying, but lately, I've stopped trying as hard."

"Is that why you said you didn't want to be left alone again?"

She nodded, wiping the tears away. "Yeah."

"If I leave, who will you annoy by calling them *Katherine* every once in a while?"

Silver chuckled. "Don't make me laugh when I want to be sad."

As she chuckled at my horrible joke, I realized that in the four years I'd known her, this was the first time I'd seen her as more than just my coworker and my roommate. I finally felt like I'd managed to peer into another layer of what made her Silver, and I felt warm inside to have been given the privilege to see her be vulnerable with me, even if it was in this single instance.

"Thanks for listening, Katherine."

All I was able to muster was a single nod, as there was this sudden realization that I had been equally secretive towards Silver about my own past. There were things she was already aware of, like the fact that my family was wealthy back in Othara, but there were other things I had kept from her. Silver had just opened up to me willingly, and I didn't want to take this moment away from her, but I also realized this was likely the only time I'd have.

"I've also kept a lot of secrets from you," I said.

"Like?"

"I have an older sister," I said, fighting a knot forming in my throat. "She was difficult for my parents to deal with. Always caused trouble, getting arrested, drugs, alcohol. My dad removed her from the will and banished her here. Bought her a one-way ticket and told her to never come back."

"Were you two close?"

I shook my head. "She was always off doing something, so I grew closer to my parents and my few friends at school. Though, in truth, I was always kind of a loner growing up. I . . . didn't come to enjoy company until I joined with the Black Snipers, to tell the truth."

"You? A loner?" Silver chuckled. "Hard for me to visualize that." She switched the hover form to the tires.

I nodded. "My dad owns a communications company back in Othara, so I had access to things most other kids didn't. I wasn't as charismatic as my sister, so making friends didn't come to me as naturally as it did to her. You'd think coming from a family with money would be incentive enough to make friends, but that is not always the case."

"Hey, you have me," she said, and I felt myself grow warm.

I muttered, "Thanks" before allowing silence to settle in the small, confined space of the van, letting the buzzing sound of the tires over pavement take over and drown the conversation that had come to a natural standstill. It was buried and forgotten, just for the moment to be shattered by Silver.

"I hope Liz has whatever information you got from the restaurant ready by the time we get back."

"There's a lot of things we don't even know yet," I said. "We don't even know why Kax joined the Lolitrons."

Silver put a finger in front of her mask, telling me to remain quiet as her gaze shifted past me. The low, signature rumbling of the engines of the technicals was the first giveaway before I realized that it was there, passing us by. Several teenagers and young adults were inside, loud music blasting from the lowered windows while a single member of the group was in the bed at the back, manning the large turret. After they drove past us, Silver stopped at one of the lights and turned onto a different street, taking a longer way home.

Liz was already asleep by the time we arrived, and the tiredness of a long day was starting to weigh heavily over my shoulders. Silver and I decided to just head straight to bed and talk to her in the morning, but sleep didn't come easily for me that night. When it did, it was filled with nightmares of Kax mocking me, and the tenuous peace we had with the Rain Enforcers was broken, the city in chaos.

The following morning, I found Liz upstairs, sitting on the couch with her laptop next to her and her gaze set on her Recaller. Only her eyes moved to look at me for just a brief moment, before going back to her phone.

"Why did you leave me to walk yesterday?"

"Good morning, Liz. How are you?" she said in a mocking voice. "I'm fine, thank you; how about you?"

I crossed my arms.

She sighed and put the phone aside. "I knew you were going to be breathing down my neck for information as soon as we came back from the restaurant. I can't get information that easily sometimes. Much less with someone hovering around my space."

"What about the reservation logbook?"

"There was nothing worth it in there. All reservations were only made under Arthur Volante's name. I managed to get a picture of the woman from the camera recordings, but aside from that, I don't have much to go on with."

"You've found people with just a picture in the past."

"It's not that easy, Kannon," she said, "Do you think I magically wave my hands and suddenly have all the information you need? I haven't even finished checking all the phones you gave me from the Lolitrons, nor looked at the laptop you brought. If you want something to chew on, I would check with Ceitr. He seems to be interested in this as much as you are."

"How long will it take you to check everything?"

Liz shrugged. "A couple of days. And no, your little hacking device won't help speed things up. I know that look."

I rolled my eyes. "And why Ceitr?"

"Well, Ceitr is one of my minor information contacts." She sighed. "I give him stuff, and he gives me some information. He's been looking into the Lolitrons for some time now, so he'd surely have something that might be useful to you."

"Might?"

"Look, you can either sit here with me and stare at these four walls for about three to four days while I work on all this, or you can go and talk to Ceitr and hope he has something for you to do at the very least. It's your choice." She leaned back and grabbed her Recaller. "I took the liberty of saving his phone number in yours, as well as the picture of the woman."

"I'll call him and set up a meeting." I turned to leave. "Thanks, Liz."

"Yeah, whatever."

CHAPTER 11

THE MIDDAY SUN barely managed to be visible in the cover of clouds that blanketed the city as Silver stopped her van directly in front of the doors of The Clockwork. The lights inside were all turned on, exposing the black service walkways that were above the lights. Some of the employees were walking around, moving tables, sweeping, and mopping. Others were restocking the bar, while from the ground, we could see Ceitr's combed-back hair as he seemed to be pacing above in the VIP area.

As we climbed, the faint sound of slow jazz music filtered through the door. We were surprised to see Ceitr in the middle of the room, hands in his pockets, while the sound came from some speakers partially hidden across the ceiling of the room. One of the bartenders was organizing the shelves behind him, but otherwise, no one else was there.

"Kannon, Silver," he said. "I'm so glad you could join me here today."

I saw the bartender shake his head as he grabbed another bottle of wine and put it on the top shelf.

"Liz said you had some information for us." I crossed my arms.

"Right to the point." He chuckled. "I like that. Well, yes, I do have some information for you. Liz has been sharing a lot with me, and she has been greatly compensated for her efforts. The Inner Circle is deeply interested in this group, you see."

The bartender pulled out a small glass, filled it with ice, and then bourbon, leaving the bottle next to it. His pressed, smoke-gray suit and yellow tie smelled of cologne, and his smile made my heart skip. *Focus.*

"Koyuki always seemed to want to remain distant from them."

"They are proving to be a thorn in her side, and ours too." He moved to grab the glass. "Now, for the piece of information you came here for, no? The woman who met with Arthur Volante manages the logistic operations of the F&L Armaments, a subcontractor of the Rain Enforcers. Her name is Adrianne Scypio. Lovely woman for her age, I might add. Never thought she'd involve herself with these people. In truth, it is a fancy title she invented. She's really the head of the company."

"Do you know this woman?" I said.

He nodded. "She's the reason I had to drop out of the Black Snipers. I thought her company would end up in shambles after the PR nightmare I caused her afterwards."

"F&L, right?" Silver said. "That's the company that makes the PLV-522 Personal Minigun?"

Ceitr nodded and drank from his glass. "You've certainly done your homework, lass. They make everything from the

Magnetic Accelerator Cannons the Rain Enforcer spaceships carry, to your standard nine-millimeter handgun, and everything in between."

"Let me guess," I said. "They also make the turrets the Lolitron technicals are equipped with?"

Ceitr nodded once more. "Most heavy ground transport vehicles from the Rain Enforcers also come equipped with one. F&L doesn't make all the armaments that the Rain Enforcers use, but they do supply about twenty percent of it."

"There is a small office near the outskirts of the city," Silver said. "Near the northeastern part. I know the way; we could drive there. It'll take us about three hours to get there, though."

"Is this minigun the thing you've been eyeing for the better part of two years now?"

Her eyes narrowed as if she was smiling, nodding in the process. "I've been meaning to get one, but it always felt like it was either too bulky, or unnecessary. Besides, I don't have anywhere to put it."

"You can mount it on your van?"

"Right."

"When you do find her," Ceitr began, "don't let her talk too long. If it weren't for her pretty words, I wouldn't have gotten my knee the way it is today."

Silver and I looked at each other before we both nodded. "Do you mind if I ask why?"

He took a sip, his gaze locked on the golden-brown liquid before he got around to swallowing the amount he had in his mouth. "Let's just say that she has a way of making you doubt yourself. So please, be a dear and stuff her mouth with something before she spits a single sentence. Deal?"

I nodded, realizing that underneath the nonchalant tone, there was a faint feeling of bitterness. And again, I regretted the observational skills that Black Sniper training forced us to learn. It was one of the reasons most Black Snipers remained single. We could detect a lot of inflections in people's voices, and we could read body language. It helped us see who was lying, who was trying to cross us, who could be a potential ally—essentially, it helped us read between the lines. It made it hard to trust others when you saw everything, when you could read people's body language and react accordingly. Of course, our training didn't make us perfect, but it was useful. It also made being a Black Sniper a difficult and lonely journey.

After he finished his third glass, he bid us farewell and sat at the bar, watching us leave. As I closed the door behind me, I caught the sudden change in his expression. Although I could've been wrong, it seemed there was a tinge of sadness in his eyes. Whatever I saw, it was all too brief for me to be certain, though the question of whether to ask him about it lingered.

During our three-hour trip, I didn't speak much, as my mind wandered, trying to figure out why everything seemed quiet on the Rain Enforcers' part, as well as with the Lolitrons. As we drove, I noticed that the number of patrols had decreased after our escape. It was an odd feeling to not see a pair of Patrol Ships on the horizon, or hovering above, at least a few times a day. Part of me found that unnerving. I didn't tell Silver about it. I didn't think she had to worry about that. Even the realization that Stella had not made contact with us was strange. It was starting to feel like we were being left to drift, to wander aimlessly through this job we'd been thrust into. I felt like something was wrong, but I couldn't quite place what the problem was.

When we arrived at the location Silver mentioned, I was taken aback at how big it was. I was expecting a small office building, several stories tall, off one of the main streets that traveled the area. Instead, it was a large, campus-like location. A large beige building sitting almost in the middle of a field, with a lake, ample parking, and from what little we could see from our vantage point, a road in the back with several semi-truck trailers parked neatly next to each other.

"You told me this was an office building."

She nodded. "Offices are in the front of the building, and the warehouse slash distribution center is in the back. They have their factories located about one hundred miles north of here, in the middle of nowhere."

"You know an awful lot about this company." I pulled up my backpack and began to check my bullets.

She shifted gears. "They make some of the best guns. Can you blame me?"

"You're such a meathead."

"And you're a socialite stuck-up, but you don't see me complaining, huh, *Katherine*?"

"Leave me alone."

She laughed. "You're so easy to tease. Now, let's go. We should move out of here. Park the van somewhere else so we can sneak in later tonight."

"We should call Liz," I said. "Maybe she can do something about the cameras."

"We'll see."

Silver drove around the campus area, almost twenty acres worth of land, looking for a place to stop the car and wait for nightfall. Eventually, she chose the parking lot of a mall that was located next to it, separated by a chain link fence and barbed wire at the top.

Anticipation and nervousness built in my chest as we waited there, staring at the building in the distance while cars came and went, along with semi-trucks dropping off trailers and picking up new ones. Several Rain Enforcer Patrol Ships hovered above us, moving somewhat lazily across the sky, one of them being followed by a sheriff.

My several attempts to contact Liz were fruitless. I was only able to get a hold of her minutes before the sun set. Aside from her usual irritation, she agreed to help us, but she said that it would take her some time to set everything up on her side. It didn't matter much about the time since Silver and I were planning to break into the facility closer to the middle of the night.

"What do you think will happen if the Lolitrons up the violence against the Rain Enforcers?" Silver said.

Her question was somewhat unexpected. I wasn't going to lie and tell her that I didn't think about it, though. After getting over the initial shock of the sudden inquiry, I exhaled. "Another Cleansing Day-like event most likely."

The fabric of the chair rustled as she moved on it. "I don't think I will be able to stomach another one. And if it's how I expect it, it will be far bloodier than the last."

I allowed silence to settle, the wind moving the leaves of the trees outside as the last rays of the sun finally disappeared over the horizon. The world of night and starlike lights that covered the cityscape in the distance were left behind. Between the buildings, we could see the flashing red and blue lights of the patrolling Rain Enforcers, their sirens drowned out in the cacophony of the city sounds, becoming an afterthought by the time I heard them.

"Do you have an idea of what Stella could be?" I found myself saying as I stared at my own reflection in the glass. The very nature of what she could be, haunted me. Who, *or what*. The only thing we knew was what Liz told us, or implied, that she was a Wraith.

"No."

I took a deep breath, briefly becoming aware of the glow of my wine-red eyes, reflecting off the glass.

"I'm trying to make the time go by," I said. "I'm also nervous."

She turned to look at me, her eyes holding their place for a moment as if she were trying to think of something, or was looking past me, before she went back to her old position without saying a word. But I could tell how she was feeling. The stiffness of her shoulders spoke volumes on how exhausting this had been. The insistent vibrations of my Recaller made us both sit up, and I saw Liz's name set on the screen.

"I'm ready," she said. "The Wraiths had a back door into their servers installed almost eight months ago, and a few friends of mine were tasked with keeping an eye on it. We have taken control of the camera feed, so you both can sneak in."

"Thank you, Liz."

"Just don't get yourself killed. Don't you hang up."

My blood was pumping, and the time between us leaving the van and reaching the chain link fence was almost lost. Only one task was in our heads, so we were just following it, opening a hole in the fence, running across the trailer yard, and avoiding detection by the last few truck drivers as we went. The cold of the night was beginning to set in as the heat that was still lingering on the concrete roads dissipated into the air. Sweat formed on my forehead, and my heartbeat settled in a steady rhythm, as if following a metronome.

Silver and I tried several of the unoccupied dock doors for any renegade open ones, finding one at the fifth attempt. Silver went first, putting her backpack in before I helped her crawl inside. I was right behind her, and although we were in a distribution center, Black Sniper training always told us to assume everyone could have a way to shoot us, and this time, it made more sense.

Polished concrete floors, stacks of wooden crates of varying sizes, forklifts of different makes, sizes, and models, and towers of empty pallets dotted the area. There were also desks scattered in certain places, and the distant honking of a few leftover employees driving forklifts echoed through the eerily quiet space. Silver cleaned her jacket with one hand while she had her shotgun in the other as I tried to orient myself.

"There's the entrance to the front," I said, grabbing Silver's sleeve.

Most of the lights in the warehouse were turned off, and the musty scent of years-old layers of dust over the wooden crates began to clog up my nose, making it run. *I can't sneeze here.* I stifled it, but I got a headache as a result.

As we reached the entrance to the hallway, the figure of a security guard was reflected off the blind spot mirrors for the drivers. I stopped dead in my tracks, grabbing Silver by the arm and pulling her back as I kept my gaze locked with the reflection. It was too late. His eyes met mine, and he was already reaching for his handgun.

Instinct took over. My hand wrapped around the collar of his white-buttoned shirt, my leg swept his, knocking him off his feet and onto his back, knocking the wind out of him. His eyes were wild and he was wheezing, gasping for air as Silver grabbed his handcuffs and tied him to a nearby set of pipes for the fire lines. She then took off his shoe and sock, cramming the sock into his mouth as deep as she could before she knocked him out with her shotgun.

"Was that necessary?"

Silver just flashed me a look before she walked away; I shook my head and followed.

The hallway was different from the warehouse. Tiles instead of concrete floor, and office roofing and lights in the ceiling with matching white walls that held advertisements for their next corporate event coming in the next few months. There was also promotional material for the weapons and equipment they sold.

"Liz, are you still there?"

"Yes."

"Where to next?"

"Adrianne's office will be located on the third floor," she said. "On the eastern side of the building, or your right when you get off the elevator. There are about three more guards inside the building, so keep a close eye out. I'll call you when you get to the office."

We arrived at the lobby, standing right behind the reception desk manned by a single guard focused on her Recaller. A set of stairs were to our left that led to the second floor, and another on our right. The elevator was to our right.

As the mirror-like doors closed before us, the reflection of my slightly unkempt, wavy auburn hair and wine-colored eyes decorated with lightly dark circles felt like the weight of the contract was beginning to ooze through my skin. Whatever desire I had to take care of them as I stared at my reflection, handgun in hand, disappeared as the face of another security guard appeared as the doors opened.

We all stood there for a moment, looking at each other, before we reacted. His hand went for his handgun. I grabbed his wrist and collar, tightening my grip as I slammed him into the wall, metal clattering as he grunted. I kicked him to force him to kneel, but the sudden hit of electricity made me fall to my knees. Several shots from Silver's shotgun drilled into the pain that gripped my body, and a flash of white was on the floor farther inside of the building as he backed away with his handgun.

The kick of mine felt familiar as I fired it three times, and blood stained his leg and dominant hand. He fell to his back next to one of the cubicles, breathing heavily as his body shook with pain. His gaze shifted between Silver and me, teeth gritted, brows furrowed. I didn't even think about it. No thought, no hesitation as I shot him three more times, killing him.

I don't know how long I stared at the dead man. I just know Silver grabbed me by the arm and forced me to follow her at a fast pace for a moment as the rush wore off enough for me to get back into rhythm with her. The face of the man, his worried and scared expression, just stayed with me, fresh in my head as we both ran through the building. *He was just doing his job.*

"We don't have the element of stealth anymore," she said as we reached the door to Adrianne's office. "But I'm not kicking this door."

I didn't blame her. The door was made of knotty alder wood, and the lock was the standard secure knob common in many buildings across the City of Laohz. Opening the door with the lockpick set was harder than previous times, as my hands were trembling, and I couldn't keep myself focused. I gritted my teeth as I kept struggling to get the right pressure into the pins. I bit my lip until I tasted blood, forcing myself to stop and breathe.

"You have to be a master of your emotions," I said under my breath. "You have to control them." I breathed in, then out. After repeating this several times, I took one last deep breath and unlocked the door.

The inside of the office was painted peach, with chic paintings on two of the walls, a map of the City of Laohz on another, and a wooden desk in the middle with a desktop on top. Several stacks of books and folders lay on top. The office chair was padded with a seaweed-green cushion. The Recaller went off in my pocket moments later, and I set it on speaker.

"Since you killed that guard," she said, "we don't have as much time as I would've liked. Try logging into it."

I pressed the keyboard. "It's password protected."

She groaned on her end. "Try typing 'Password,' uppercase p."

"Liz, do you really think someone like her will have that kind of password?"

"You wouldn't believe me how many times I found someone using a stupid password like that before."

I rolled my eyes but tried it, but the computer remained locked. "No."

"Try 'Password1' then."

"No, it doesn't work either."

"You two better hurry up," Silver said as she moved to the door. "I don't like our odds at this point."

"Look around. Some people keep their passwords written down in their desk drawers or underneath the desk."

I did, opening drawers and searching through all the papers and notes she had, moving the folders and all the files aside, as well as searching under the desk and her office chair, but found nothing.

"Do you have any better ideas?" I half yelled.

"Look, let's not start this right now. Try 'admin'?"

The screen changed to 'Welcome' before loading onto the desktop. "Yes, that worked, now what?"

There were things being moved on her end, papers fell, as well as the sound of distant cans falling to the floor. "Read me her email. Most people in corporate leave their accounts logged in, so it should be easy to find."

"Okay," I said, "the address is avillanova@fandl.clz."

There was only typing on her side for a few moments, then a can being set down. "I just sent you a file. Open that and let it run."

Anticipation and excitement were rising as I opened the email Liz sent and clicked on the link that was attached to it. "Why does it look like an advertisement?"

"It's an old phishing template. It's much easier to set all this up when someone is inside. Just let me know when it finishes downloading."

"Time's up," Silver said from the door as a pair of security guards were coming in our direction, hands reaching for their handguns. Silver opened fire.

"It just did," I said. "Now what?"

"Don't fucking die. All the work I had to do will be wasted effort if you do. It'll take me a bit to get all the data copied, so I suggest you leave!" She hung up.

Several shots hit the door and several things behind us, and I don't know what compelled me to slam the door shut and lock it, but before I even realized I was doing it, it was done. Silver began to reload her shotgun, while I looked around the office for a way to leave, as I had effectively trapped us in that room.

"What's the plan?" Silver said.

At that moment, the memory of Blacklight, the leader of the Specters, came to mind as his voice repeated the words that he told me when I got my mods for the first time. My attention turned to one of the windows hidden behind several cabinets and a set of blinds.

"Do you remember what the maximum height is that we can jump down with our mods?" I said as I raced to push the cabinets away.

"Katherine," Silver said, "whatever idea you just hatched, it's not one I want to follow."

I moved one of the metal cabinets aside. "Do you want to get arrested by the Rain Enforcers again?"

She rolled her eyes and strapped her shotgun on her backpack as she came to help me. After we made a big enough space, Silver went for her handgun, but I stopped her, pointing out the sliding rails that were installed as a fire safety standard.

The soft wind threw up our hair as we looked out and down, then at the distance to the avenue that ran next to the distribution center. Silver climbed the edge first, letting out a small yelp as she looked down.

"I really don't like this idea, Kannon." She turned to me, eyebrows furrowed in worry. "I really don't like it. Are you sure our mods will let us survive?"

"I don't think Blacklight would tell me that our mods can help us survive a fall of a maximum height of four floors if he wasn't sure it could work. Trust me."

She nodded, then turned back to the fall, closed her eyes, took a deep breath, and jumped. She was on the ground seconds later, losing balance and falling face-first to the floor, but she managed to get up.

I would be lying if I said I wasn't scared as I climbed up, vertigo slithering in quicker than expected. The cool wind that wafted by, the distant zooming of cars in the street, excitement, anticipation, fear, all were jumbled inside my chest. The door began to unlock, and I had no time to think before I forced myself to jump.

The knot of fear that you get when you go down a roller-coaster grew within me as I felt the rush of wind, and the ground approached fast. Pain shot through my legs, belly, chest, then shoulders and arms as I landed, and like Silver, I was unable to keep myself standing, so I fell forward with barely enough time to put my hands out first. Almost immediately, Silver dragged me back to my feet and pulled me behind her in a full sprint back to the van.

She said something to me that I didn't understand, and I heard voices behind me. Sirens echoed in the distance, but the sprint from the building to the van, what happened during it, was lost in my mind, almost as if someone turned off the recording in a camera. We both reached the van as the guards seemed to yell from the building. Unable to make out their words, Silver and I closed the doors, then she shifted gear and burned rubber as we drove away.

"That was too close for comfort," she said as she forced herself into traffic. "I would like to avoid life-threatening situations for a few days."

I looked back at the building. The window was still open as one of the guards seemed to be there, probably following us with his gaze. "The Lolitrons will know we were there now."

"At least the Rain Enforcers didn't catch up to us this time."

Red and blue lights flooded the street around us. Silver lost control of the steering wheel as two pairs of thrusters appeared around us, kicking up debris everywhere, hitting the windshields.

"Rain Enforcer Impound Ship!" I said as we realized Silver's efforts to leave the underside of the ship were fruitless. The ship's claws wrapped around the van, then it began to gain altitude, until the van's wheels were no longer touching the ground. At that point, Silver let go of the steering wheel and leaned back, rubbing her temples.

"By the Bloody Oath." She breathed out a deep sigh. "Why did I have to speak too soon?"

"We're not escaping this time," I said. The ship that had grabbed us was gaining altitude with each passing second. "We'll just have to wait until they let us go to get our answers."

CHAPTER 12

WE HAD BEEN CAUGHT in the Impound Ship's claws for almost three hours now. Dawn was just three hours away as the ship holding us captive darted between buildings and other small air-traffic. It was evident that the ship was heading for the outskirts of the City of Laohz, our van rocking gently in its claws. After some time, the high-rises gave way to the outskirts of the city, mostly residential and low-density buildings, with the forest visible near the edge of the skyline and drawing closer.

Several Patrol Ships hovered near a particular area, lights flashing, while a Sheriff Patrol Ship was grounded on an overlook, several black cars parked at the opposite side, with people standing around. Even from the distance we were at, I could tell their heads had turned to the ship that was holding us hostage. The shifting sound of the engines, and the sudden drop in altitude, was tell-tale enough sign for me that this was our destination.

"Where are we?" Silver said, breaking the silence as she sat back upright and looked around.

"Black Cat Overlook," I muttered.

Black Cat Overlook was an important location in the City's history, where The Cleansing really started, at the height of the tensions between the Black Snipers and the Rain Enforcers.

Wraiths had pulled data from their servers, and we had seen the Rain Enforcers mobilizing forces into the City from off-world for almost two months. We all knew something was going to happen. Many of the documents stolen had several instances of the word *Mentalities*. A secret project with no other information other than the bits the Wraiths stole.

A meeting was convened between some of the Black Sniper Elders and Colonel Harris and his closest men. Sadly, the meeting didn't go as we hoped, and he ordered the slaughter of everyone present before the sirens went off all over the City of Laohz. The day became known as the Blood Flag Incident by the Black Snipers.

After the crisis reached a standstill during the fighting, Black Cat Overlook was the place where the initial steps of ceasefire were taken. Troops still alive stood down, and the violence receded. The Rain Enforcers put down any looting and rioting, and in weeks, everything was running as if nothing had happened, but the scar was there, invisible across the entirety of the city, and surviving Black Snipers still remembered the Rain Enforcer's betrayal at the overlook. No one in The Oath had been able to forgive them for it, even after two years.

Her face turned to me, then forward, and her eyes widened briefly. Then, she sat back and passed her hands over her eyes in what seemed to be frustration. Her gaze seemed lost, looking for a way to get out of this situation, but there was none.

It's not that bad. I knew what this was about as we got closer and were able to distinguish the faces waiting for us to be delivered.

The ship began to descend in the middle of the overlook, turning to make us look back at the City. I turned the van on, moments before the ship released us, in just enough time for the thrusters to brunt the landing as Koyuki's face appeared to our left, surrounded by ten of her men and her personal Black Sniper bodyguard.

Stepping out into the cool night, we moved into the area flooded with the lights of the hovering ships.

Surrounded by faces that hid more than just resentment to the opposing group, it felt like walking out toward the eye of a storm as the cloud of dust that was kicked up by the Impound Ship as it flew off dissipated.

This was the meeting Koyuki Akikawa had told us about the day after Kax tried to kill me. The meeting with Colonel Harris, the Rain Enforcer in charge of all the Rain Enforcer patrol units in the City of Laohz. The man who orchestrated the boots on the ground during The Cleansing.

"Everyone is here," he said as Silver joined me. "Now, I hope you're open to explain why my men are being killed by your Black Snipers despite the agreement the Rain Enforcers have with you and your forces.",l

Koyuki crossed her arms, her amber-colored turtleneck tugged by the wind as she moved forward, her bodyguard following closely. Once she stopped, she called us and Colonel Harris closer.

"Always so impolite," she said. "We meet here at your request for an open space, and you so rudely skip introductions."

"I want answers, Miss Akikawa."

"I can't believe this is how you bring us to this meeting, Colonel," Silver said, crossing her arms. "We would've come willingly."

"One can never be too careful with people like you."

Koyuki shifted her weight. "Colonel, I invited you to a meeting to discuss this matter that is plaguing our City, not as an enemy, but as a potential ally. And yet you come to me demanding answers as if the Black Snipers owed anything to *you*. You have no power here to demand answers from me, Colonel."

"Then why did you—"

Koyuki held up her hand. "You will learn to listen when you are in my presence, Colonel. I invited you here to discuss the violence that has been brought to the men and women who serve under you, not to be ordered around as if I was one of your soldiers." She gazed at me briefly. "I will dismiss this indiscretion just this once and tell you this: I did not order such an affront that would jeopardize the agreement all the members of The Oath have with the Rain Enforcers. We are not *stupid*."

"What about the cargo ship your accomplice here shot down two months ago? The men she killed when she destroyed it? Expensive military hardware was lost because of her rash actions!"

"It was an isolated job requested by a client," I said. "The agreement states clearly that such jobs will happen, and they will be executed. It is also stated in the agreement that you are free to try to stop us from completing jobs targeted at any and all Rain Enforcers. We are doing our job, just as you are doing yours."

"No one in the Black Snipers sanctioned the free killing of Rain Enforcers," Silver added. "No one is funding the rogue group called the Lolitrons to do so either."

"So you expect me to ignore it? My superiors are asking questions about this, Miss Akikawa! They are demanding results!

Not to mention the pressure they are applying for the apprehension of Miss . . . Kannon here. I cannot wave my hand and dismiss everything they have brought up against *you* nor against *her* for the events that have happened in the last two months!"

"I believe we just gave you the answers your bosses are looking for, Colonel Harris," Koyuki said. "Do what you will with it. But you have a choice to make before you leave today. Break the agreement, and be besieged on two fronts, or accept the truth that has been presented to you for what it is. In the end, Colonel, the only head that will roll is yours."

Silence fell among all of us, wind rustling the leaves of the trees around the overlook as his eyes moved between Koyuki, Silver and me.

"If you care for your men as much as you say you do," Koyuki added, "you will know what to do. This meeting is over."

Colonel Harris stood straight, saluted Koyuki Akikawa, turned on his heel, and walked back to his ship, followed by his co-pilot. After they both climbed on, the two Patrol Ships hovering nearby moved some distance away and waited for him to take off, following him shortly.

We all stood there in silence, watching the ships get smaller as they flew back to the City of Laohz, the echoing of the ship's engines fading to the background, getting drowned in the wind combing through the leaves of the trees nearby, and the bugs of the night that chirped in the dark, peppered with the occasional crunching of loose asphalt beneath our feet as some of us shifted in place.

Koyuki was the first to break the silence that had settled between all of us present, giving me a pleased gaze before smirking.

"You are free to go, Miss Kannon, Miss Silver."

"Why did you need us in this meeting?" I asked.

She smiled, looked at her bodyguard, then back at us. "You're free to go, Miss Kannon. I'll have further work for you soon."

She didn't allow me to utter another word, as she went back to the black sedan, her men following suit. Engines joined the cacophony of sounds around us, and in moments, they were gone, leaving me and Silver alone in the overlook.

"Let's go home," Silver said. "I don't even know why Koyuki dragged us to this meeting in the first place." She pulled out her keys.

I didn't have an answer for her. Nothing came to mind as we both walked to her van. Whatever Koyuki was planning by inviting us to that meeting, she never shared it with either of us.

Silver started her van, but it stalled. "Of all the places to take us for this meeting." She tried a second time. "It had to be Black Cat Overlook!"

She slammed her hands on the steering wheel, eyes glaring at the trees in the distance as she grumbled under her breath and tried to start it for a third time.

"Fina-fucking-ly!"

My Recaller vibrated as she shifted gears and began to drive.

"Liz," I said, "do you have something new?"

"Where the fuck are you two?" I've been trying to find you for the better part of an hour, and I can't find your Recallers anywhere!"

"We're at Black Cat Overlook."

She sighed. "By the f—why are you there?"

"Liz, do you have something for us?"

There was silence for a moment, then a heavy sigh. "I did find something. That laptop you gave me had a detailed record of all the invoices that mechanic Vitis did for the Lolitrons. Two accounts were used to pay for all the repairs and custom jobs. One belongs to Adrianne and the other to F&L Armaments' direct accounts.

"I followed her spending habits with her corporate card and cross-referenced it with the scraps I got from her online shopping, which allowed me to get her personal credit card information. Thanks to that, I was able to follow the paper trail of receipts and expenditures across the city and built a somewhat detailed picture of her schedule."

"Thank you, Liz."

She scoffed. "Just make sure you deal with Adrianne. We can't have her fund the Lolitrons anymore." She hung up.

Silence fell as I put my Recaller away. Silver's gaze remained focused beyond the windshield, hands on the steering wheel, shoulders tensed until she exhaled.

There were a lot of groups now involved in the mess the Lolitrons were stirring. The fact that the Rain Enforcers started to take a more direct approach with the situation didn't bode well for all involved, and they were going to do everything in their power to keep the City under their control, even by force if they needed to.

Koyuki Akikawa, in the meantime, would most likely sit on the sidelines and watch as the whole situation unfolded. She would only take direct action if she was forced to. As for the Wraiths and the Specters, they most likely would take their usual support role to whatever the Black Snipers deemed necessary.

The only thing Silver and I had for a solid lead was the clue Liz gave us, and as such, our next target. After we took some time to talk about what happened, we left the overlook to search for Adrianne and get answers from her. It would take us several hours to make it back to the city, so stopping to rest was not an option.

CHAPTER 13

THE TENSION WAS PALPABLE the next morning as Silver and I drove out into the streets with Adrianne's schedule in our Recallers. Several times during our drive to one of her first stops, patrol ships sped past above us, low enough to the ground to make the whole van shake. Sirens echoed somewhere in the distance, hidden away by buildings.

"This feels like the Cleansing all over again," I muttered as I saw the third Patrol Convoy speed over us.

"Even the news is talking about it," Silver said as she pointed at the subtitled screen with the news.

". . . Harris has declared an Orange Level Alert across the City of Laohz and has issued a mandatory curfew from 8pm to 6am after several Rain Enforcer squadrons have been found dead, killed by what appears to be a new gang that has taken a foothold in the City. When asked if the Black Snipers were involved, this is what he had to say: 'The idea of the Black Snipers being involved in this crisis has been looked into, but so far, our investigations have proved that the M.O. of this rogue group does not match that of the Black Snipers. We will continue to monitor the situation and make arrests when necessary. The safety of the people of the City of Laohz comes above all else.' The Colonel is also—"

We drove away, cutting off the rest of the broadcast.

"The broadcasts are similar to when tensions were rising two years ago," I said. "I'm afraid that this conflict with the Lolitrons will lead to another Cleansing. I still can't forget those days."

Silver nodded. "The first few days were difficult for me. I still remember the first firefight I was involved in. I killed way too many soldiers during those months. All I could think of was my brother, hoping I wouldn't be the one to end his life. In the end, he just died in the aftermath. No matter how much I try, though, it's hard to forget those days. What becomes hard to remember is just the events that led up to it."

I slumped on my seat, looking up at the moving skyline as the fading memories of all the news broadcasts that had been fabricated by the Rain Enforcers in order to raise tensions between us among the people of the City. It was effective, to a certain extent, but during the Cleansing, it was the Black Snipers who protected the civilians the most. Everyone in the Black Snipers knew that everything had just been used as an excuse by the Rain Corporation, not that the reasons mattered much now, two years later.

We fell into silence, driving along the city for another hour until we managed to see the iconic sports car that Adrianne drove. It was not where we expected it to be, instead parked in a packed parking lot between buildings. She stood there next to it in a glittery white jacket and black pencil skirt, her hands crossed as she talked to members of the Lolitrons, their technicals surrounding the car.

"Keep driving and keep low," I said as I looked back. Silver turned around and into a nearby alley.

Once parked, we moved in as close as we could, sneaking between the cars in the lot. Though there were only about five cars between us and Adrianne, we could barely hear what they were talking about. Clicking and a hand reaching for my spare magazine made my heart jump, but my focus was on the somewhat distant conversation.

"And what are you gonna do?" Adrianne barked. "You and your men are pathetic. You wouldn't be armed the way you are if it weren't for my help and my company. So why don't you take that misogynistic ego and swallow it? I'm giving you surplus merchandise that was deemed to be discarded but is in good condition. Count yourselves lucky. Otherwise, you'd all be just another petty gang playing under the feet of giants."

There was a yelp and the slamming of something against a car. "Condescending rich bitch. You're *lucky* Fate and Vahar want you alive. I would have put a bullet through your skull if I could."

There was some groaning from Adrianne, as well as some words, but we couldn't hear.

"Should we go?" Silver mouthed.

I shook my head. She rolled her eyes, then made a notion with her fingers to sneak closer.

". . . think that hurting me will help you?"

"The weapons better be delivered to the drop-off location, Adrianne. You made a deal with *us*, and we expect *you* to deliver. Got it? Good. We're leaving." Doors opened then closed as engines were turned on, leaving shortly after as tires screeched and they merged onto the avenue.

Adrianne was sitting on the ground, coughing hard as she held her stomach with both hands as we left our hiding spot and moved closer to her, guns drawn.

Not even your money can protect you, it seems.

"Adrianne," I said. "We need to talk."

She chuckled between coughs, one of her eyes beginning to swell. "You think waving a gun in my face will scare me?"

I sighed and put it away as I crouched before her, moving her face to look at her injured eye. "Why are you helping the Lolitrons?"

She looked at me from head to toe, her expression somewhat twisting as she seemed to be looking at every inch of me, then she swatted my hand away. "Who are you?"

"Kannon," I said, taking my backpack off. "This here is Silver. We're Black Snipers."

"Shit," Adrianne said flatly.

I looked into her eye and put some ointment on it, making her wince. "Why are you helping the Lolitrons?"

Everything fell silent between us, with only the sounds of the city rushing around us, the constant breeze that wafted by, and the wincing sounds of Adrianne as I applied ointment to her bruises and scratches. Several of her manicured nails were broken, her makeup was smeared in some places, and her white jacket was tussled. At least it wasn't damaged, which was more than I could say for her pencil skirt and broken heels.

"I don't have to say anything to you."

I stopped and just held my stare. "No, you don't. But it'd be in your best interest if you did. Who are Fate and Vahar?"

"I'm not telling you anything, Kannon. Now, if you're done bothering me, I have a busy schedule today, and I don't need any more no—" She fell to the ground unconscious, a large gash opening on her cheek, where Silver had hit her with the stock of her shotgun.

"Seriously? Why did you do that?"

Silver rolled her eyes as she knelt next to me and searched the pockets of Adrianne's jacket. "We can't stay here in the open talking to her all day, Katherine."

"What makes you think I was going to let that happen?"

She stopped and locked eyes with me briefly, then went back to the task.

"Now you're mad at me?"

She pulled out Adrianne's Recaller and gave it to me. "We can't play nice anymore, Katherine! Why are you losing your edge now? This is not the time for it, not with all that is going on!"

"I'm not losing my edge!"

"Then act like it!" She rubbed her temples. "Show me you're the Black Sniper you were before all this started."

Silver was pacing away, hands balled at her sides, as I held Adrianne's Recaller in my hand. This job was creating more tension between us than we had previously. I had to admit to myself that the more this developed, the harder it was becoming to tap into my training. She wasn't the enemy, and anger clouded my senses whenever we butted heads, but I never told her about these thoughts, or the fact that I could tell the stress of this contract was getting to her.

"What do you want to do with her?" I ended up saying, instead of any of the other things on my mind.

"Let's just take her with us," Silver said. "Liz can work on her Recaller, and we can work on something else while we figure out how to deal with her."

I nodded. "Go get the van. We—" My words were cut short by the vibrations of my Recaller, and I felt my skin go cold as I saw the name on the screen.

"Who is it?"

"Stella."

CHAPTER 14

MY NERVES WERE RATTLED, I felt myself break out in a cold sweat, and the hairs on the back of my neck suddenly stood on end. I didn't understand why I felt like that at the sight of Stella's name on my Recaller, but there was no denying my body's reaction. By the time I decided to answer, the ringing had stopped, and the screen was glitching as the iconic shaped fox face of Stella appeared on the screen with a black background.

"K-Kannon," she said as the phone went to speaker mode by itself. "The capture of the asset: Adrianne, has proven valuab-b-ble. New directive: Eliminate Adrianne. Asset value has been deemed negligible."

"She has information that we need to extract from her," Silver said, carrying her in her arms.

The screen glitched, a low, synthetic hum coming through. "Your progress has exceeded projecte-e-ed expectations. Elimination of assets, Adrianne estimated-e-ed to destabilize Lolitron organization by further 21.16%. Reward to be dispensed upon completio-o-o-on."

"Stella," I said, "she has information on what we believe to be two high-ranking members of the Lolitrons. We need to talk to her to—"

"Request denied," Stella said, interrupting me before I could even explain our plan. "Fail-safes have been implemented to ensure the permanent destabilization of the organization. Your orders have been issued. Comply, or be subjecte-e-ed to correctional disciplinary action."

Pain began to pulse through my jaw as my grip tightened around the Recaller. I wanted to ignore her orders, but something in me wouldn't let me speak up, and a quick glance at Silver told me she was equally hesitant. In the grand scheme of things, we didn't know what the fail-safes Stella implemented were, and questioning her about it would likely yield no answer from her, so I had to swallow hard and take a deep breath.

"How are we supposed to get information on Fate and Vahar?"

"Eliminate Adrianne. Asset value proven to be negligible. Elimination proves the best course of action for the best resu-u-ults. Reward will be dispersed upon completion of the contract. You have five minutes."

I turned to Silver, whose eyebrows were furrowed, knuckles growing white as she tightened her grip on the unconscious woman in her arms. Her teal gaze met mine, and her eyebrows furrowed even further. She didn't have to tell me she didn't like the idea of killing our only lead, but the correction that Stella was talking about was not something we were willing to find out about, so I nodded, and she rolled her eyes.

"Put her in her car," I said, putting the Recaller in my pocket, trading it for the handgun strapped to my thigh.

"It feels wrong to kill her while she's out cold," Silver said.

I nodded and tried to wake her up. As her eyes opened and looked around, I had to harden myself, push everything aside, and call back on the words of my trainers. *Dehumanize the enemy. They are just targets.* My breathing grew deeper as she slowly came to, but it all ended as soon as her eyes met the barrel of my gun, and widened, then a shot rang out, echoing in the parking lot that was nestled between the buildings we were in. The cream-colored leather seats and glittery white jacket were drenched in blood, the air flooded with the smell of rust and gunpowder.

Silver sighed and paced a distance away, arms crossed. I took several deep breaths, trying to keep myself from succumbing to the rush of emotions washing over me like a tidal wave. Frustration, anger . . . I closed my eyes and took a deep breath to keep myself from gagging, pulling everything together to regain my composure as I went back to Stella.

"She's dead," I said. "I hope the loss of information was worth it."

There was only the synthetic hum emanating from her end of the line, lasting a few moments. "Reward has been dispensed. We are pleased with your progress. Information of Fate and Vahar has been granted. Further tasks will be allotted as necessary. We will be watchi-i-i-ng." The call ended, returning my Recaller's screen to normal.

I fell to my knees after putting my Recaller away, and I couldn't hold myself back from retching. Cold sweat and the sudden wave of dread, guilt, and regret almost overwhelmed me. *I shouldn't have done this.* The words just echoed in my mind over and over as I gagged, then retched again, sweat forming on my forehead, and my body suddenly feeling warm as I closed my eyes. Adrianne's face staring up at me was burned into my mind.

I felt Silver's hand on my shoulder, squeezing it lightly before she let go, and I heard her footsteps recede in the direction of the van. Tears welled up in my eyes, and I wanted to cry, but I didn't know what emotion was calling them forward, so I just did my best to stop myself as I stood and followed Silver.

"Do you think Stella should be trusted?" Silver said, eyes meeting mine.

My Recaller vibrated twice, and on it was the information Stella had provided. "I don't know. She is an unquantifiable unknown that is paying us good money to deal with this situation. Whether she'd be involved in this or not matters little in the end. Koyuki would've likely assigned us, or someone else, to deal with the Lolitrons at some point or another. No one wants to see chaos engulf this City again. Not so soon."

Silver didn't speak; she just shifted gears and took off.

"Do you think Liz has managed to get any information from the Recallers?"

She shrugged. "I'm still trying to find out what Stella's angle is. Ugh, thinking about it gives me a headache, and I'm tired of running around in circles trying to find out where we stand in this storm we managed to wander into."

"I know it's my fault," I said. "All this fucking mess started with the contract we took from Stella."

She sighed, rubbing her forehead with her free hand as she turned on a corner. "I'm not trying to blame you, Katherine. I'm just frustrated. I miss the easy missions."

"Yeah, but easy missions get boring after a while. You'll wish you had another mess to clean before long."

"I hate it when you're right."

"If you don't want me to be right, you can ask Koyuki to reassign you to another partner."

She gave me a sideways glare. "You're not getting rid of me that easily, Katherine."

"And I wish you'd stop using my real name," I said. "I wonder if I should start using your real name too?"

"Don't you dare."

"Don't force me, then." I grinned.

"Just go ahead and call Liz. I want to know where we need to go next."

I stifled a laugh as I looked up Liz and called, the line ringing a few times before she picked up.

"By the Oath," she said. "I thought something had happened to you both!"

"What made you think that?"

"I've been trying to call you both for the last twenty minutes! I couldn't even find your Recallers!"

"I'd rather have the annoying Liz back," I said.

"Look, Stella gave me a quick message that disciplinary action was to be taken against you two. Just promise you won't let that happen."

I could feel the tremble in her voice as she said the last few words. I heard her taking a deep breath away from the line, barely audible. The thought of asking her what Stella's discipline entailed flashed through my mind, but I never mustered the nerve. It was one of those things where ignorance about the subject was better than knowing the details.

"Did you get anything from Adrianne?"

"Yes, she won't fund the Lolitrons anymore," Silver said.

"Good. She'll be a valuable asset to us in the future. Hopefully cutting them off from Adrianne will hamper them."

"Adrianne is dead," I said.

There was silence on her end for what felt like minutes, allowing me to notice the several Patrol Ships as they sped past us and stopped one of the Lolitron technicals farther ahead. Silver took an alternate route.

"What did you do, Kannon?"

"Stella's orders."

She sighed.

"Why are you mad now?"

"No, it's . . ." She breathed in. "It's just Wraith stuff. Don't worry about it. Stella sent enough information here on Fate and Vahar. It'll take me a bit to organize it into something that makes sense to a non-Wraith member."

"Did you get anything from the Recallers?" Silver said.

"Most of the Recallers had junk in them. Nothing that would be of interest to you. However, one of them had a lot of talk about that Military outpost in the southern part of the City. I think it was the Kostic Military Outpost."

"Why would they talk about that place?" Silver said.

"I don't have a lot of information on why, I'm afraid. Just that it was a location of much interest to them."

I turned to Silver and saw her eyebrows furrowed. "We'll have to ask Koyuki."

"I can get the information, but it will take too much time. Time we don't have."

"Well, we need information on that military station. We'll go visit Koyuki, see if she can glean a clearer picture on what could possibly be there," I said. "Perhaps she can set up another meeting with Colonel Harris if she doesn't have it."

"I'll reach out to my contact network and dig around some more. I'll keep you both updated."

"Thanks, Liz."

"Save it, Kannon." She hung up.

Charming, as always.

Silver didn't say anything, just switched the blinker on and got on the highway toward Hanabatake Block Host, to Koyuki's house.

▲ ▲ ▲

The rays of the sun cast a combination of reds, oranges, and grays across the sky as Silver drove through the gates of Koyuki's mansion, the crunching of the tires giving a soft comfort as we parked behind two black sedans.

"I recognize that motorcycle," I said. "Rui's here today."

Rui Kuwabara was one of the few people to have known Koyuki Akikawa long before she was a Black Sniper, and the leader of the organization. Before she was in control of sixty-seven percent of all the ACCENT drug trade in the City of Laohz. She was also the one who approved and gave the final word on who was to join the elite members of the Black Sniper Hunters, and it was she who oversaw the logistics of the chaos that had been the Cleansing. I had only met her once before, and the only way I could describe her was with one word: bitter.

"She's probably mad at Kax's betrayal," Silver said. "What do you want to do, Katherine?"

I knew she wasn't mocking me this time, her voice carrying with it a tinge of fear. I didn't reply, just left the van and climbed the steps, though the loud opening of the double doors made me stop midway up as a woman left the house. She had waist-length, ink-black hair tied in a ponytail, amber-modded eyes burning brightly, and tattoos that covered her arms and neck. She stopped in her tracks, eyebrows thin and furrowed as she eyed everyone present, then exhaled.

My heart was racing, my chest contracting as anticipation and a dash of dread mounted as she walked over to me, eyes set and glaring, the same sharp, predatory gaze that Koyuki had. Rui managed to make me feel defenseless, as all the stories of her exploits flashed across my mind. Deep down, I knew some of them were pure fallacies, but even among the lies, there were nuggets of truth. Like when she killed one of her old classmates and hung her corpse from a tree at the entrance of the school she used to go to. I had seen the pictures, and her cruelty and brutality were something I was never going to match.

"How close were you to Kax?" she demanded, her tone matching her demeanor.

I thought for a moment. "We grew up together, but we weren't that close."

"Good," she said, "because that motherfucker you call a cousin has killed *half* of the Black Snipers under me, and he turned Fate and Vahar into fucking *traitors!*"

"Wait," Silver said. "Vahar was a former Black Sniper?"

Rui turned to her, crossing her arms as she nodded. "I trained them both. I put up a bounty for both of them, but seeing as you two are already working to kill Kax, Koyuki decided to give you exclusive rights to them as well."

"What about Kax?" I asked.

"What about that piece of trash?" She lit a cigarette.

"Does he have a bounty on him?"

She shook her head. "We all want him dead, but Koyuki wants him brought in alive if possible. Now, I guess you're here for information? Koyuki's busy right now, so you'll get what you need from me this time. The Kostic Military Outpost is a lightly manned station near the southern outskirts of the city. It's located near one of the main train tracks that connects to the other military installations across the city, and it's home to one of the Rain Enforcer's main ordnance depots, mainly for explosives and other large weapons."

"How did you know we needed the information?"

"Everything Koyuki knows, I know. Make sure you give me proof that Vahar is dead. I have instructed the other Black Sniper Hunters who remain to assist you in this, per Koyuki's orders." She tightened her jaw, then took a deep breath, and her expression relaxed. "Anything the Hunters find will be sent to Liz. But don't expect much. They are busy trying to contain the Lolitrons."

"Who's sending it to her?" I asked.

"All you need to know is that any information we give her will be checked before it reaches her hands. All eyes are on you both. Fuck this up and it'll be your heads that will roll next. And I'll make sure I'm holding the fucking ax." She got on her motorcycle and put her helmet on. After idling it for a minute, she left, leaving behind the lingering scent of nicotine and exhaust.

Silver rubbed her forehead, letting out a loud sigh.

"How are you feeling?" I said.

"I'm okay."

"Can you breathe? Do you want to take the mask off?"

She glared at me.

"It was just a joke!" I said. "You can take a joke, can't you?"

"I know what you're thinking, and I will stop you right there, Katherine."

"You're going to keep doing that?"

"Only way I'll take this mask off is if it breaks."

I grinned. "That can be arranged."

She rolled her eyes. "I'm not sure if I trust her."

My train of thought was brought to an abrupt stop as my Recaller vibrated, but as I brought it up, all that was on the screen was Stella's fox image.

"Move-vement of asset target Vahar has been located," she said. "Compiled information of CCTV footage from across the city-y-y-y confirms Lolitron rogue group to have attacked Kostic Military Outpost. Attached is the most efficient route for ambush and suggested location for effective elimination of target Vahar."

"So much for finding out what that outpost was for," Silver said.

"Location: Kostic Military Outpost deemed low-priority target by Lolitron rogue group. Reminder: Job priority is to eliminate-te-te-te all leadership of the Lolitron rogue group, not prevent their activities, unless otherwise specified. Failure of this task will warrant corrective measures. We are watching your progress." The connection ended.

"Do you trust Stella?" Silver said as she walked back to the van.

"I don't know. So far, she has come through, though we don't even know what the Lolitrons wanted from that outpost in the first place. We don't even know anything about Fate and Vahar, aside from what Rui just told us."

"Does the information say how long we have to complete this?"

I shook my head. "Just the trajectory and location." I rubbed my forehead. "I'll call Liz and Ceitr. They may have more information on them."

"Try calling Stella again. We need a timeframe."

Not long after Silver said it, a text message came in. "We have six hours."

"Long enough to make one stop." She shifted gears.

"Let's pay Ceitr a visit, then," I said. "He might know how to set up an ambush better than Liz would."

"I hope he also has the manpower to spare for it."

CHAPTER 15

"DO YOU THINK this is a good idea?" Silver asked as we rode the elevator to Ceitr's penthouse.

"No," I said, looking at the flashing numbers as we climbed. "But we don't have time to run around the City to meet at a different location."

Ceitr had agreed to meet with us in his own apartment at the Sunlit Towers, five miles to the center of the City of Laohz. The elevator bell rang, and the doors slid open to a small circle with four doors. We knocked on his door, and he opened it moments later.

He stood there, wearing his usual combination of relaxed suit and dress pants. Beyond was his apartment, a luxurious semi-circular living room one level lower than the floor with a fireplace against the wall, and a TV set up against it. Floor-to-ceiling windows that gave way to a terrace, lay beyond a full kitchen with an island in the middle. Polished marble floors gleamed as a scent of vanilla was lingering as an afterthought in the space, along with a faint melody of jazz.

I always thought that all members of the Inner Circle had high-end real estate, but I never thought that Ceitr would live in a place such as this.

"It reminds me of my place back in Othara," I said, catching myself once I saw the confused gazes of both Silver and Ceitr. "I had an apartment like this when I lived back there."

Ceitr chuckled. "No need to apologize. Welcome to my home. Please, make yourselves comfortable."

"We're not here to socialize, Ceitr," Silver said. "We have a deadline of five hours, and we need to plan a way to deal with Vahar. We don't know how to set up an ambush for what we believe will be a convoy of heavily armed Lolitrons."

Ceitr didn't say anything, walking across the open-floor space of the apartment as he grabbed a set of glasses and a brand-new bottle of whiskey.

"Let me guess, ladies," he said as he set the glasses down. "You think I know how to plan one?"

We both nodded.

He sighed. "You ladies give me too much credit. What information did she give you?"

I brought up the map and showed it to him on my Recaller. He rubbed his chin for a moment before he chuckled, somewhat dryly, before serving the drinks.

"The location she chose for this mission is rather straight-forward." He handed me a drink. "All you have to do is have two teams to block the two points of travel in front and behind them."

"Do you have men to spare to post on the buildings around this space?" I said.

He nodded and gave Silver her drink. "Silver can use her van to get some of my men on the ground and have them surround everyone. I have a few semi-trucks I can use to box them in while you go in and surround the main target. Can you get in contact with some of your Black Sniper buddies and have them pick off all the turret operators?"

Silver nodded. "I'll make a few calls and cash in some favors."

"Remember, we owe them for the museum event," I said.

"Yeah, I know, Katherine. We'll pay them back when they ask for it."

I rolled my eyes. "The main target is Vahar, an ex-Black Sniper Hunter who was turned by Kax."

"We don't know what they look like, or anything about them, really."

"Don't worry about that," he said. "Once they're cornered and their lookouts are taken care of, it should be fairly easy work to get them to comply. What's the bounty Rui put on their head?"

"How do you know about that?"

He chuckled and drank from his glass. "I've known Rui for as long as I've known Koyuki. I'm the one who trained them both. So, does she want Vahar alive or dead?"

"Dead."

"She never said anything about wanting them back alive, except for Kax." Silver crossed her arms. "The bounty is five hundred-thousand rullians."

"Good." He finished his drink and poured some more. "I'll tell my lieutenants the plan and have you meet them there. Make sure you tell your contacts."

"Will do," I said. We finished our drinks in one gulp and left, making calls as the elevator took us down to the parking lot.

▲ ▲ ▲

Thunder rumbled above us as a storm brewed in the skies. The ambush point had proven to be a small stretch of road with buildings around and only two ways to enter, not counting the alleys in which we had hidden blockades to stop them. Everyone else, Black Snipers we now owed favors to, and Ceitr's men, hid inside the buildings, crosshairs aimed at the streets below.

Silver and I were manning the semi-trucks we were going to use to close them in, she in one and I in the other. Despite all the planning and trust we had in everyone carrying out their tasks, I still had nerves about this working. Stella had only given us six hours to get everything in place, and I wasn't confident that everything would go according to what we hastily planned.

The reports our Wraiths gave us were four technicals and a stolen military cargo truck from the Rain Enforcers, hardware they were going to want back.

I tightened my hands around the steering wheel, eyes locked ahead as the man next to me took a deep breath.

"Are you ready?" Silver said through the comm in my ear.

"You know the answer to that." I sighed. "What's the ETA?"

"Rounding the corner," Ceitr said. "Just breathe."

"Don't remind me. A lot of unknowns are riding on this."

I began to regulate my breathing. *In. Out. In. Out. Silence. Just . . . breathe.* The first pair of technicals passed, a black truck with two trailers attached to it, followed by two more technicals.

I shifted gear and floored the pedal as soon as the hood of the first of the last two technicals appeared, then hit as we slammed into the second one and felt something roll underneath the right tires. The next moment I was out on the street, assault rifle in hand, shooting everyone who stepped out of their vehicles, snipers picking off those on the turrets.

My mind was steady, focused on the task as instinct kicked in, the feeling of the kick of the rifle on my shoulder a steady rhythm as members of the Lolitrons fell dead on the street. The rush steadied as we surrounded the cab of the truck, where the person we thought was Vahar sat at the steering wheel. He matched the picture that was provided to us by Stella, pulled from a snapshot from a CCTV camera.

Vahar opened the door from the outside after rolling down the window, and he stepped out onto the street. His nose and mouth were covered with one of the dual-cylinder gas masks the Lolitrons wore, but it was sleek black, topped by purple modded eyes and matching hair.

"So like all of you," she said, hands raised. "Typical puppets of Koyuki. None of you even understand the reasons behind this, do you?"

The voice made me stop, my brain pulling on a string of memory. "Tamara?"

Saying her name out loud brought a mixture of confusion, anger, anxiety, dread, and revulsion. It was a cocktail of emotions I was not prepared to deal with, not so suddenly, not in front of everyone present.

"Katherine," she said smugly. "Still with the Black Snipers? How's the little rich bitch doing as she keeps playing assassin? Gotten bored yet? Finally see the truth of the organization?"

"I don't go by that name anymore." I aimed the rifle at her. "You know that."

"You know her?" Silver said, moving closer to me, keeping her shotgun aimed at her.

I nodded. "She's my older sister."

"I'm still your sister? That's so sweet. Why didn't you go back home where you belong?"

"Don't bring family into this, Tamara."

"Or what? You were always a crybaby growing up, and Mom and Dad always favored you over me. You got the privileges, the grants, the latest cars and toys, while *I* always got second best! I'm the eldest! *I* should've gotten the best things!"

"Tamara," I said, "please don't make this about our family. This is more than that, and you know it."

"Well, this right here, right now, *is* about our family. You know it's been a long time coming since you gave it all up, all the opportunities, to come here and study photography instead of using those open doors that should've been mine!"

"Tamara, stand down and drop this drama. You know full well that I'm not here to fight you over me rejecting Dad's wish to take up the mantle and continue the legacy of the company. You betrayed the Black Snipers, and, as much as it pains me to say it, I need to kill you."

"Like you killed Dad's dream," she said. "Because of *you*, Dad won't give *me* the company. Instead, *he* decided to just declare *you* as the owner, and appoint someone else as the CEO of the whole operation!"

"Shut the fuck up!" I shot several rounds at the ground. "Will you shut the fuck up? You've been this whiny bitch older sister who took everything for granted growing up. You got into trouble all the fucking time. Every *month* Dad had to bail *you* out of jail because of some stupid *bullshit* you pulled! The principal had Mom's cell phone number on speed dial because she got tired of being called at work. We went through *four* groundskeepers in six months because you crashed five cars through the gardens more than ten times! You always stayed out late, got bad grades, got drunk, and you even stole several company vehicles! Why else do you fucking *think* Dad willed the company to me? Tamara, you're the biggest financial drain Dad had.

"Do you know how many times I caught him crying in his home office after picking you up drunk from the police station? How many times have I heard him *apologizing* for the ungraceful display you made each and every time he had company over—"

"Dad didn't care!" she yelled. "He *banished* me from the house. He kicked me out, remember? When he gave me a one-way interplanetary ticket to come *here*, and told me to not come back? He never cared, Katherine! He never fucking cared about me! And you know that's the truth!"

I had to swallow as hard as I could to hold back the tears as I reaffirmed my aim at her. "Do you want to know what happened after the ship left that day? What he said once the ship was gone?"

"No."

"After the ship left, and all that was left was the small picture he always kept in his wallet of the two of us when we were kids, he cried. He cried and he said, 'I wish I could have my little girl back.'"

"Liar."

"It broke his heart, Tamara. It broke him, and he hasn't been the same since then. And now." I wiped a tear from my eye. "Now, I'm standing here, with orders to kill you, because you couldn't *stop* yourself from betraying another family that took you in, and *cared* for you, because *nothing* in this universe is fucking *enough* for you."

I had no time to react to her pulling the rifle from my hands, her fist connecting with my head, knocking me to the ground. Somewhere, Silver yelled "Don't shoot!" over the ensuing chaos. The scent of exhaust and asphalt as I fell to my hands and knees, the sensation of it on my palms moments before I moved my head, Tamara missing her punch, giving me the opening to hit her side, then her gut and face as I got to my feet.

Her eye was turning red as she regained balance and threw more punches, which I only managed to block two, the last hitting my side and finishing on my face, knocking me back to the ground. Her fingers wrapped between my hair and pulled me back, sending jolts of sharp pain through my scalp as she dragged me. My mind raced. I was vulnerable, and in the next thought, my knife was through her boot, forcing her to kneel as her eyebrows furrowed in pain.

I didn't want to kill my older sister. I didn't want to break Dad's heart again, but at this point, there was nothing else I could do for her. She refused to change, and I couldn't make her change.

"Please, Tamara, just give up."

"I'd rather die."

Everything happened in a flash, and my mind barely recorded it. She threw herself at me, a knife clattered on the ground. I pulled her mask off and threw it aside, as my next punch broke her nose, making her fall and hit her head on the door of the truck on her way to the ground.

"How will Dad feel," she said as she spat blood, "the moment he hears you killed your sister?"

I felt my face flush when she said that. Her ungratefulness and all-deserving tone made all my feelings well up. I grabbed her by the hair and forced her to look at me, handgun pressed against her ribs.

"I'm not going to be a big fucking *disappointment* to our parents like *you've* been for the past *sixteen* years of our lives." I pushed her back to the ground, knocking her out with the grip.

Everyone stood in a semi-circle around us, handguns and rifles lowered as they all stared at me, though Ceitr was the first one to break the silence as he stepped out.

"Are you okay?"

"Tie her up and take her to Koyuki's," I said, giving the gun back. "We'll head there at a later time. Silver and I need some rest." I began to walk away, but Ceitr grabbed my arm and pulled me close.

"I know what you're thinking, and I have to say that it is a bad idea. Are you sure about that?"

"I'll see you at Koyuki's mansion." I pulled myself free and walked a distance away, Silver following close behind.

My mind was burdened, digging up the memories from long-forgotten altercations and arguments, depressing thoughts and disappointments that Tamara caused over the years. All the family friction, the secrets that I kept hidden from everyone, spilled for all of them to see. To people I didn't even trust, or like. Old, buried memories and scars unearthed and reopened, I was left feeling naked and vulnerable as I walked away. In my mind, all I wanted was to hide, to let the ground open wide and swallow me whole.

I leaned against a wall, my gaze set on the operations as they bound and dragged Tamara's unconscious body away. Other Black Snipers opened the trailer to look inside, while the others searched the pockets of those who died in the ambush, which was most of the Lolitrons. I knelt, digging my fingers through my hair, everything looping in my head.

"Are you okay?" Silver said, joining me.

I just sighed. "How can you be okay after that?"

"I don't know. Why did you never tell me your sister was a member of the Black Snipers?"

I knew how she felt when she asked, it was palpable in the tone of her voice. The tinge of hurt for not trusting her with the information.

"I don't know," I said. "I wish I could give you a valid excuse as to why. A simple one that will neatly cover all the reasons, but in all honesty, instead it's a messy bowl of goop poorly packaged with barbed wire." I chuckled. "It's a poor reference.

"When I moved here, I never intended to even see Tamara again. I never searched for her and never bothered to look her up. Time passed, and I joined the Black Snipers and lived up to this now. During all that time, I forgot, ignored it, pushed the memory of her as deep down in my mind as I could. She had hurt our family too much, and I didn't want to bring her back into my life. I wasn't ready. *I'm still* not ready."

"Why did you spare her? Stella will come after us for not obeying her orders. Katherine, I do *not* want to find out what the corrective measures she has for us are."

Quiet joined the murmur of voices as the men and women searched the vehicles and opened the trailer of the semi the Lolitrons had captured. Bodies were moved aside, guns and Recallers pried from their corpses.

"I don't know." I detached myself from the wall. "I guess I'm hoping that the next step I take makes sense in the end. We are trained to lean on our skill and cold calculation. Emotion takes over sometimes. I can't help it, I suppose."

Silver sighed. "Emotion has driven you more lately than all the years we've worked together."

I shrugged. "I suppose."

A distinct ball of orange light appeared before us, hovering as the crackling of electricity, fading lights, and popping of streetlamps happened all around us. Dread flooded my mind as the multitude of ways that Stella would have to inflict pain rushed through my brain.

All the lights around us went out, and Stella's body came into form moments later. Even though her eyes were hidden away behind her mask, depicting a fox with neon orange triangles, I could almost feel her burning stare sear my soul.

"Fuck!"

CHAPTER 16

"WARNING. WARNING. Implementi-i-ing corrective measures," Stella said, electricity crackling beneath her, arcing to the ground as she moved closer to us. She said nothing as she closed the gap between us, intent in her movement, and fear rooting me to my spot as my gaze was locked with her flashing mask. There was no dialogue, no hands of hers grabbed me, but I felt my skin burn, heat coming from under it as I fell to the floor, writhing in pain.

I heard nothing other than my own screams, and I couldn't see anything, as whatever Stella was doing to me felt like being seared from the inside out, pain forcing my eyes shut. Silver's screams came next, then I heard her fall to the ground. It was hard to describe. A feeling of tendrils slithering through my body, as if burning metal rods coiled around like hot iron snakes.

"Black Sniper Kannon," Stella's voice boomed over our screams, "your failure to kill asset Vahar, has been noted by all. We-e-e will provide corrective measures to ensure that further failures are avoided, and errant behavior is corrected in accordance with our directives. Due to your failur-r-re, reward for the task shall be withdrawn from the agreed upon amount per our contract."

The pain stopped, the burning feeling fading away as a passing breeze as tears coated our cheeks, and we both gasped for air. Then, after several moments, I felt my extremities pull me to the air. My vision blurred, and I saw cufflinks on my ankles and wrists, pulling me up and manipulating my body until I was facing Stella.

"Reminder: Job priority is to eliminate-te-te-te all leadership of the Lolitron rogue group, not prevent their activities, unless otherwise specified. Failure of this task will warrant *further* corrective measures."

"There are . . . things that take precedence over obeying your commands," I said.

"Objective: Elimination of any and all leaders of the Lolitrons. Calculating: Elimination of all effective leadership of the rogue group Lo-o-o-olitrons will cause a destabilizing effect on the collective. Fail-safe-e-e-es are in place for this eventuality. Priority task: Unchanged."

"Fuck . . . you, Stella."

She kept silent, her mask flickering for a few moments as her face and whole body remained still.

"I will remove Tamara from the equation," I breathed. "But I will not kill her."

Her mask flashed several times. "Response has been logged. Reminder: Job priority is to eliminate-te-te-te all leadership of the Lolitron rogue group, not prevent their activities unless otherwise specified. Failure to comply with the parameters of the objective will warrant further-er-er-er corrective measures.

Further tasks will be allotted as necessary. We will be watching your progress."

The lights all around us began to flicker once more, her body turning back into a ball of light, the cufflinks disappearing and allowing me to fall to the hard floor. The whole block went dark as soon as Stella was gone, and silence fell over us, only the echoes of distant sirens and the murmurs of those who were around the Lolitron convoy. Silver groaned next to me, her eyes shut as she breathed heavily.

"Are you ladies all right?" Ceitr said as he and one of his men came to us. He knelt next to me and put my head on his knees, pushing a strand of hair out of my face. I would have blushed at the sweet gesture, were it not for the lingering pain and the lack of air.

"I need to rest, Ceitr," I said, voice close to a croak.

He nodded. "We'll get you looked at by the Specters before we get in contact with Liz."

I tried to sit up, but the faint, distant feeling of what Stella did to me still ran under my skin, so I had to resign myself with just nodding, and hoping that soon, I would find myself underneath a few layers of blankets. *I don't want to go through that again.*

▲ ▲ ▲

The steady, low hum of the air conditioner coming out of the vents and the comforting feeling of being tucked away in the bed were the first things that came into focus as I woke up. The light was turned on, albeit dim. Liz was standing near the door, her glare steady and arms crossed, joined by a straight set of lips. She sighed as soon as my eyes met hers.

"We don't have room for sentimentality, Kannon," she said. "The Lolitrons will not do the same for us."

"Nice to see you again," I mocked her. "How are you?"

"Tsk. I'm not in the mood for bickering, Kannon." She moved closer to the bed, grabbing the nearby chair and sitting next to me. "Now, you know why I don't like to talk about Stella. You *never* cross Stella, Kannon. You do as she says, and don't ask why."

"What would you have done if it had been your brother?"

She looked away. "This isn't about that."

"It's about loyalty." I sat up. "I know. To show that I can be trusted. That I am *loyal* to the Black Snipers. To The Oath. Silver questions it every chance she gets; even if she's not direct with her words, I know the intent. I can sense it in her tone."

"This whole mess is not a test for you to prove your loyalty, Kannon. But you can see why everyone is on edge. Looking for any excuse to root out traitors that would *be* a threat to us."

"I have a lot of reservations, Liz, about all of this. Many that I don't speak about with anyone, not even Silver. Not due to a lack of trust, but because there are things I'm still figuring out myself. I don't have all the answers yet."

"Can we count on you to kill Kax when the time comes?" Liz didn't stop. Her tone was steady and direct, her red modded eyes meeting mine and resting still as she waited for my answer.

"I know Stella has some influence over you. Your questions are looking for answers that you yourself are certain of, Liz. And maybe Stella is immune to what I'm about to say next, but you yourself ask and think on this question: Would *you* be able to kill your own brother? Sister? Cousin? Family?"

She sighed, her body shaking as she looked away. "I don't know."

I stood up and stretched. "I'm loyal to the Black Snipers, Liz. This is my family, but I have to save the remainder of what little I have left back in Othara. I will not break my father's heart by killing Tamara."

She said nothing else, just stood and left the room, taking with her the weight that had settled between us, leaving behind only silence. This small measure of respite was broken when the desire to wander spurred me out toward the hall. It was unchanged, lights Illuminating it at equidistant intervals, while the hum of the AC just filled the silence in between.

Silver stepped out of her room before I was halfway to the stairs to the ground floor, her teal eyes meeting mine, my gear in her hands as she walked to me. She sniveled as she gave it back.

"Show me the Black Sniper I know you are."

"Did you ask Liz to do that for you?"

She shook her head. "I did hear most of the conversation. I'm . . . sorry for pushing you. I know this has not been easy on either of us."

I couldn't help but smile as I took my backpack and rifles. "Thanks for trying to keep me focused. There are a lot of unknowns that we have been thrust into. Making heads of it all in the middle of all this chaos and stress . . ." I trailed off, fingers caressing the fabric of my backpack. "I think we should get ready. There's a meeting we have to attend with Koyuki and Ceitr, and then we have to deal with the fate of my sister."

She nodded.

▲ ▲ ▲

Silver and I arrived at Koyuki's mansion in the evening, and the tension was already palpable as we walked inside. Hushed voices from the guards and the maids slithered in the halls as we moved past them to where Koyuki had decided to keep Tamara, the Training Room.

Reaching the doors, I stopped short of grabbing the handle to slide the door aside. Anticipation, then nerves, fear, dread. In my mind, I was determined to go through with my choice, but it didn't make it any easier to push forward. In those moments, my heart began to race, and I hadn't realized I was frozen in place until Silver put her hand on my shoulder and gave it a light squeeze. I slid the door open.

Tamara was kneeling in the middle of the room, chains and cuffs holding her tied to the floor, while Koyuki stood over her, arms crossed over her favorite, amber-colored turtleneck, matching her modded eyes. Ceitr, on the other hand, stood near the doors that led to the garden, leaning against one of the many wooden support beams, hands in the pockets of his dress pants, his lips uncharacteristically straight.

"Miss Kannon," Koyuki said, "I believe the task was the elimination of Vahar and Fate. Nothing was said of live captures. Though I have to commend you for the feat. She has proved useful in finding information regarding the activities of the Lolitrons. Good work."

"Thank you, Miss Akikawa," I said.

"Now, Miss Kannon, I believe you have not come to my home to just receive praise for your accomplishments. There are further matters that you wish to discuss about Tamara that seem to be troubling you."

I swear she's psychic. I nodded. "I wish to use the Token to spare Tamara's life."

At least Ceitr and Silver gasped at my proposition, while Koyuki remained unfazed. But the most vocal of all was Tamara, whose voice almost drowned out everyone else with her loud, "What?"

"Do you think I will stop? You'd better kill me right now, Katherine, because sparing me will not stop me from going back and re-joining the Lolitrons!"

"In exchange," I continued, "she will be expelled from the Black Snipers and exiled from the City of Laohz and the planet of Rhode, to be sent back to Othara, where my father will receive her."

"You can't do this to me, Katherine! You can't send me back!"

I met Koyuki's gaze, who nodded in Tamara's direction. Aside from my sister's protests, the room was silent as I moved over to her and took her combat knife, along with its sheath, from her belt. This was a symbolic ceremony that showed that the person deserved a second chance but would have to earn their weapons, and the trust of the members of the Oath, back if they were to be accepted back into the ranks. The ceremony had only been performed once before. Treason is always punishable by death.

"Sending me back is the single worst mistake you could ever make, Katherine. Do you think I will forgive you for doing this to me? For returning me to Mom and Dad? I'm a Black Sniper at heart. I will never stop unless I'm dead."

"I'm doing you a favor, Tamara. Even after everything, you still don't get it, do you? I know Dad never learned to give you words of praise and affection. You made it hard for him as you grew up. I'm giving you the opportunity to go back home and fix all the shattered pieces you left behind. This is the last chance you will get, Tamara, to reclaim everything you lost." I gave the knife to Koyuki. "Don't squander it, like you have done with everything else."

Tears slid down her face as I walked back and took my place back at Silver's side. Her figure had slumped back, shoulders relaxed as she sobbed silently. I could feel tears form, though I refused to cry there. I didn't want to. Not in front of everyone present.

"I hope you realize that you only have one Token to give," Koyuki said. "There will not be a second one awarded to you to use."

"I understand."

"Good. I will have Ceitr's men escort Miss Tamara Ithorn before she is turned over to the Rain Enforcer authorities, who will escort her back to Othara."

"Thank you," I said. "What about Rui's request to have Fate and Vahar eliminated in exchange for a bounty?" *Great, of all the times I had to have my Recaller start to vibrate.*

"Do not worry about Rui," Koyuki said. "The bounty will be paid to the both of you. I will break the news to her."

"Thank you again," Silver said.

"Keep up the good work. There may be more work for you once this is over, Miss Kannon, Miss Silver. You're free to go. I believe you know your way out?"

We both turned and left, pulling out the Recaller as Silver closed the doors behind us, to read the text message that Liz had sent me, along with an address.

"We don't get a break," I said, following Silver as she pulled out the van's keys. My mind still lingered on Tamara, the tears breaking free as we both walked back to the entrance.

CHAPTER 17

THUNDER ROLLED AND ROILED as we met up with Liz late in the afternoon, the overcast sky darker than usual as rain clouds gathered. We met on one of the business skybridges, promenades with small restaurants that connected districts over the highways, with observation areas overlooking the distant skylines; there were only ten such bridges across the City.

We met Liz near one of the clock lampposts that lined the middle of the walkway, her usual outfit replaced by a button-down turquoise shirt and blue jeans, the tattoos on her arms and neck visible, compared to the usual coat that she wore when she went out.

"How did it go with Tamara?" Liz asked.

A knot formed in my throat, impeding me from forming words for a few moments. "I used the Token on her. She'll be returned to Othara. I hope it helps us all heal."

Liz shifted her weight, discomfort settling in over her as she looked away briefly and muttered a low, "I'm sorry."

"It'll be a while before I feel fine," I said. "I'll manage."

"Good, now come on," Liz said. "I have a limited time frame to solve this."

"What's going on?" I said. "Why did you bring us all the way here?"

"I have a meeting with one of the leaders of the rival gangs in the City. Small time. Petty criminals, but they wanted to sell an old laptop supposedly containing information on hidden caches the Rain Enforcers have scattered across the city. I need you to be my security, as I'm sure he plans to take the money and kill me."

"How does that benefit us in catching Kax and dealing with the Lolitrons?"

"Stella gave me some information regarding the contents of the containers, including the one you ambushed to stop Tamara. Help me get this done, and I'll give it to you."

"We were supposed to be in this togeth—"

"By the fucking Oath, Kannon," she cut me off. "I want you to help me with this for once. I don't know what kind of information this has, whether it is real or not, but if it contains a *sliver* of information, I will take it. Trust is a two-way street, Kannon. I've trusted you this far. Now, I need you to trust me."

I turned to Silver, who just shrugged before agreeing with Liz.

"Just make sure you don't get us into a trap we can't get out of."

She crossed her arms. "I'm a Wraith. I'm not stupid. Of course it'll be a trap. That's why Silver will go ahead and get in a good position to kill whoever comes in behind us."

"Where is the meeting place?" Silver said.

"I sent it to you just as you were parking the van."

"How do you know this is real information?"

"We don't," Liz said. "We aren't completely sure it is real, but after cross-referencing all the communications of their leaders, and most of the members of their organization, we are at least ninety percent sure it is real. Thing is, their leader is an asshole, so we can safely assume he'll try to kill me as soon as he gets paid."

"When is the meeting?"

"We have an hour. Is that enough time for you to find a decent spot?"

Silver nodded. "I'll let you know once I'm ready."

Liz sighed in relief. "I hope this works." She turned to me, her eyebrows slightly furrowed. It was the first time I remembered seeing Liz worried.

We stood there, looking at Silver as she navigated among the crowds walking through the promenade, until it swallowed her up. Then Liz turned to me, exhaling, as if she'd been holding her breath all this time.

"Thanks for helping me with this."

"You're thanking me?" I said. "I never thought I'd see the day."

"I'm being serious here, Kannon. Don't fucking ruin it." She took a deep breath. "I'm not good at . . . this. I didn't exactly join the Wraiths to make friends. So, thanks."

"Were you trying to apologize?"

She looked away, her face turning red. "D-don't go broadcasting it."

I snorted, then tried to stifle a laugh, but she punched me on the shoulder, hard.

"You're so fucking annoying, Kannon. Come on, I want to at least see them walk into the meeting place." She turned around and left, not looking back to see if I was following.

The journey wasn't long, just some distance away near the end of the skybridge, down an alleyway between two of the buildings near the highway that cut under the bridge. Liz and I stood nearby, hidden from view by tucking inside one of the stores. We kept our eyes on the entrance as we waited, but for the time we were there, we didn't see anyone walk in.

"They're already there," I said.

Liz nodded, taking the lead as she went to the meeting place with rushed determination in her stride. I, on the other hand, felt like something was wrong, but I couldn't place what.

General scents of the city turned into alleyway scents. Damp or humid concrete mixed in with the scent of piss and trash, wet cardboard and rotting animals and food.

I found the choice of location uninspired, a show of weakness and timidness on their part. A fake sense of control they really didn't have, just *granted* to them, allowed by the Rain Enforcers, the Black Snipers, and Koyuki Akikawa's enterprise; she liked the competition. I never understood the motivation behind that, and I never willed myself to ask.

The place where we met was a T-junction of alleyways, very movie-like and predictable, but not what we turned to. A group of men stood there, all wearing casual office wear, buttoned shirts and jeans. One of them had an old laptop under their arm, while two others held Silver with her arms behind her back, a gun pressed on the back of her head.

"You see, Liz," the man said, "I don't like that you sent a Black Sniper to kill me and my men. Tsk, tsk, tsk. You should've known better."

"The Black Sniper I hired is standing next to me," she said. "What makes you think she's with us?"

I stayed still and bit my tongue. I didn't want to give anything away.

"Why would a Black Sniper come here before we met? Come on, you have to do better."

"Black Snipers work independently," I said, "We don't always know when our paths will cross. Sometimes we see others scouting while on a job."

Words were cut off before they left his lips as one of the men holding Silver yelped, hopping on one foot. In one motion, she disarmed him and shot the other one in the head, then pushed the first man to the floor with one single movement as she lunged at their leader.

She grabbed him by the neck, not giving him time to react, and began to crush his windpipe. Unable to breathe, he dropped the laptop.

"P-please!" he said, fighting her grip. "D-don't k-kill me!"

"You should've thought about that before capturing a Black Sniper and threatening to kill them in the first place. Coward."

"You had such potential to be of use to the Wraiths," Liz said as she picked up the laptop. "Yet you had to let your own ego and fake sense of superiority get the better of you."

"Fine! Fine! Just take the laptop, okay? No payment, no nothing. I'll leave with my last man, and you won't see us again."

I pulled my handgun and shot the first man five times, then turned to the leader. "You're not going anywhere."

"Pleasepleasepleasepleasepleaseplease! Pleaseeee don't kill me!"

"You can release him, Silver," Liz said, standing next to her; she did. "You think we can trust you after what you did today? The Oath doesn't take kindly to traitors and those who can't be trusted."

The man fell to his knees, coughing as he nodded. "I understand. I can be useful to you."

Liz grabbed Silver's handgun from its holster. "How so?"

"You should know by now what I do." He coughed some more. "I have access to servers of information that can be useful to you. I can sell you whatever I can find. No one will even know."

"We already have access to your servers." She shot his leg. "We have access to every company here in the City of Laohz in some shape or form. Your petty attempts at negotiation do not sway the Wraiths so easily. Now, leave."

"Y-you won't kill me?"

"Not unless the information you promised us turns out to be useless. Now go, before I change my mind."

He didn't think twice, and with a lot of painful groans, he managed to stand up and limp away to the street. She didn't shoot him anywhere that would kill him. There was still a possibility that he could bleed out, if he didn't manage to get any medical attention in time . . . and this city could be very unforgiving.

After he was gone, Silver's eyes shifted to us as she breathed heavily. The small pocket of silence was short as she took her handgun back from Liz and pushed past us, barely saying, "I'm going."

Reflex made me act before I thought about it and grabbed her arm. "Are you okay?"

She freed herself with a gentle movement of her arm, nodding. "We'll talk later, Kannon. I just need to think."

With that she left, passing a hand over her scar as she walked away.

"Good," Liz said. "It's not damaged, at least. Now, I promised you information, didn't I?"

"You're not going to acknowledge the fact Silver's acting strange?"

Liz shrugged. "Do you really want me to waste time discussing that? We have more important matters to take care of."

"Nice to see you back your old self."

"Shut up."

"Well?"

She rolled her eyes. "All the information that was gathered, Stella forwarded to me. I guess she is still mad at you for disobeying orders. Don't do that again."

"I can't make any promises, Liz."

"You don't want to find out what she can be capable of. Aside from useless information to you, there were mentions of future plans to attack one of the air bases from the Rain Enforcers, but the details were vague. I have to hand it to Kax for keeping some form of operational security with a ragtag band of mostly teenagers without discipline."

"What about the trailer Tamara was in charge of escorting?"

"It was filled with explosives. Enough to destroy a Rain Enforcer cruiser. Whatever they're planning is bigger than what we thought. Very few important targets under Rain Enforcer control come to mind, but I can't start making assumptions without more information."

"Was that everything the Lolitrons stole?"

Liz shrugged, eyebrows now furrowed as her eyes averted mine. "I don't like what this means, Kannon. I can reach out to the Colonel and have him give us a manifest of all the munitions that were stockpiled in that base, to get a better sense of what they were after, but it'll take some time."

"Have you heard anything about the Black Sniper Hunters?"

"Koyuki and Rui brokered a temporary alliance with the Rain Enforcers to deal with this instability the Lolitrons have caused. They are moving troops, but I don't know the rest of the details. They didn't give them to me. Perhaps I will know more later."

I rubbed my forehead, the thought of being stuck, having nothing to go on, and not being able to stop whatever depravity Kax was planning quickly became overbearing. "So we don't have anything to follow up on?"

She crossed her arms. "Could you let me fucking finish?"

"Get to the point."

"All of it was important, Kannon! By the fucking Oath! Stella also found a contact that would be willing to talk. I was going to give you the name, but you're being your annoying self again, so you'll get it *after* I verify the contents of this laptop."

"I guess that apology doesn't mean much anymore."

"I meant every word, Kannon," she said, pushing past me as she walked back to the street. "I'm not going to repeat myself. Now come on, Silver's being annoying too, and I can't have you two on a rut."

"It's not me who was upset."

"Whatever," she said, almost muttering as we reached the exit. "Either find out what's wrong with her or don't. But just make sure you two stop this whole moping bullshit you have been getting on all this time." She rubbed her forehead. "It's getting on my damn nerves, and we have more important work to do!"

"Look, I don't know what's going on with Silver, okay?"

Liz crossed her arms. "Then what the *fuck* is going on?"

I shrugged. "Beats me."

She sighed, rubbing the bridge of her nose as she took a deep breath. "Do you want to get her, then?"

"I'm fine," Silver said as she walked up to us. "I've never been captured before. This was a . . . first. I have a lot to think about how I should approach things going forward."

Liz sighed heavily. "Really? Look, we have work to do, and I am *done* dealing with you both having this bullshit. Now, get your fucking shit together and your fucking head in what we have to do, because, by the fucking Oath! I'm going home. Come find me once you two solve whatever stick you both have. We'll talk more about that contact once you get back."

Silver and I looked at each other as Liz stormed off, leaving shortly afterwards.

CHAPTER 18

SEVERAL PATROL SHIPS darted overhead as Silver and I drove down the avenue, as in my mind I wrestled the urge to ask if she was okay. Her shoulders were relaxed, she was breathing normal, and her hand was resting on the edge of the window as she rested her head on her fist while she drove.

"I'm fine, Kannon," she said, not turning to look at me, her teal gaze somewhat reflecting the small glow off the window next to her, fingers tapping rhythmically on the steering wheel.

"I haven't said anything."

"Liz's words are bouncing inside your head," she said. "I just felt vulnerable when they caught me."

"Then something is wrong."

She shifted on her seat, the tapping getting faster. "You're just going to keep pressing."

I nodded. Liz was right; we had to stop having these issues between us if we were going to deal with the Lolitrons, and subsequently, Kax. Looking out the window at the other people walking down the street and those driving around us, it was obvious that the spiraling aggressions against the Rain Enforcers was growing out of hand. The dawning and looming notion that everything was being rested on our shoulders was daunting at best.

"Kax and the Lolitrons are not going to stop and wait for us to get our act together."

"Now you're starting to sound like Liz."

"Because she's right. What happened?"

She took a deep breath, her eyes darting to look at me briefly before returning to the road. The tapping of her fingers slowed down, and the rhythm she had was lost.

"I wasn't expecting anyone to be there yet." Her tapping fingers stopped. "As I reached the alley, chuckles came from around the corner, and before I was able to draw my gun, a pair of hands had grabbed my arms, and a knife was held against my throat, and I just froze. Stood there like a deer in the headlights. They took my rifles and knives afterwards, and it made me feel naked. I don't like feeling like that. That is part of why I became a Black Sniper."

"Thanks for telling me."

"You didn't have to worry about it," she said. "It's not important, at least not compared to this contract." She stopped, allowing silence and the muffled noise of cars around us to sink in. "Do you really think the Rain Enforcers are sending reinforcements?"

"Most likely. The City of Laohz is important to their business. I don't see the Rain Corporation letting a group such as the Lolitrons seize control of it. A lot of money and equipment flows from here off-world, a money pit they won't allow to be disrupted rather easily. And the Black Snipers, nor anyone else in the Oath will allow the balance to be shaken further."

"I guess you're right. Even Koyuki is feeling the effects of the instability." She turned to me. "Do you know where we're meeting this contact Liz spoke about?"

"No." I pulled out my Recaller. "But I can send her a message."

She nodded; I texted Liz. She replied almost instantly with complaints, followed by a call.

"I reached out to some of my contacts to get more information about this person that wants to talk, and, Kannon, believe me when I tell you this is not someone you want to go to unannounced. The person you'll be meeting with is a member of the Lockhart family. They're known for being a procurement organization. Black Market so to speak, but they have legitimate business that acts as a front for most of their illegal shipping. They have done business with almost every criminal aspect in this city to obtain things that would normally be impossible to get. Even Koyuki and the Rain Enforcers have done business with this family."

"Do they have that much power?" I said.

"No. But it is an organization you don't want to fuck up with. The person you'll be meeting with is a man named Edwin Lockhart. He'll be expecting you at this address. Don't mess it up. And learn to have patience, the both of you."

Liz sent the address after she hung up, a place that was located almost at the other end of the city, The City of Laohz National Conservatory. The trip took us four hours, leaving us arriving at the location an hour before dawn.

The City of Laohz National Conservatory was a four-block large indoor arboretum that contained almost every plant found on the planet of Rhode. It was a location many schools visited from across the world, and it was also one of the main tourist attractions in the Ccity. Entry was free since maintenance income was taken from the taxes of the citizens and funneled into the facility. Despite the animosity, it was one of the few things most members of the Oath, and Koyuki, admired and supported from the Rain Enforcers, and some actively donated to keep it in service.

The Conservatory was mostly empty during the night, and most maintenance was done during that time. Workers silently shuffled through the gravel paths, carrying plants, nutrient mixture, fertilizer, and shovels while the small assortment of animals and insects that were allowed to reside within chirped and cried, hidden among the leaves of the small forest inside.

Edwin Lockhart was waiting for us atop one of the observatory balconies, leaning on the veranda, looking at the scenery.

"I was assured Liz would be showing up for this," he said. "And yet, two Black Snipers come instead."

"Edwin Lockhart," I said. "You're not what I imagined."

He hid his hands in the pockets of his black jeans, his posture relaxed as he smiled. He was young, barely older than I was, with a buttoned shirt and was wearing shades.

"I like it that way. Easier to blend into the background and be ignored when things don't go as planned. Now, I know you came here for information that Liz requested from me."

"Requested?" I interjected. "I thought you came forward to give it willingly."

He chuckled. "Does it really matter? In the end, you need my information. It doesn't matter if I offered it, or she requested it, or it came in a letter, or with a pigeon. All that matters is the impact it will offer. Right?"

Silver and I looked at each other before I nodded.

He took a step forward. "One of my associates seems to be in bed with this new group that you're fighting. The Lolitrons, is it? I saw some note entries in one of his personal journals while I was visiting the other day. Just a passing glance, really, and mentioned something about renting one of his warehouses to one of their members."

"That's all the information you have?" Silver said. "How is this supposed to be useful?"

"I run a business, Silver. Things need to be done. The information I gave you is not all there is." He strolled back to the veranda and leaned on it. "He also keeps a lot of notes around his personal residence; writes everything down, you know? I will give you the address if you bring back something from his home."

"We're not thieves for hire."

Edwin raised an eyebrow.

"What's the item?" I said.

"It's a small wooden statue. He keeps it somewhere in his living room. It won't be hard to miss. It's about five inches tall."

"How does stealing this statue help us deal with the Lolitrons? And why do you want this item in particular?"

He shrugged. "Man owes me money. He won't pay, so I'll collect some other way. I'd rather avoid breaking people's bones to get my messages across. Helps keep business lines open with less animosity. Unlike Koyuki's methods, right, Kannon? As for how it helps you in your campaign against the Lolitrons?" He chuckled. "You need to pay more attention. If you had been reading between the lines, you would have come to the conclusion that you'll have access to this man's notes. Journals, information he may have scattered about, all there available for your perusal."

I shifted my weight, loathing that he was right. Pride would not let me admit it in front of him, though. "We never introduced ourselves to you."

His smile was relaxed, warm almost. Though instinct told me, along with how connected and informed he was, that his smile was just the same as a Venus flytrap's. Enticing, sweet, and deadly.

"I'll have to admit that I cheated." He chuckled. "Liz sent ahead your names."

"It's all just business for you, isn't it?"

He smiled. "It always is, Kannon. I can't collect money from someone who's in the hospital or dead, now, could I?"

Silver and I looked at each other. I didn't know how to feel about his odd demeanor. "No."

"Well, I expect to see you back soon." He pulled his Recaller and sent the address. "And be careful with the statue; it is rather expensive."

"What's the catch?" Silver said.

"There's no catch," he said, pacing about. "I'm being as straightforward as I am able to be. Is she always this suspicious?"

"We've had a rough few months," I said. "How soon do you need this?"

"How soon do you need this information?" he replied.

"Come on, Silver." I motioned her to follow as I headed for the stairs, pulling up the address in the map as we walked away from him.

"So we're really doing this?" Silver finally broke the silence as we left the Conservatory.

"I want this to be over. I am tired of being on the road, and of having to sleep at Liz's place. I need a break from all of this so I can go back and build my photography portfolio. And if doing this, and helping Edwin Lockhart, gets us closer to that goal, I will take it."

"Fine, but once this is over, you need to completely focus on your photography. You're letting that talent go to waste!"

"I've been thinking about that all this time. This has been too much for me to deal with. This is not what I signed up for when I joined the Black Snipers. I never thought that Kax would do this to us."

Silver closed the door and turned on the ignition. "I want a vacation once this is over."

"To where?"

"Anywhere that is not here." She pulled out of the parking spot. "Somewhere sunny for a change."

▲ ▲ ▲

The location was a place called The Crystal Tower, an upscale apartment complex where the average unit was about the size of a penthouse somewhere else in the city. This man's unit had two floors with triple the square footage.

The late morning sun barely managed to break several rays through the blanket of clouds by the time we arrived, taking in the pearlescent whites, accentuated chromes, and translucent, blue-tinted glass of the lobby as we heard our footsteps echoing over the

tiled space. After a quick elevator ride, and several minutes finding the apartment, breaking in was a minimal task. Once inside,
we stopped in our tracks as we admired the open floor-to-ceiling,
twelve-foot-tall windows. There were stairs to one side leading to
a second floor, and a veranda overlooking the living room, and a
large patio-like balcony spread outside, beyond the windows.

Chrome accents and wooden floors, white walls and beige
couches, the odd potted plant here and there, as well as abstract
paintings hanging on the walls, expertly placed to accentuate the
space.

"This place is amazing," I said.

"Come on, we need to find this statue," Silver said, going in
deeper. I followed.

The apartment was quiet, as if all the sounds had been sucked
out of the world, leaving just our footsteps and rustling of clothes.
Things were neatly organized, and the countertops were clean;
yet, there was no statue in the living room we came into.

"I almost feel guilty thinking about opening anything," I
said as I opened some drawers in the kitchen. "I don't really think
Edwin knew where the statue was."

Silver scoffed, opening the pantry and moving things. "I
don't. Do you think he cares that he's working with a group that
will eventually get him killed?" She slammed both doors and
moved to another room.

"It's all so . . . organized and clean. I can't help feeling all sorts
of wrong moving things out of place."

"So?" she called back. "I still don't see how that affects us."
There was silence for a few moments. "Found the statue! Edwin
was right! It *was* the only wooden thing for decoration!"

"Good. Anything on where the journal might be?"

"Hmmm? No. I'll go check upstairs."

There was silence after that, though I heard her move through the apartment above me, as did I on the ground floor, but we didn't speak. I didn't find it odd. We often did this when we had several months of downtime between jobs. Dry seasons, we Black Snipers called it, and contrary to popular belief from some of those who romanticized what we do, they happened more often than anyone wanted to admit. It was the reason we charged exorbitant amounts for the jobs, why we had Initial Fees. Some Black Snipers charged so much they only took three to four jobs per year. It was during these times that many of us pursued our hobbies. I had wasted the last one we had, lounging around and not practicing my photography. I was starting to crave one, just so I could have a couple of months where I felt normal. I wanted nothing more than to forget that I was a Black Sniper right now.

As I finished searching through the last cabinet, something grabbed my backpack and pulled me back, as an arm wrapped around my mouth. I was too startled to react, but the words that broke the silence next froze me to the spot.

"I thought I made my intentions clear to you, Kannon," Kax said. "It seems you still lack the common sense to stay out of other people's business."

CHAPTER 19

MY HEART BEAT like a locomotive, and my breathing became shallow as he held his hand over my mouth. My thoughts went to Silver, who was still upstairs, but it seemed she didn't hear anything of what was going on. *I* didn't even hear him come into the apartment or walk up behind me, so that was understandable. Was this real? Was this a nightmare? Did I pass out? The wild gaze he held at the gala when he stabbed me flashed before my eyes, and dread washed over my body as the sudden thought of him coming back to finish what he started back at the gala flooded my mind.

Focus! You're a Black Sniper! Focus!

I bit his hand, pushing him away as I drew my handgun, making distance between him and I, a good five or six feet between us. "You tried to kill me, Kax. I won't forget about that detail as fast as you'd like me to."

He had a thick black beard now, along with a trench coat, open to reveal his bandolier and black jeans, but his sunglasses remained the same.

"You should've taken the fucking hint and stayed out of my affairs," he said, pulling out his knife. "You were inconsequential then, a footnote in my plans, but now you're a thorn in my side, and it seems I have to teach you another fucking lesson. Meddling any further will put people I have no quarrel with, in danger. Do you really want to do that?"

"Really?" I took another deep breath, trying to focus. Reminding myself to remain calm, keep my aim steady as I backed away from him. "I'm not the one ordering teenagers to attack the Rain Enforcers out in the open like that!"

"Says the woman who downed a chemical cargo ship in the middle of a congested avenue during rush hour. Such hypocrisy coming from a Black Sniper."

"Silver will be here shortly, and you'll be outnumbered."

"My men took her while you were busy searching through pots and pans." He took another step forward, and I took another one back. "Easy to do when you have a tranquilizer gun. Now, I suggest you back off and let me and my men go about our affairs, and you will be able to see Silver again. Don't, and I will return her to you in a body bag."

The words felt like a punch in the gut. My air was gone, focus lost for a brief moment, before everything else began to blend together. The feeling of my handgun going off several times, the disorienting force that made me fall to the floor, the handgun no longer in my hands, clattering off somewhere. I felt his punches hitting my face as he sat on top of me, training kicking in on the second hit. His sneer disappeared when I grabbed his fist and punched his nose a few times, then pushed him off me.

In my attempt to stand, his hand grabbed my hair and pulled me down on my back. Using the momentum, I wrapped my legs around his neck and pulled him over. At some point during the movement, I grabbed my combat knife and tried to stab him. I don't know what happened, but I know I didn't hit him, and I was on my feet again, running for my gun. He tackled me before I was even close and put his boots over my wrists while his hands wrapped around my neck.

His eyes were wide and wild, his shades no longer on his face, irises modded to a mixture of bright blue and deep red. His mouth turned into a snarl as he tried to choke me; I spat in his face, and he released me for a moment before pressing my own knife against my throat.

"Take heed, Kannon!" he said with gritted teeth. "My fight was *never* against the Black Snipers or The Oath, but today, you have made them my enemy. Once I'm done with you, I will deal with the Rain Enforcers. Then I will deal with everyone else. You could've had Silver back in mint condition, but you chose to resist. I *will* finish what I started, Kannon, and you, and everyone else, will watch as we take control of this *fucking* city and make everything fair. No one will stop me!"

He fixed his grip on the knife, pressing the edge to the base of my throat, but a shotgun blast brushed his arm, and blood pooled on his shirt. I heard the distinct pump reload before another shot went off, and he jumped off me and ran. He used his handgun, then I heard the breaking of glass. Another shotgun blast, another reload, then the frantic face of Liz appearing over me as she pressed against my neck.

"I can't leave you two alone for five fucking minutes!" she said as she tore a large chunk off my plaid shirt and tied it around my neck. "You won't die, but you need to keep pressure on it. Where's Silver?"

"He . . . has her."

"*Motherfucker!*" She helped me sit up and then put my arm over her shoulder. "Why are you so heavy? You're not supposed to be this heavy!"

"I have body mods, remember?" I steadied my feet, lifting some of the weight off her shoulders.

"Right. Fuck! You two are so *fucking* annoying." She grabbed my free hand and put it against my neck. "Keep pressure on! Dammit, Kannon! Let's just go!"

As we reached the elevator, I felt my leg grow warm, and in the polished walls of the elevator, I saw blood caking the left side of my body, plastering my clothes to my skin. I didn't even feel the pain of the injuries due to the adrenaline, my heart pumping and head throbbing. Everything went dark as soon as I looked down at my injuries, a wave of cold washing over me just seconds before I felt my body give in to gravity, then darkness.

I woke up to Liz over me, her hands digging through one of my wounds, and I couldn't hold myself from wincing from the pain.

"Do you have to be so rough?"

"By the Oath!" she said, hugging me. "I'm so glad you're okay! Sorry, I had to get the shotgun pellets out so I could apply the concentrated biogel."

We were in a storage closet, an assortment of cleaning materials and tools towering above me on the two racks of shelves on either side. The smell of blood was starting to linger in the air, and I felt my blood-soaked shirt detaching from my skin as Liz applied a gauze over the injuries that felt familiar and gross.

"Who are you, and what did you do with Liz?"

"Stop making jokes." She applied more gel. "We have bigger things to worry about. The sirens are going off outside, and the Rain Enforcers have their sirens blaring and flying way too low! Now stop moving about, for fuck's sake! I only got half of them out, and you're not helping!"

"You couldn't use your handgun?"

She glared at me, then I felt a flash of pain as her fingers dug around inside my skin. "I tried my best, Kannon. Even a choke is not enough to reduce spread."

I winced as she pulled out another pellet and applied more biogel. "You have a *handgun*!"

"Yes," she said. "You also know I'm not a good shot like you are. Now hold still while I pull out the last ones."

"Did you get the information?"

"Yeah," she said. "I almost had to beat Edwin Lockhart for it when I was trying to track you."

"Speaking of which," I said, trying to sit up, but she forced me back down. "How did you even manage to find us?"

Liz sighed as she stood up, her tattoo-painted hands covered in my blood. "Stella came to me and told me that Kax was planning to ambush you. Sadly, she didn't give me any other details, so I had to run around the whole city trying to find you."

"Why didn't you call us?"

"I tried. But you never answered the phone. You didn't hear it ring at all?"

"No."

She rubbed her forehead, shifting her weight. "Anyway, here is the journal. Find the address of that stupid warehouse. It's the only lead we have at the moment. I need to clean off my hands. I don't like how they're feeling now with all your dried blood."

The piercing and pulsating of the wounds made my head hurt as I sat up and leaned against one of the shelves with the journal in hand as I flipped through the pages, reading as fast as I could.

"Did you find anything?" Liz said as she came back, wiping her hands with something, a strong scent of soapy odor filling up the small space.

"Yeah. I have the address." I gave her the opened journal. "Now, please, take me to the Specters. I . . . need proper medical attention, Liz. Not bleeding out is nice, but I would rather avoid an infection. And the pain is just making being awake impossible."

"I don't know how to do stitching. And I can't carry you on my motorcycle."

"I have a spare key for Silver's van."

She rolled her eyes before she helped me up, putting my arm over her shoulder. Every move felt like a jolt of lightning flashed through my muscles, and anything and everything I did as I was helped by Liz to the exit was just torture, until the anesthetics of the biogel began to kick in.

It was afternoon, and the chaos of gunfire, flying ships, and the curfew sirens merged together in a cacophony of noise. The now-empty streets and low-flying patrols from the Rain Enforcers brought back memories of the chaos the Cleansing had included.

"Where's the van?" Liz yelled over the noise.

I gave her the keys and pointed at the old van a few cars away before we ran for it. A patrol ship turned around a corner farther down the road, its weapons readying as it sped toward us, exploding in a ball of fire as we got in the van, and crashing somewhere behind us.

The dread started to crash over me, but I had no time to process, or focus on it. My nails dug into the leather of the seat as Liz changed gears and pulled out onto the street. Everything was bad. It was like war had hit us, and we had no idea when it started.

The clanking all over the van snapped me back to reality, survival taking the spotlight as gunshots peppered the fuselage; one cracking the windshield.

"We're sitting ducks here, Kannon!"

"You're the one driving!"

"I can see that! Thanks for pointing it out, smartass! Where should we go? What's the nearest place?"

"Why are you asking me?" She took a sharp turn, and my elbow dug into one of my injuries, pain running all over my body as Liz maneuvered to avoid crashing into another parked car.

"I don't know the city as well as you Black Snipers do, remember?"

"Fuck me, Liz." I tried to think as she avoided the sudden flood of people rioting in the streets along with Lolitrons shooting at the Rain Enforcer patrols. "Go to The Clockwork! It's the nearest place I can think of!"

"Damn you, Kannon! The highway is the least safe place to drive on!"

"You think I don't know that?"

"Pick someplace else!"

"There is no other place, Liz!"

She groaned as she took another sharp turn to catch the exit just as a patrol ship fired its main gun at a group of Lolitrons surrounding a technical. The last thing I saw was through the rearview mirror as the ship's engine began to smoke.

"This is the Cleansing all over again." Liz's voice dripped with the fear of someone watching everything fall apart. It wasn't hard to imagine, as the sky was covered with more patrol ships than what you usually saw during a regular day.

The few cars left on the highway were just other civilians, trying to reach safety as violence, more so than usual, and now unchecked, spilled onto the streets as people looted, and overall engaged the Rain Enforcers. Several of their patrol ships sped above the highway ahead of us, lights flashing, sirens blaring as smoke began to coat the skyline before us. Explosions were happening here and there. An oncoming Lolitron technical was destroyed by an errant missile from somewhere between the buildings.

"No," I said, passing the now-burning car. "This is worse."

▲ ▲ ▲

Night had fallen, and distant sirens echoed in the darkness, as the columns of smoke rose up all around the city, visible from The Clockwork. It was as if an entity of chaos had reached down and touched the collective subconsciousness of the population, spurring them all into acts of rebellion.

"We can't do anything now," Liz said, stopping the van. "Come on, I'll help you inside."

Ceitr greeted us at the entrance, taking me in his arms and carrying me inside, despite the fact that almost all of my clothes were covered in blood. His cologne was intoxicatingly sweet yet subtle as his hands held me tightly. I felt myself blush.

"Can you do something?" Liz said as she followed us. "I couldn't sew her up."

He carried me upstairs to The Gears VIP area and set me down on top of the bar. He took off his suit and rolled up his sleeves. He didn't speak, just reached over the bar and grabbed a bottle of alcohol, eyed it for a moment, then tore my shirt with one hand as he poured the bottle over my still-open, but not bleeding, injuries.

"You did a good job," he said, "but we have to do the whole process again. Once this is over, you *will* take classes to sew up injuries. Now hand me the med kit. It's somewhere behind the counter. Wait, where's Silver?"

She nodded once as she jumped over it and opened some cabinets. "Kax kidnapped her. In which cabinet is it?"

Ceitr just pointed to someplace before he took off his belt, bent it, and jammed it into my mouth.

"I already took out the pellets," Liz said.

I began to do breathing exercises as I heard him rummage through the kit, but my mind started racing. I was trying to decipher what Kax had said to me before Liz showed up, wondering if Silver was okay, and what the Elders thought about the whole situation. What the plan was to deal with this. Koyuki was not going to be pleased.

"Probably," Ceitr said, and I realized I had said that out loud, though my voice was muffled. Yet, before I had any chance to speak further, the needle dug into the first wound. That tugging feeling, the jolt of pain as he passed it through my skin each and every time wasn't something I ever got used to. You *never* adjust to something like that.

Quite honestly, I don't remember how long it took for him to finish, only that it was painful. The biogel had stopped the bleeding, but the injuries needed to be closed to avoid infection. It was the reality of being a Black Sniper—the needle would become your second-best friend. But once he was done, his shirt was covered in alcohol, and his forehead with sweat.

"Don't do that again," he said.

"You can thank Liz for that."

She crossed her arms and looked away.

"Never mind whose fault it was." He wiped his forehead. "What the fuck is going on?"

"Kax kidnapped Silver, and the Lolitrons are running rampant," I said, sitting up. I would've been embarrassed that he was seeing me in my bra, but after the day I had, it was the last thing on my mind. Silver's safety was monopolizing my thoughts.

He shifted his weight and clicked his tongue, his hands on his hips while he shook his head. "This is bad."

"And you think we don't know that?" Liz yelled. "The whole fucking City is falling around our ears, and you have the fucking audacity to fucking say that?"

"Liz!" I said. "You're not helping!"

She threw her arms in the air and paced around. "I was hoping *he* would have a better plan than what *we* have. The Rain

Enforcers are getting their asses handed to them out there by the Lolitrons! A bunch of punks! Kannon, you and I know that what we have is not a solid—"

I grabbed her arms and held her still, my eyes meeting hers until she shut up, then she began to cry, her black eyeliner running a bit as she fell to her knees. The usual tough demeanor of Liz broke at that moment, and all we could do was let her cry in that small window, a pocket reserved just for her. That was the first time I had seen her break down. Up to that moment, I thought she was the toughest one of the three of us. As I knelt and hugged her, I realized that she had just been trying to be strong.

"I can't deal with another Cleansing, Kannon," she said between sobs, her face digging into my shoulder. "I can't do this again. It was too much last time, and I don't think I'll be able to push through this again!"

"We'll figure something out," I whispered. "You told me Koyuki and Rui were working on an agreement with the Rain Enforcers. It'll be okay."

She pulled away, drying her eyes and smearing her makeup as she said between sobs, "If any of you ever tell anyone about this, I'll kill you both."

"Have you heard anything about that deal with the Rain Enforcers, Ceitr?"

He shook his head. "I've been rather busy dealing with the aftermath of Tamara's convoy. I'll reach out to them and see what they have and let you know. Do you have any other leads? Something to tell us what Kax's ultimate goal is? Other than sowing anarchy all over the City?"

I shook my head. "We do have an address for a warehouse he was using to store things, as well as needing to find Fate, his second lieutenant."

"You've yet to do that?"

I nodded. "Are you okay, Liz?"

She nodded as she finished cleaning her face. "I'll be fine. Just get your shit ready. I want—"

The lights began to flicker before the luminous ball of orange light appeared in the center of the room, Stella materializing seconds later. Her triangular, symmetrical fox-shaped mask's orange neon lights flashed for a moment before she turned her head to each of us.

"G-g-greeetings, Kannon," she said in her usual, glitch-filled, multifaceted synthetic voice. "We have further instructions for y-y-you."

CHAPTER 20

THE LIGHTS KEPT FLICKERING as she hovered in place, almost as if deliberately allowing silence to settle in before she deemed it necessary to speak again.

"Your actions have been noted. Kax's behavior has been logged-d-d-d. The Lolitron rogue group actively engaged the Rain Enforcer group across the city. This act of aggression has been deemed unacceptable. The current location of rogue actor Fate has been noted. Reminder: Job priority is to elim-inate-te-te-te all leadership of the Lolitron rogue group, not prevent their activities unless otherwise specified. Failure of this task will warrant *further* corrective measures."

"How long have you known about their location?" I said.

The lights of her mask flashed. "Objective: Elimination of any and all leaders of the Lolitrons. Calculating: Elimination of all effective leadership of the rogue group Lo-o-o-olitrons will cause a destabilizing effect on the collective. Fail-safes are in place for this eventuality. Priority task: Unchanged. Once rogue actor, Fate, has been eliminated. Further instructions will be dispensed. We will be watching your p-p-progress."

Without another word, or giving us time to ask questions, the lights all over The Clockwork began to flicker, several lightbulbs exploding before her body turned back into an orange ball of light before disappearing in a flash of light. Moments later, the address was sent to both Liz's Recaller and mine.

"I don't think it's a good idea to go now," Liz said. "You can't afford to get hurt again, Kannon."

I ignored her, pacing as I looked at the information in my Recaller. I couldn't stand around doing nothing while Silver was out there, a captive of Kax. If this was the only lead that would help me save her, I was going to pursue it.

"Isn't this the same address as the one we got from the journal?"

Liz nodded. "You should get used to it. Sometimes it feels like she knows more than what she lets on. And she lets on a lot. That bitch. At least she was kind enough to give us a picture of Fate. Or as much as you can call it when whoever Fate is has a mask on."

"I need another shirt. I'm not going back out there topless."

Liz took off her jacket and gave it to me. "We'll make a quick stop at the safe house before we head to the warehouse."

Liz's jacket was mostly a waist-long beige-colored coat, something she always wore to hide her tattooed arms whenever she went out. She now stood there in the middle of the room, eyeliner smudged across her face, black sleeveless buttoned shirt, and red jeans that matched her lipstick.

"That sounds like a good plan," Ceitr said. "In the meantime, I will pay a visit to Koyuki to find out what her plans are.

And probably find out what Rui and her Hunters are doing in the streets. I feel like this will be something we'll have to clean up afterwards."

We all nodded once and left, Ceitr closing the door behind us, bidding us farewell with a single wave, then the locks falling into place from the inside as Liz and I got back in the van.

The streets were empty as we drove through the City, fires burning in almost every street, while rioters and looters caused property damage. Rain Enforcer patrols often flew past, opening fire on Lolitrons, while many of their vehicles were there set ablaze, bodies charred.

"The Cleansing was never this anarchistic," Liz said, her voice carrying worry as we left the highway.

"No," I said, passing several crashed cars. "It was a controlled event. This is not."

The passenger rearview mirror was gone before I saw it. A technical was speeding behind us, blaring its horn, then there was the sound of the shattering of glass and the roar of the strained engine as Liz floored it. Next was the hit as they nudged us from behind, before pulling up next to us. Muscle memory took over, and I had my handgun in hand and was opening fire as their colorful masks came into view, blood splattering the inside of the cabin after one of my bullets killed one of the passengers.

"Kill the bitches!" one of them yelled as they stepped out of the window. "We'll cut off your throat just like we did the Rain Enforcer patrols!"

I didn't think at that moment, ingrained training kicking in, fueled by rage and anger. I don't remember feeling pain, just reaching out, grabbing the jacket of the kid, and pulling him out of their car as Liz pulled away. The next thing was the cracking of their skull as Liz ran them over with the rear wheel, then the technical disappeared. Looking back, they crashed into a concrete pillar, limp bodies falling onto the ground.

"This is not safe," Liz said. "I can't believe I'm being reduced to fieldwork! I fucking *told* you I didn't want to do *fieldwork!*"

The van was pelted by several more shots, glass exploding on Liz's side, and my brain raced to process her scream of pain as she almost lost control. Her left arm was bleeding, her eyebrows were furrowed and her teeth gritted. Her shotgun was in my hands the next moment. I only remember firing at the driver, missing once, then killing one of the passengers.

There was screaming next, and arguing, but we didn't stay to find out what they were arguing about, even as we were peppered with more gunshots. Heat washed over us as an errant missile from an unseen ship hit the technical, breaking all the glass on the driver's side. Liz lost control of the van after that, with several of the thrusters damaged, and the mechanism to lower the tires was broken, the screeching of metal over asphalt echoing in my ears moments before we flipped over, tumbling across the road several times before stopping with a traffic light.

"This is what you call driving?" I felt my head as it throbbed, the warmness of blood covering my palm as I pulled it away to see. "Fuck me, Liz!"

"You're not the only one hurt," she said, several pieces of glass embedded into her arm along with the errant bullet that had hit her earlier. "I'll have to get these tattoos fixed now, by the fucking Oath."

One more technical pulled up next to us, and after I saw them get off, their footsteps crunched over the glass scattered all over the intersection. Their faint voices could be heard speaking over the distant echoing of gunfire and explosions. Kax had managed to recruit more people into the Lolitrons than I had expected.

I'm not dying here. I turned to look at the street, and I could see the feet of the Lolitrons as they walked around the upturned van. *I'm not letting Kax get away with this.* "I'm making this motherfucking dipshit pay."

They laughed until I opened fire with my handgun. Two were dead before my magazine clicked empty, and the others ran for cover. I reloaded. Liz fired her shotgun, but my attention was on the Lolitron climbing the back of the technical to man the turret. I wasn't going to let them kill us that easily. He pulled the bolt back, but I was quicker, and a mist of pink sprayed behind him. His body falling over the gun was enough to make the others hesitate.

They spoke among themselves, and some asked if there were snipers around, calling for information among each other. The distance was short enough to be accurate with my gun, but I had to time my shots if I wanted them to think there was another Black Sniper around. It was easy enough, minus the hot casings that fell on top of me each time I shot a head out of cover.

I don't know how long it took to kill them. I was lying on the upside-down roof of the van, looking out the crushed window, waiting for them all that time. The last one to die was one that made a run for the driver's side of the technical, but all he managed to do was plaster his brain against the yellow paint of the vehicle.

"Liz." I put the gun down and twisted to see her. She was still tied to her seatbelt, struggling to cut the fabric with a piece of broken glass. "You'll cut yourself."

"Just get me down."

I pulled out my knife, albeit with difficulty, trading it to her for her shotgun. Seconds later, she was free, falling to the ground with a metallic thud and a groan as I twisted and turned to leave the van.

My muscles ached, my skin was cut and bruised, and my head throbbed from the hit and the airbags. Liz limped for a moment, putting her weight on my shoulder as she looked at her leg, her jeans torn to show skin and some superficial wounds, but nothing that would prevent her from walking on her own.

"The Lolitrons have made a mess of everything," she said, stepping away. "I don't think Silver will be happy with me when I tell her about her van."

"Forget about it. We need to find another way to get to the warehouse."

"I don't think Fate will be there at this point."

"Search the bodies and get the keys for the technical," I said. "I'm getting my gear."

The PSA sirens went off as I crawled into the van, going off for about a minute, before a bell followed, then the announcement: "Be advised: curfew is now in effect. Repeat, curfew is now in effect. The Rain Corporation would like to remind you that anyone found in violation will be shot on sight. Have a nice day."

I pulled out my backpack and slung it over my shoulders, then grabbed my sniper rifle and ran to the technical truck, which Liz had managed to get running.

"We're going to be a target in this thing," she said as she pulled one of the bodies out of the truck.

"I know." There was one dead member in the backseat, so I pulled them out, keeping their rifle, checking the bullets as I climbed on. "There is still one Lolitron dead in the back bed, so that at least should make them think twice. Otherwise, let's hope we don't stumble into any patrol ships."

Several Rain Enforcer ships sped above us, sirens blaring and echoing all around us, and I thought about what Kax must be putting Silver through. His wild gaze, now burned in my mind, only showed me what cruelty he was capable of inflicting on her.

Liz shifted gears, looked back at the corpse, and floored it. "That was too fucking close. I hope we get to leave this fucking mess alive."

We spent the rest of the trip in silence, avoiding most of the main roads, and applying biogel to our wounds to stop the bleeding. Several of my stitches had reopened, and I had to deal with them as well before we arrived at the safe house. After a quick re-supply of ammo, biogel, and a fresh set of clothes, Liz sent a message to someone before we got back on the truck.

The drive was long, lasting about an hour before we got to the district the warehouse was at, and another ten minutes to find it. It was a small building, nestled between two larger edifices. Just brick and mortar, a side door, and two large double doors in the front, all closed and no windows. Effectively, we were blind to what was going on inside.

"Stay here," I said, taking the safety off the rifle. "I'll go inside. You hear any shooting, get on the gun and open fire."

"Kannon, you know I don't know how to use anything other than my shotgun and a handgun. And even if I did, how am I supposed to know what I'm shooting at from out here?"

A brief glance over my shoulder to the blood-splattered window and turret was all I gave her as I said, "Fine, then shoot at whoever comes out. As for using it, just pull the side lever, aim, and shoot. It's already pre-loaded with the belt. Shouldn't be that hard."

She rolled her eyes, whatever words she had said next drowned out in the dissonance of sirens and gunfire. Everything else was the noise of my gear as I ran to the door and tried the knob; it was unlocked.

I heard voices inside, clanking of metal over metal, and the engine sounds of a forklift moving about in the interior, then the movement of Lolitron members. A large semi-truck was partly inside toward the back, backed up to a loading dock, where they were loading something into it. There were crates on wooden pallets stacked against the wall, most already pulled out and loaded. Above was a catwalk with a floating office pod and stairs that let up to them at the other side of the room.

Only seven.

I snuck inside, regulating my breathing, letting instinct and training take over. *Breathe in. Breathe out.* One by one, each one on the ground floor fell dead before they had a chance to react. An alarm went off in the building, then a metal clanking, and the truck began to leave, the doors at its back closing as it pulled out.

There were two more on the catwalk above, their shots ricocheting off the metal until someone yelled at the other.

I poked my head out and opened fire. One of them fell, their gun hitting the ground floor, and the other one fell back inside the pod, blood splattering the wall. I exhaled and started to check the bodies on the ground floor, but none of them were Fate, per the picture Stella gave me and Liz, so I took their masks off.

A groan from the second floor made me jump back into alert. Climbing the stairs, I saw that the first one I had shot on the catwalk was dead, blood dripping to the floor below between the metal grate, but the feet of the second one moved near the door of the pod, writhing in pain.

My blood was pumping, and my breathing grew shallow as I approached the man bleeding on the floor, his hand held over his side to try to slow it down.

"I should've known you'd survive," he said, his voice too familiar to forget.

"Edwin Lockhart." I took his mask off. "I wish I could say I'm surprised. Kax ambushing us now makes more sense than I thought it would. What do you even stand to gain from this mess he created?"

"The Rain Enforcers have been in charge of this fucking cesspit of a city for too long now." He groaned. "Draining the pockets of everyone to make themselves and everyone they deem their friends and investors rich. Their board of directors and their fucking generals lining their pockets with our money. It's time the rich each get a fucking bullet through their brains."

"I thought you and your family were rich."

"You said it," he said. "Were. Increasing taxes and prices on everything, as well as all the political scandals and backroom deals that fucked us over time and time again over the years reduced us to just an old name forced to do business with the scum of this fucking city. All the power we had was just information we had gathered over the years. Luckily, our businesses kept us afloat enough for us to not sink deeper, if just barely. But if you're asking for information, you've come to the wrong man."

"What's Kax's plan?"

"You're living through it." He chuckled. "Talk to him if you want the details. I just made sure the supply line was still running."

"Where's Silver?"

He chuckled. "With Kax, where the song of the moon meets the Tower of Darkness."

A wave of cold ran through my skin like a pulse as he breathed his last breath. The Black Spire was the local name given to the Rain Enforcers Headquarters, the main military base located in the center of the City of Laohz. In the city's center, it was a large tower with special glass that made it look like onyx. It was where most of the Rain Enforcer forces were housed. Where all their patrol ships came from most of the time. Their center of power, it was located at the heart, so to speak, of the city.

"He's planning to attack the base." I ran back to the truck, the sudden wave of dread crashing down as the chaos that would follow if he were to succeed in destroying the Rain Enforcers played in my mind. Whatever outcome I could conjure up, everyone ended up losing in the end.

"Did you find Fate?" Liz said as I got back on.

"It was Edwin Lockhart," I replied, throwing my gear in the truck. "But Kax is planning on attacking The Black Spire.

"And Kax?"

"Watching from the Moonsong Hotel with Silver."

CHAPTER 21

THE FIGHTING WAS WORSE as we got closer to the center of the City. The streets were littered with the charred and burning remains of patrol ships and technicals alike. Columns of smoke covered the skies, and the echoing of gunfire and explosions was always present.

As the Moonsong Hotel came into view, Liz pushed the engine to its limits, running over some of the Lolitrons that were in the way, blood splattering the windshield. Liz turned on the wipers.

"Slow down!" I said, but my request fell on deaf ears.

Roaring of jet engines closed in quick, as well as the front door of the hotel, all the while the technical truck we were in was peppered with gunshots, the windshields shattering, the warning bell of a malfunctioning engine pushing up the dread and anticipation toward the pit of my stomach as the entrance drew closer.

"Duck!" was all Liz said before she grabbed my head and pushed it down seconds before the shattering of glass and metal erupted around us as we drove right through the lobby doors. One of the tires was pulled from its axel, the truck skidding through the reception area and crashing onto the back wall and desk.

Muscle memory took over once we stopped, and my gun was in my hand and opening fire on Lolitrons coming in from the street to investigate. They were dead before they were able to make it ten feet into the building.

"What the fuck were you thinking?" I yelled, cutting the seatbelt with my knife.

"Thank you, Liz, for saving my life," she said mockingly. "We were being shot at, and a patrol ship was right behind us!"

I gave her a protesting groan as I jumped over her, feet crunching over the broken glass and wood. The fighting continued outside until a missile went off, followed by an explosion moments later. The ship was gone after that.

"How are we going to find your cousin?" she said, climbing off the truck.

"I don't know."

The Moonsong Hotel was the biggest hotel in the Central District, riddled with opulence, all hidden away now behind the errant gunshots that decorated the walls, grafiti, as well as the mess Liz made with the Lolitron technical we stole.

The pink granite floors were scratched and soaked with the spilling fluids of the vehicle, as well as smeared blood. There were bodies lying around, many who appeared to have been killed before we even arrived; the stench of decay was now digging into the lingering mix. The interior was dark, the power apparently cut in the building, and the emergency lights were the only illumination inside.

"You just don't know how to fucking quit," Kax said through the intercoms. "Your constant meddling in affairs that will benefit everyone but the Rain Enforcers is starting to get on my nerves. You want to kill me? Come to the roof, then. I will grant you a show before I kill you. *Properly* this time."

My first instinct was to flip him off, then my mind kicked into gear. Training took precedence as I grabbed the rifle and reloaded it with a magazine from one of the dead Lolitrons. Focus. Breathe. Breathe. Breathe. It was all that I could think as I walked to the emergency stairs with Liz in tow. I felt pain as I moved, my whole body ached, but I willed myself to ignore it as I emptied my mind. Every noise came into focus, and was filtered and analyzed before being discarded as not being within the building. There was no resistance as we climbed up. No Lolitrons, no guards, no guests. Just the emptiness and the distant echoing of gunfire from the outside.

It took us about twenty minutes to climb to the top, stopping at the last landing to catch our breath. I stared at the doorknob, heartbeat accelerating as the inevitable confrontation with Kax, my cousin, my blood, was just steps away.

"Are you sure you want to do this?" Liz said. "We can call the other Black Snipers and have them eliminate him."

I shook my head. "Stay here. I'll be the one to finish this."

It was a problem I was tasked with solving. A job *I* needed to complete. It was the only way I would have enough money to pursue my photography. I couldn't let sentimentality and emotions get in the way of my duty as a Black Sniper. I opened the door, the wind taking it from my hands and slamming it against the wall. Beyond, stood Kax, staring at The Black Spire, Silver next to him, tightly tied with rope to a chair. Two armed Lolitrons stood next to him.

He looked over his shoulder, and with a nod of his head, motioned me to come forward.

Even with the flowing wind, it felt as if all the noise in the world was muted, with the exception of the crunching of my feet over the gravel laid on the rooftop, and the shuffling of my gear. The walk was short, but it sure didn't feel like it. It was that proverbial feeling of walking to your death. That feeling when the teacher calls you out in the middle of the class for passing notes, or being pulled over by a cop. That anticipation that builds in you as you are walking to face the music, the consequences of your actions. I got closer and stopped, with probably five, maybe six feet between us, and on the chair next to him, eyes set in a glare, was Silver. She was mostly unharmed, just a bruised eye and scratches across her face. Though I was happy to see her alive, the joy was quickly fading. Kax turned around, his modded eyes glowing in the dark as he stared at me, and inevitably looked at me from head to toe.

Steel yourself, Kannon. "Are you okay, Silver?" I asked.

"Yes. I've suffered worse. I'm still shaking off the effects of the tranquilizer."

"You should've heeded my warning when I told you to stay out of my affairs, Kannon." Kax grabbed his spiked baseball bat off the ground, while he held a radio in the other. "You're stubborn, just like everyone else in the Black Snipers."

"What did you do to Silver?"

"We just roughed her up a bit. I had to restrain her after she killed ten of my best men. I had to make her stay put by tasing her several times. She was sturdier than what I imagined."

"You should've let me kill you," Silver said, a snarl almost in her voice. "It would've made this mess you made easier to clean up afterwards."

"Those who fear change, oppose it the most. I am the herald of change in this city, and change hurts, while cleansing the impurities present. Just like a forest fire clears the way for new trees to grow, culling the old. I will raze this place to the ground to build something new!"

"What do you hope to accomplish with this, Kax?" I asked. "What do you hope to gain by attacking the Rain Enforcers? Sowing all this chaos?"

He chuckled, albeit dryly, then stifled it. With one simple move of his head, his two guards aimed their rifles at me. "Now you want to understand? After getting in my way all this time?"

"Is all this destruction and unchecked death really necessary?"

"Even if I explained it to you, you wouldn't understand my motivations! But in order to move forward, blood has to be spilled now."

"For what?" I yelled.

"To make this city better! To give people who don't have anything to eat a chance to live without having to beg in the streets! When I got to this city from Othara, I marveled at how everything was, but the stars quickly faded from my eyes. Jobs paid close to nothing. Education was near impossible to attain, and general living was just a simple struggle for survival. So I joined the Wraiths in order to afford food and a roof over my head.

"But I wanted to do something about it. I was tired of sitting on the sidelines, installing ransomware and Trojan horses in the networks of all the companies scattered across the city and then doing nothing with them! So I joined the Black Snipers, and it gave me hope that we would one day eradicate the Rain Enforcers. I mistakenly thought that they were fighting the rich *fucks* that control this place. The generals and the CEOs and board of directors that run this bloody place!

"Then the Cleansing happened." He stopped, turning around to look back at The Black Spire. "And I thought that we were finally doing what I hoped we would do. But I was proved wrong in the end. We decided to fold over and make a peace with them, just to keep our fucking business running! To make a quick buck from killing others that probably didn't even deserve it."

"That's it?" I said. "That's your fucking reason?"

"The Black Snipers weren't willing to do anything about it." He turned back to me. "Do you think these people will rise up and oppose these tyrannical fucks on their own? The Oath has the training, the weapons, the know-how to take up arms and remove them from power! And all we fucking do is play hired hitman to anyone on the street!"

"Because that is what the Black Snipers stand for! The Cleansing didn't happen because we instigated it, it—"

"Do you think I give a *fuck* about who started it, Kannon? I only care about who could've ended it. The Black Snipers failed to step up to the plate, so I did. And I *will* finish what I started. The time for talking is over. You will stand there and *watch* as I bring the Rain Enforcers to their *fucking* knees."

"And then what?" I yelled. "What will you do once you destroy the Rain Enforcers? Have you stopped to think that a revolution takes more than the will of a single group acting alone on behalf of everyone else in the city? Do you really think you will be able to establish a suitable replacement for the Rain Enforcers as a body of government just because you fucking will it?

"And never mind the fact that the Rain Corporation will not allow this city to be taken from their grasp as easily. Do you really think they will not send their reinforcements to bring back order? The goal you are aiming for is doomed to fail, Kax! Even if you succeed at bringing the Rain Enforcers to their knees, all you're doing is hurting everyone else you've set out to help! There is nothing in this plan that will lead to the results you wish to accomplish!"

"I wouldn't be doing this if the Black Snipers had finished the job during the Cleansing, Kannon. Contrary to them, I *will* finish the job."

There were plans that had been set in motion by Koyuki Akikawa and her Inner Circle. Reasons why the ceasefire was put in place, and only a certain few outside that group were allowed the knowledge of her plans, and even less the knowledge of the idea of a contingency that had been set. I had not been allowed to know the details of it, just that she had a bigger reason why we didn't finish the job, and it seemed Kax was unaware of it.

"Do you really think Koyuki would do something without a plan?"

"Shut up! Your lies will not be enough to stop me from achieving my goals, Kannon. This conversation is over!" Kax said, and he motioned the guards.

One of the Lolitrons took my rifle, while the other forced me to kneel. Kax walked back to the edge of the building, bringing his radio to his mouth. There was silence for a minute, then the first explosion inside the walls of The Black Spire's military base that surrounded it. Several more followed, shattering the silence, piercing the sound of the wind as it flapped my clothes. Kax raised his arms, almost as if taking in the destruction and chaos being sown by his men.

"You will be the first to witness the first moments of the fall of the Rain Enforcers in the City of Laohz, Katherine! For the first time in your life, you will see what victory looks like! What it *should've* looked like when the Black Snipers decided to sign that treaty with them."

Thunder flashed across the ever-cloudy skies of the City, rumbling as a light began to shine through, then they were pushed aside by the force of the first ship coming out of hyperspace, revealing the imposing form of a Rain Enforcer Destroyer spaceship entering the city. Kax lowered his arms, taking a step back and shaking his head as the second destroyer came into the city, followed by a third.

I heard the door behind me open, pulled back by the wind as gunshots rang out in the air around me. Survival took over, and my hands grabbed one of the rifles and pulled it away as I armed myself with my knife, sinking it into one of the Lolitron's throat as I took hold of the other rifle and pulled, throwing them out of balance and into the path of Kax's spiked baseball bat in full swing; blood splattered my face as I ducked, the hit connecting with the Lolitron's head.

"What did you do?" he yelled.

"Koyuki Akikawa, and all the members of The Oath, brokered another treaty with the Rain Enforcers," Liz said, waving her lit-up Recaller in her hand. "They had their military command send reinforcements to take back control of the city."

"I will kill you *both*." He pulled the baseball bat from the Lolitron's head. "Starting with you, Liz!" His gun was in his hand before I could react, and by the time his third shot was fired, Liz had fallen to the ground, pulling the door closed.

There was no time to think at that point, just act, so I tackled him as the last two shots hit the steel door. My hand held back one of his wrists while I punched him, whatever moment in-between was lost from my memory. He pushed me off, blood falling from my nose as pain made my head throb.

"Do you fucking realize what you just did?" Kax yelled as he stood over me, bloodied baseball bat in hand as he looked at the destroyers deploying their own patrol ships. "You've just given away the only chance this city *had* to be free from this tyranny!"

"Nothing you did would've changed that, Kax," I said. "You should've listened to me when I told you the Rain Enforcers were not going to just hand over this city to whoever asked for it nicely. They have the largest production of military hardware here on this planet, on Rhode. Their largest export dock is two miles from here!"

"Unlike the Black Snipers, Katherine," he said as he raised his bat over his head, "I don't give up easily."

Everything slowed down at that moment, as the downward momentum of his baseball bat began to gain speed, and my only thought was to kick him in the crotch. His bat missed my head, probably by mere inches, as he fell to his knees, both hands on his balls as he groaned.

The wind carried with it the scent of blood, fire, oil, gunpowder, and smoke. Gunfire was carried faintly by the wind. I don't know how hard I had hit him, just enough to make him stay on the floor groaning. I could've tied him then and there, but I was not willing to risk him leaving that rooftop alive. So I stood up and grabbed my combat knife, which had fallen some distance away during the struggle, and pushed him on his back. My blade was still dripping blood.

"Go on," he said between groans. "You've taken everything. Sell yourself to the powers that rule this cursed city. This *cesspool* of crap and corruption. I'll have no meaning after this. You said it yourself, only one of us will be leaving this rooftop alive."

I knelt next to him, a sudden wave of grief washing over me, and no matter how much I tried, I couldn't push that feeling down. I could not suppress it as we were trained to do. My human nature took over.

"You know what the hardest part of it all is, Kax?" I put the tip of my knife between his fourth and fifth ribs on his left side. "Having to remember all those childhood memories I shared with you, as I am faced with the reality of having to kill someone that is flesh and blood."

"Save your tears, Katherine," he said. "At the end of the day, what you and I do is business. Everything else is just a distraction." He grabbed my hands and forced the knife into his chest. Blood covered his shirt almost instantly as his arms grew limp, allowing me to pull the knife out. Tears seemed to slide from his eyes as they grew distant and lost their shine, his body gasping for air several times before he stopped moving, dying a minute later.

Anger, sadness, and regret spilled over me, and a shiver ran down my spine as tears formed in my eyes. I looked up at the Rain Enforcer ships in the distance as I held back the desire to cry. In anger, frustration, longing for a lull in the wave of everything going on around me, yet my hand still held onto the bloodied knife.

A knot formed in my throat as I looked back at his body, lying there before me as Patrol Ships deployed from the destroyers flew past the building. I couldn't hold myself back, and I put my hand over my mouth as tears began to fall. I tried to force myself to sob silently and failed. Despite everything, my heart was breaking, and all the memories we fostered growing up, albeit few, rushed back into my mind as the wind seemed to caress his hair. I don't know how long I sat there staring at him, just that the crunching of footsteps made me look up at Liz, her arm covered in blood and her hand over her wound.

"I'm sorry."

I didn't reply.

She walked around Kax's body and squeezed my shoulder. "I'll take care of Silver."

I nodded.

After she was gone, the distinct orange ball of light formed, electricity crackling on the ground as it grew, until, with a flash, Stella came to form, hovering in place, her clothing seemingly unaffected by the gusts of wind blowing on the rooftop. She remained still for a few minutes, her mask flashing as it always did until she moved her head.

"Rogue Actor Kax has been removed. Analyzing: Destabilization of rogue group Lolitrons: 83.78%. Warning: Additional Lolitron forces have been detected across the city-y-y-y-y."

"I already did what you hired me to do, Stella," I said. "Just pay us and leave us the fuck alone."

Her mask flashed several times. "Task Complete, pa-a-a-yment dispensed. Your progress has fallen within projected parameters with a 96.23% accuracy. Further jobs may be provided."

"I'm not taking any more jobs from you." I stood up. "Now, unless you have anything else to say, I suggest you leave us alone."

Stella tilted her head, her mask flashing again before she turned back into a ball of orange light. "We will be watching your progress."

The crunching of gravel sounded behind me, then I felt a hand on my shoulder as Silver stood next to me, taking a deep breath. "Are you going to be okay?"

I nodded once.

"I'm sorry you had to kill him."

"I tried to reason with him, but he was too far gone to be saved. Though nothing he ever did was going to change the City of Laohz for the better."

Silver sat next to me and put her arm over my shoulder, pulling me closer to her as she wrapped me in an embrace. She said nothing, spoke no words, and just allowed me to stay there.

Tears fell down my face as the knife that was in my hand clattered to the ground, all the weight I had been carrying seeming to lift from my shoulders. "I just want to go home."

EPILOGUE

WE WERE PICKED UP from that roof an hour after Stella left, by a Rain Enforcer cargo ship. We passed several Black Snipers who were aboard with a wave of uneasiness. Rui Kuwabara was also aboard, her pleased expression fading as the ship pulled away, leaving Kax's body behind to bleed on that roof. It would not be retrieved for a week, and he was cremated, before the ashes were returned to Othara.

The violence and chaos that had engulfed the city took six months to bring under control, and the Black Snipers were given special immunity to bring anyone into justice; few participated.

In the end, the estimated death toll had been projected to be about 100,000. There were hundreds of downed Patrol Ships, and an astronomical amount of Rullians in damages. It took longer for the city to recover from that. Even our apartment was destroyed, possibly ransacked by Kax's men and his desire to eliminate us.

We came back to destroyed furnishings, broken glass, and dried spilled wine everywhere. Our gun rack was looted, and Silver's cello was shot and burned in the middle of the living room. There was nothing left for us to go back to, not even our motorcycles.

Silver's and Liz's injuries healed quickly, and Liz's tattoo parlor was mostly intact, allowing her to go back to work in a rather short amount of time. Silver had to go to therapy for a while to deal with the stress that the job had caused.

As for me, I left the Black Snipers a year later. Unable to deal with the memories that The Cleansing, and The Moonsong Incident—as Kax's insurrection came to be called—left in my mind, haunting me every waking hour. I moved to the City of Sunsets, following a job opportunity to become a photography teacher at a boarding school given to me by the agent I met in the gala, Alinor. Silver followed months later, also unable to cope with being a Black Sniper anymore.

Whatever remaining members the Lolitrons had were absorbed or eliminated by the other gangs. The power vacuum that the death of Kax and his lieutenants left behind was never filled, and it left the organization too weak to sustain itself, eventually collapsing.

I would like to say that Kax's actions accomplished something. Spurred some kind of change in the rhythms of the City of Laohz, that hope reached it, even if a small glimmer, but I'd be lying. After two years, everything was back as it was before, as if nothing had ever happened. The constant patrols, the murders, the struggle for power that was always present in the background, the uneasy truce between the Rain Enforcers and The Oath. The only difference now was the scars Kax left behind, and the hollowness Silver and I will always carry. In the end, nothing will ever change the nature of The City of Laohz.

▲ ▲ ▲

Liz closed the door to her apartment, throwing the keys in a small wooden bowl next to the door as she blindly searched for the light switch. Her injuries, although stitched together and healing, still ached with every movement she made. Her feet dragged, her shoulders felt heavy, and part of her still resented Kannon for dragging her into the clusterfuck that had been dealing with Kax and his men.

"Next time she drags me to one of her escapades," Liz muttered as she grabbed a beer from the fridge, "I'll fucking charge her hazard pay. I'm a Wraith, by the Oath!"

She grabbed the bottle opener and turned to the couch, stopping in place as she saw a figure, white cloak, ethereal in movement, and hooded with a white mask covering its features. It hovered atop her coffee table, no sound, no movement as the flat mask turned on with a single white line where both eyes would be.

"Wraith Liz," it said, a singular synthetic, yet guttural voice, almost like a low rumble. "I am EN-71Y. You may call me Entity. The Collective has watched your progress. We are pleased with the results. Further tasks will be assigned."

Her hand tightened around the neck of the bottle. "What's next?"

ACKNOWLEDGMENTS

I WANT TO START by thanking my friend Jonathan Otero, who helped me figure out the many basics of human psychology and how to apply it to my writing, and who gave me many pointers and feedback on my early drafts and ideas. Without him, I would not have taken the leap to write this series.

Thanks to Emily Hitchcock and Clair Fink from Columbus Publishing Lab, who managed my project from start to finish.

Huge thanks to Sara Herchenroether, my editor who was amazing with her feedback and pointers with this book and the several drafts it took to bring it to get the story to shine.

Special Thanks to Kiersten Sprague, Tony Maggio and Rosa Enid, who took the time to read the drafts of this book in its early stages.

ABOUT THE AUTHOR

ERICK J. FALCON is a Puerto Rican native whose writing is deeply influenced by the political climate in his homeland. This backdrop serves as the foundation for the socio-political conflicts faced by the Black Snipers in his debut work, which he has been developing since 2012. Falcon blends real-life themes with a touch of otherworldly magic and technological flair, creating a modern-futuristic setting that resonates with readers.

Passionate about computers and IT, Falcon explores dystopian elements to examine their potential exploitation, although his first book primarily focuses on the journey of Kannon. An avid tabletop role-playing game enthusiast, he enjoys games like Dungeons & Dragons, Pathfinder, and Starfinder, along with video games rich in dystopian themes, such as the Fallout and Watch_Dogs series.

Falcon also appreciates narratives that delve into human emotions and psychological pressures, often gravitating toward thrillers and detective stories like *Girl on the Train*. Currently, he is focused on completing the second book in his series, with the ultimate goal of engaging readers and reflecting real-life complexities through a dystopian lens.